THE CHAMP

a novel

by Daniel Martin Eckhart

Dedicated to my wife Nathalie and our children Nick, Milo and Eliza for all their love, laughter and patience. Thank you for letting me be part of your journeys.

Copyright © 2012 by Daniel Martin Eckhart

All rights reserved.

No part of this book may be reproduced in any form or by any electronic or mechanical means including information storage and retrieval systems - except in the case of brief quotations in articles or reviews - without the permission in writing from its publisher,
Daniel Martin Eckhart.

CHAPTER ONE

LIFE

STOP

One hundred and fifty-nine feet.

Maybe a bit more. Maybe a bit less. Wilber's steps weren't exactly accurate measurement anymore, hadn't been for quite a few years now. He used to stride back then, but his striding days were over. One hundred and fifty-nine. It felt about right, it looked about right and he liked the sound of his inner voice saying it. One hundred and fifty-nine. The old man smiled and said it out loud.

"One hundred and fifty-nine."

Wilber was certain that the young woman standing in front of him had heard his creaking voice. She didn't move, didn't look back, didn't react at all to his incomprehensible garble. It didn't take much to know that she ignored him.

Wilber's smile widened, lines like canyons creasing all across his face. His voice had a lovely habit of bringing back the present. He liked to remember his voice as the young one, the strong one. But his spoken words brought back reality in a flash - life, now, old - very old.

His own voice cracked him up at times. Speaking wasn't easy, with lips constantly quivering, shaking up a storm at times - that and the fact that his dentures had been state of the art about forty years ago. With every movement of his jaw, his teeth clacked against the gums and fought a monumental battle with his tongue. Still, those dentures were better than no dentures and he was used to them.

He could make himself understood, when required. But in truth, he mostly talked to himself anyway, and he knew what he was saying ... he was still pretty sharp for an old fart.

"Yep, that's right," Wilber mumbled out loud and watched the woman's back tense up just a little.

Wilber knew what she was thinking, she thought he was nuts, a senile weirdo who would hopefully stay in his place and not bother her with his antics. That made Wilber smile even more and that, in turn, forced his tongue to press the dentures back in place. For those rare occasions that required clear communication, he did have a trick ready. Chewing gum - always available in his right jacket pocket. You chew it, you stick it in between dentures and gums. Just like glue. Absolutely no clacking, snapping or slurping then. Nope, with the gum, he could talk just like the young Wilber.

Except for the energy, of course.

Weirdo - yep, that was him alright. He loved this place, loved the people who came and went every day. Wilber never forced anybody to speak to him ... sooner or later they all came to him anyway. What he did, however, was play with them. He would make faces at little children, he would grin at old ladies, he would start into a song just to make people stare and, inevitably, laugh.

Sometimes he even simply burped as loud as he could just to get a rise out of a stony face. Wilber immensely enjoyed himself, just as all those men and women and children did enjoy his presence ... well, one way or the other.

Wilber thought of the retired teacher he had met the other day, a bitter face hard as a rock. She had been about to sit down next to Wilber - which of course had been the perfect moment for Wilber to break into masterful yodel.

∞

The startled woman missed the bench by an inch, landing flat on her buttocks. She stared at Wilber in disbelief - her face wide with emotion.

It took her a moment to regain the composure of the frozen face. Only her eyes remained alive, livid - eyes that exuded waves of sternest disapproval - a look practiced and perfected over a period of thirty-six years at junior high in Ellisburg, PA. When she stood up she quickly checked around for people laughing at her, people she would stare down.

... but she found only Wilber's eyes looking at her - eyes that showed no malice, eyes that shone. The teacher ended up sitting next to Wilber for three and a half hours, telling him half her life and a few things she had never told anybody before and had planned on keeping to herself until her dying day. Three and a half hours that had been reserved for urgent errands.

But most things had a way of losing importance when compared to time spent in the company of one Wilber Patorkin.

∞

Wilber now remembered the teacher's face again, the look of disbelief when he had felled her with his yodel. He cracked up, his sudden laughter loud and clear and only the hand that went up to cover his mouth kept the dentures from spilling onto the asphalt.

The young woman had been standing at the edge of his world for three minutes now. Monday through Friday, every day, same time. Wilber knew her, even though she had never even so much as nodded in his direction. Her name was Ann Riker, daughter of the local baker, bakery two blocks over. Two blocks that were too far for these old bones to get to. She was on her way to work and she didn't look happy. She hadn't looked happy for a long while now and Wilber knew that it was bad, it was dark - and it was getting worse.

He would have to do something about that sometime soon.

Bus coming.

He could hear it a long way off, long before seeing the sleek blue lightning bullet its way through the narrow tunnel. The highway passing above the tunnel, loud like a river rushing by, a constant flow of droning steel. Wilber had decided long ago that he liked that sound very much. He tilted his head just slightly, bringing his left ear up in the direction of the tunnel.

Bus coming.

ANN

Ann Riker had been watching the old man from the corner of her eye. Just like all the regulars of the stop she would take her cue from the old man's movement. It was common knowledge. Despite the trucks roaring past on the highway, despite the children screaming on their way to school, it was a fact that the frail looking little man on the bench always heard the bus before anyone else did. People would watch him, wait for him to tilt his head and then get up, pick up their bags, their briefcases, close the book and get ready. Ann Riker picked up her bag.

She wanted to talk to him. She had no idea why, but she felt drawn to him. Every day she saw him here, every day he was cheerful, wild, weird ... and every day people took time to talk to him. Drawn to him ... no. Too many things on her mind, too much going on, no time.

Bus coming.

BUS

Exactly one hundred and fifty-nine feet down the street the 93 shot out of the tunnel, racing toward the bus stop. Not slowing down yet, always too fast. Something would happen eventually ... had happened before, Wilber thought ... it would happen again. Most things had a way of repeating themselves, no point worrying about it.

Yellow leaves blew from the tall birch trees, blew across the street, past the bus stop. Wilber watched as the bus flew closer and slowed down. And he watched the bus driver watching him. Wilber knew him, although they had never spoken.

Walt Wirowsky had been driving the 93 for a year and a half now. He was a heavyset man, married with seven children. Wilber knew that responsibility was dragging the man's shoulders to the ground. Still, Wilber had caught a hint of a smile once, about a month back. He hadn't imagined it. And he had smiled back at the driver. But until he had formed a smile on his gray lips, the bus had already stopped a few feet ahead. It sometimes annoyed Wilber royally. This was simply the wrong place for a bench. From where he was sitting, he could never see into the opened door to the driver.

Then Wilber smiled. He was looking forward to the day the driver would shut off the engine, step out, sit next to him for a few and just talk.

Ann got on the bus, nodding to the driver, it seemed. Then she was out of sight and the bus sped away. Wilber gingerly leaned forward, his hands trying to support his weight on his knees. Wilber always watched the bus disappear. A kid in the back of the bus waved at him. One of the boys stuck out his tongue. He wanted to wave to the children, but by the time he managed to raise his arm without losing his balance, the bus had vanished in the distance.

WALT

Walt Wirowsky kept looking back in the mirror. He could still see the old man leaning forward. He was always there, every day of the year ... always there and never once did he get on the bus. He would always sit there on the bench, tucked in like a sandwich between Calvin Klein poster boards ... lookin' happy. A glow about him.

Walt still felt the wonder that always crept up on him when approaching the stop. It was as if something warm was caressing his heart. It was as if for a moment, he didn't have to worry about the family, the bills. Somehow, when he was near that bus stop, near that old man, life seemed just fine.

One day, he thought. One day he would stop for a few seconds, shut off the engine. Yes, he'd get out then, he'd talk to the guy, find out his name at least. Then he had to take his eyes off the rearview mirror. See ya tomorrow, old man.

GONE

There'll be another bus, then another. And someday soon I'll watch my final bus go by, Wilber thought.

That girl Ann. She reminded him of Paula ... Of course she did. Everything and everybody reminded him of Paula. Everybody had always tried to make it better, assure him that it would get easier in time. But they had never understood. Nothing needed to get easier. It was as it was and that was fine.

He had lost his wife in 1946, fifty-two years ago and he hadn't forgotten one single thing. Quite the opposite. Every passing day, week, month and year made the memories more vivid, more detailed. Wilber's wife had always had a silly streak in her. She had made him laugh a million times, and it still made him laugh, thinking about the things she used to say and do. Always unexpected, always full or surprises ... until the surprise had killed her. It had been a bus, the killer, but that didn't make Wilber hate buses or anything. That was just a plain fact, the killer had been a bus.

∞

Paula Patorkin snuck out of the baby store ahead of him, their Buick waiting for them, parked in a tight spot right out front. Wilber followed her, pretending to look for her, well knowing how she always jumped up at him from all kinds of unlikely places. She crouched behind the car now, ducking around it. Wilber went for his keys as he walked to the driver's side, waiting for her ambush. He knew it would happen any moment, he loved those little games, loved playing along. Bus coming. Wilber looked up, frowned at it ... He felt a cold wind blow down his spine. And he suddenly knew, knew before it happened, couldn't get a word out, couldn't do a thing, frozen in place as his wife jumped out from between the cars with that mischievous glow on her beautiful face.

∞

It had not been crazy, not careless, really. Just a matter of timing, a matter of distance. Just an inch too far out into the street, just an inch that left Wilber without Paula for fifty-two years. The bus driver hadn't seen her. He hadn't seen how the side mirror had swiped Paula's head, had spun her around like a ballerina. Swan Lake on Michigan Avenue. She had fallen hard and fast, breaking her jaw on the fender of the Buick. Even now Wilber could hear that sound.

Crack.

The fall had not just broken her jaw, it had broken her neck, too. Dead on the spot. No wife, no children, all gone. One inch. Wilber still frozen, still standing there. Fifty-two years ago. He still remembered every second of it.

"Could have been worse," Wilber said to himself as he dug up another smile. His eyes focused again.

He'd been staring into the trees across the street. Hadn't noticed anybody come and go. Buses must have passed. But it didn't matter, he liked spending his time with Paula. He even liked being with her in those final moments. Yes, it could have been worse. He could have never known her in the first place. Imagine that, a life without Paula. A life without fifty-two years filled with shining memories. Not all peaches, those memories, but they sure had a way of looking more and more glorious as they passed into ancient history.

Paula.

It was raining now, cold and raining, late afternoon. There would be tea and crackers. And Frank would be in his wheelchair waiting by the door, waiting to play another losing round of chess. Time to head back to the home. Ninety-three feet, that one, from his bench at the bus stop to the entrance of the Eisenhower Memorial Veterans' Home. Ninety-three feet ... It would take him a while.

Wilber looked left, looked right. The street was deserted, nobody coming, nobody walking by. He'd walk back on his own, as always. Yes. It would take a while, but that didn't matter. It was his time, good time.

TIME

She watched Wilber 'The Champ' Patorkin from the window. Amazing, really, she thought. Every day, and goes nuts every time I try to give him a walker. The old man wouldn't even take a cane, nothing ... He should use one, at least the cane. But until he stumbled, she had no argument.

Amanda Griffin had been head nurse at EMV for seven years now. It was a good place, despite the ever-present scent of death in the building. They came here broken, they left here dead. But she was doing her best to make the place as pleasant as possible. She wasn't perfect, she wasn't a saint, she could be hard at times, she had to. But in all, she tried to make them feel good. The home was Nurse Griffin's pride and she personally took care that even the difficult cases felt good around here.

And it didn't just stop at the vets. She pampered the personnel, too. She made sure they felt like family - made sure they passed it on to the old guys. Amanda even made time for the plants, they needed talking to just like everybody else. That fichus in the back of the canteen, for instance. It needed attention, had lost leaves.

Amanda would find the time, later.

She was up on the seventh floor, her office, watching Wilber. He had already been here when she had taken over. And they had already called him Champ back then. The oldest living person in the State of New York.

Back then there still had been a woman in Florida, one hundred and eleven. Now? Now it was Wilber, country-wide. Wilber Patorkin, the US champion of age. Looking at him, she marveled. He was so slow, so incredibly slow. Probably ninety feet to the home, and that distance usually took him a good ten minutes. He didn't so much as walk anymore. It was more like a tiny shuffle, barely lifting his feet, pulling one just slightly ahead of the other. He'd always do about ten of these, in quick succession, then stop and take a breather. He had it down pat. The 'Wilber Shuffle', Amanda called it.

And Wilber had never stumbled once, yet.

Amanda always took the time to watch him leave for the stop and return to the home. There were two reasons for watching him. One, she wanted to make damn sure he never stumbled and ended up lying down there on the sidewalk without anybody running to his aid. And two, she loved this time. This was her time, watching Wilber. Personnel knew about it and would bite their tongues rather than disturb her.

Watching Wilber was like meditation to Amanda, a good time to think and let thoughts fly, a good time to breathe and breathe deep. There he was, shuffling closer, at times talking to himself, at times laughing out loud for no apparent reason. But there was nothing senile about Wilber Patorkin, Amanda knew just how sharp his mind was.

Despite his sometimes odd behavior, his jokes, his pranks, there was something resoundingly peaceful about him. Nothing she could put her finger on. But it was there. Wilber made her feel good. Just watching him made Amanda Griffin feel good.

LIFE

Good to be alive, Wilber thought.

"Great to be alive!" he suddenly shouted, scaring a lone pigeon into panicked flight. „Make noise", his father had said ages ago. For most of his life Wilber had misunderstood his father's wisdom. He had always thought he was supposed to make that noise to be heard, to be noticed, to be somebody.

The truth was, as always, so much simpler, so much closer to home. „Make noise, be loud", his father had never been concerned with what other people might have thought.

Aaron Patorkin had been a farmer in Bulgaria, in the time of kings. He had developed that particular piece of wisdom while working in the field. Sometimes he would simply stop, lean his head back and shout out loud - anything that came to mind. It had never been for anybody to hear him, or for anything he tried to communicate - he had shouted simply because it felt fabulous. The inside mattered, one self mattered.

Wilber closed his eyes and smiled. His memory could bring back any given moment of his long life. He could see everything, smell everything, feel everything, as if it was happening right this moment. Now he was watching a young boy and his father in the middle of a small field in Bulgaria. The wind strong and cold, the morning fog trying to cling to the ground. The sun breaking through. A father and his son leaning on their shovels, tilting their heads back, out-screaming each other. How they had laughed.

He set his feet in motion again. The home was in sight, the distance shrinking at snail's pace. Frank wasn't at the door yet, but he would be within moments. Frank ... Wilber decided then and there that this was going to be the day. Today he would tell his best friend.

Today he would tell him everything.

HOME

"Where the fuck you been?" Frank was waiting by the door, shifting in his wheelchair to give a fart some room.

Wilber smiled at him, shuffling past the rail guards by the entrance. He could grab the rail, of course, but he always made sure not to fall into that trap. Wilber had been walking, on his own, no help, for most of his one hundred and fifteen years now. It was a nice track record he planned to improve on for another while. Besides, he liked his arguments with Nurse Griffin, her trying to get him to use a cane. She had even tried a walker on him once. Wilber knew that she liked those arguments as much as he did. It wasn't really arguing between them, it was just good time spent in each other's company.

It took Wilber another minute to get past the rails and stop next to Frank.

"Bus stop," Wilber finally replied.

"What?" Same old routine.

Wilber continued his shuffle as Frank turned the chair and followed next to him. Wilber glanced at Frank. Yep. Today was the day to open the windows of the old-routine-house, let a little fresh air inside. Frank would always ask where he'd been and Frank would always pretend not to understand Wilber's mumbled reply. Things would be a little different today.

"What's it gonna be, Frank? Black or white?"

"Fuck you, I ain't no slave. You probably think I pick white, 'cause I got a problem being black. But this here is one proud nigger, proud to be black, you see? Even had them paint the chair black, see? So no, I ain't picking white - I pick black." Frank vigorously nodded to himself as he wheeled forward in slow-motion next to Wilber.

Wilber gave it a shrug.

"Good." It wasn't worth saying anything more about it. The truth was, Frank's wheelchair was black all right, Jerry the janitor had done him the favor, had spray-painted the whole thing, a nice and shiny black. Frank, on the other hand, was as pale as Wilber was, a regular whitey from Hammond, outside of New Orleans.

Frank had spent most of his life as a cop, chasing criminals in Louisiana, then later in San Francisco. And Frisco - Chinatown, to be exact - left parts of his brains scrambled. Frank didn't talk about it to anyone, and he had said just a few words to Wilber once, that Frank had 'gone after a mugger and that's where some things happened'. Frank's words.

Wilber knew more. He knew that Frank had gone missing for three weeks, then had come out of Chinatown a black man ... Wilber knew the whole story. He never mentioned it, though. He looked at Frank again. Good guy, Frank. The funny thing was that Frank actually was blacker than a lot of the other black men at the home.

Frank really was proud.

CHESS

Losing again. Frank knew it and it didn't matter.

Best time of the day. Sometimes he'd feel guilty for cursing Wilber's feet. He was so damn slow. All he wanted was for Wilber to get back to the entrance, get their thing going, their routine, talk, play, be. Best time of the day. Sometimes he'd curse that fuckin' bus stop, too. That place took up most of Wilber's day, took Wilber away from him.

"Check," Wilber muttered.

"What?" Neither man looked up from the board. Routine, good routine. "Why don't you put the gum in, Champ? 'Least I can understand you then. Know when I go down, know what I'm sayin'?"

"You understand everything I say, gum, dentures and words aside." Frank looked up at Wilber, who didn't take his eyes off the board. Frank cheated. He knew he never got away with it, but he tried all the same. It was part of the fun between them. But Frank had noticed that lately Wilber had to work harder at keeping an eye on him.

Wilber's eyes were still sharp, not glazed over as many of the other men's eyes were, but bright green. Startling green, people said. And yet Wilber was getting slower, and it made Frank uneasy. And, besides his worries about Wilber's health, cheating just wasn't as much fun if Wilber didn't catch him at it.

"What'd you say?" Frank couldn't help getting another one in there.

"I said 'Check' my friend."

Frank grunted and moved his king to safer waters. He wanted to beat Wilber someday, he would beat him someday. After all he was thirty years younger than Wilber. Thirty years. Jesus, Frank thought. I mean, I'm old, but Wilber ... thinking about it sent an icy jab into Frank's side. How much longer, Wilber? How much longer are you gonna live?

"About three months," Wilber answered to unspoken words.

∞

Boom. There it was, Wilber had done it. This would be fun, this would also be hard. Either way, he thought, he had to tell Frank sometime before he went. As always in life - the best time was now.

∞

Frank didn't look up, Wilber didn't look up. A silence like a winter's day dawning over a frozen pond.

Nothing moved.

It was as if nothing had happened. Any closely watching observer would have noticed just one little difference.

Frank didn't ask his usual 'What?'.

WHAT

Frank was watching the pieces on the board like he had never watched them before. His eyes were clinging to the sanity of those squares, that game where everything made perfectly logical sense. His mind was spinning.

Had Wilber just answered his thoughts? But that was crazy, absolutely fuckin' brain-fried-booby-hatch-crazy. Wilber made another move, but Frank wasn't paying attention, Frank didn't give a crap about chess right now. Frank was somewhere else, thinking hard. He had been wondering, just thinking to himself, goddamnit, just thinking about how much longer Wilber was gonna live. And then Wilber had said right out loud, "About three months". Like that, just like that ...

Nah, bullshit.

It was nothing, had to be. Frank probably misunderstood, it was almost impossible to make sense of Wilber's garble anyway. Misunderstood, yes, that was it. Or maybe it was just a stupid coincidence that got him freaked for no reason. Wilber had probably just commented on how long it took him to change his diapers these days - about three months.

Frank smiled, always keeping his eyes on the board. He moved his king again, frowning with fake concentration, moved away from another 'Check' he'd heard mumbled. He didn't have any dick problems, not Frank Wilkinson. He could piss all day if he felt like it and no white-coat was ever gonna put a diaper on his dick. He still had it, yeah, he could do Nurse Griffin anytime, anywhere, anything she wanted, if he could only -

"Frank, please. I'm trying to concentrate here."

Frank looked up now, straight at Wilber, who didn't seem to notice.

"What?" Frank said and all that cherished routine was gone from his voice. He glared at Wilber, glaring like a mad dog and shit-scared inside. "What the fuck did you say?"

"I said, I'm trying to concentrate, Frank. That's all. And with you day-dreaming about Nurse Griffin, it gets a little difficult, you know?" Wilber was still keeping his eyes on the board, but to Frank it looked as if Wilber was trying to keep from laughing out loud. Wilber moved his Queen again.

"Check."

Frank swiped the board, one sudden move, always staring at Wilber. The pieces, black and white, went flying across the hall. A few of the others looked up, but the heavy bulk stayed glued to a rerun of 'Wheel of Fortune'.

An orderly, Jerome Rudders, started picking up the pieces - Frank's temper was well known - and so the orderly calmly picked up the chess pieces as if this were happening all the time.

TRUTH

"Easy, Frank." Wilber was looking up now, looking into Frank's frightened eyes, suddenly realizing just how scared the big man in the wheelchair was. "It's okay."

"What's okay?" Frank said menacingly. Wilber got out a piece of gum, chewed it for a moment, then stuck it up onto the roof his dentures.

"I want to tell you a few things, my friend." He had taken his time placing gum and dentures, he was taking his time now, speaking at a leisurely pace. Frank needed time to get this.

"Yeah, you better tell me what the fuck is going on here. 'Cause I was just thinking, thinking to myself, man. Nothing you could have heard 'cause I was just thinking, you hear me now? This is me talking, that was me thinking before, nothing you could have heard, get me? So you go on and fuckin' tell me or I'm gonna shove your teeth with gum and all up your ass!"

This time everything stopped in the hall - nobody watching Vanna White's legs anymore, nobody staring blankly out the window. Time had stopped and Frank had made it so. He had been yelling at the top of his lungs, his head a deep purple, ready to explode. Every ancient set of eyes on him, even Jerome had stopped looking for the missing pieces, still on his hands and knees, staring to where Frank was sitting.

Wilber didn't say a word, he just looked at Frank and waited for him to breathe again, feel his pulse come down, let the searing blood drain from his head. Wilber knew his buddy, knew when it was time to continue. So he and Frank stared at each other for a full minute, then Frank nodded.

∞

"Alright, I'm calm. So tell me," Frank said quietly. He had realized all eyes on him - scanned the room - Vanna White clapping to no audience, Jerome on all fours, looking up at him like a confused puppy. Made a damn fool of myself, Frank thought. Keep it together, keep it together now, no matter what Voodoo-shit Wilber is gonna toss your way. I'm gonna stay calm, I'm gonna be strong, be proud, like a real man, a black man ... Man, if Wilber can read my brain ..., no, stop thinking.

Within moments most of the crowd had simmered back into their routine and dozed off again.

"I can hear people's thoughts," Wilber finally said.

How the fuck's that possible, Frank thought and before he could say it Wilber replied.

"How? I don't know. It just happened. I can't - "

"Don't you fuckin' do that! Stop reading my head, you hear!?" Frank could feel that he was heading into vein-popping-territory again.

"Sorry, Frank. Won't do it anymore. Promise, Scout's honor." Wilber made the sign and Frank couldn't help but smirk. "It started a few years back, maybe around a hundred and five, somewhere there. I just sort of broke some mold, I guess. So now I can hear people's thoughts, like yours, like Nurse Griffin, I just - "

"Griffin?" Frank had been listening, wide-eyed, but now a different interest glimmered behind his eyes. "You been checking the woman's mind?" Frank was grinning now.

"She's been thinking about you," Wilber said, returning the grin and doing a little Groucho Marx with his eyebrows.

Frank was stunned again, good stunned this time, as if suddenly seeing a whole new world before him. Frank was thinking about Nurse Griffin, all the things he'd imagined, all the places, Jesus H. Christ, maybe with Wilber's help he was gonna - ...

"You're not doing it right now, right?"

"Promised I wouldn't, didn't I?"

"Right, right. But how do I know, right? Ain't exactly like a bell going on in my head when you do it, right?" Frank was torn. He really wanted to hear about all this ... but Nurse Griffin passed by the door and his mind did a warp speed one-eighty that way again. Without a word Jerome walked up and carefully placed the chess pieces back onto the board.

"Thanks, Jerome," Frank said. "Sorry about the mess."

"No problem, Frank." Jerome nodded to both of them and casually walked off again.

∞

Wilber's smiling eyes followed Jerome and he listened into the young man without even realizing it. Chess, piece of cake. Bet I could beat Wilber if I wanted to. Wilber Patorkin - always smiles at me with that funny smile, like he knows something ... Whatever. Time to do the floors. Start on nine, work my way down, shit detail, no problem. Shit detail's clean compared to some of the stuff I ... before Nurse Griffin gave me this job.

Wilber waited until Jerome was a distance away.

"Frank, I don't have to listen to your mind to know what you're thinking about. I never had to do that. You're my friend, my best friend. I know you."

"Yeah I thought I knew you, too."

"You do, Frank. I'm the same old fart, same old Wilber Patorkin."

"Yeah right. Same old, with a few extras. The Champ reads minds, man ... Hey, what am I thinking right now?" Frank said with a sound of playful challenge.

"You asked me not to read your mind."

"You got permission for the moment." Frank's face closed down and Wilber realized with hidden amusement that Frank was trying to go blank, trying not to think of anything at all. So Wilber played along, his face showing a sudden strain, seemingly getting more and more frustrated.

"Ha! Reading minds - can't beat this black mind. I got the power," Frank said gleefully. Then his face slowly sagged as Wilber's voice spoke inside his head.

"We'll have to work on your telepathic barriers, my friend. You wanted to know if I could hear your thoughts.

Well, you're not making it very hard. Nurse Griffin, Frank, Nurse Amanda Griffin. You're wondering if I - "

"Shit!" Frank gaped at Wilber.

"I can't just hear other people's thoughts, I can also talk to anyone I wish. And you can talk to me, of course. Say something, Frank. Give it a try."

"I don't - I think, I - " the words kept coming from Frank's mouth. He was greatly frowning, trying to force his head to project thoughts.

"Frank, relax. It's as easy as thinking. Just think to me, simple as that," Wilber's mind said.

∞

They were just sitting there now, not even playing chess, just looking at each other. To any set of interested eyes they appeared to be two old men, two vegetables, just waiting for someone to bring them back to their beds, tuck them in for their nap. Yet Frank was thinking furiously.

" ... I ... can't ... how the fuck, this is bullshit, I mean ... come on, Frank, can't be that hard, can't. Hey, Wilber! You hear me? This shit ain't working. Wilber!" Frank thought as loud as he could.

Wilber smiled broadly.

"No need to shout, my friend. I can hear you loud and clear."

"You heard me?" Frank said inside and a bright glow started spreading across his face. "Holy Mother - we can just talk like this and nobody knows about it? Man - I mean, Man! This is fuckin' great, Wilber! So can I read minds, too?"

Wilber shook his head. "Maybe later, maybe in your next life ... whenever you're ready for it, Frank." Then Frank, without noticing it, switched back to using his voice.

"Figures. Frank Wilkinson's not ready. Damn. Still, I think you and me we're gonna have lots of fun with this."

"So, what do you want to know about Nurse Griffin?" Wilber said. Two regular old guys at the chess table again, just sitting there, just talking. Frank looked around, a bit uncomfortable about this.

"She's really been thinking about me?" Frank said quietly, his voice no more than a whisper.

Wilber simply nodded.

Jesus, Frank thought. What if she has the hots for me, what if I actually ever get the chance to ... Man, it's probably twenty, fuck that, thirty years since I last soaked my ...

"So what's she thinking about me?"

"To tell you the truth, I've been trying to tune her out," Wilber said with a straight face. "Some of the stuff is just plain disgust - "

"What does she think about me, asshole!?" Frank was loud and laughing now, having fun with this.

"You know the couch in her office?"

Frank nodded eagerly.

"That's where she's been thinking of spending a little time with you."

"Time?"

"Yep. Quality time, as they say," Wilber said with a massively exaggerated double-wink.

"You shittin' me, right?" Frank's joy suddenly evaporated. "What the fuck are we talking about here. I'm a cripple, man. I'm an old cripple. I can move my dick, but that's about it."

"Doesn't seem to worry her."

Frank was eyeing Wilber inquisitively. "How does it work, Champ? Do you hear her speak? Do you see pictures she makes up in her head?"

"It's different every time. Sometimes it's just images, sometimes simply words, sometimes I get colors or smells. And sometimes I get the works, everything. But, to calm your worries, my friend - no, I did not see you and Nurse Griffin doing the wild thing on the couch." Frank had gripped the rail of his chair, gripped it painfully tight. He let go and rubbed his hands. "I just know," Wilber continued calmly, "that she's been thinking about it. I know she's wondering about you. I know she wants to get to know you better."

"Shit. Wants to get to know me better. Get to the interesting part. What about the couch?"

"That, too, my friend. That, too."

∞

Wilber sighed with hidden relief when he knew Frank to be all right again. Wilber's 'thing' wasn't troubling him anymore, at least not for now. Frank didn't even think about it, he was busy thinking Amanda Griffin thoughts.

A picture drifted across Wilber's mind. Frank and Nurse Griffin walking hand in hand through the park, fall leaves moving, all beautiful colors.

"You should go up and see her, see what happens," Wilber said casually.

"Yeah right, fuck that. What I'm going up there, roll on the couch and say 'Hi there Nurse Griffin I heard you wanted to hump my wiener so here I am let's do it', that what you want me to do?"

"You may want to try a slightly different approach," Wilber said with a gentle smile. "Maybe try talking a little first. About the weather, for example. The weather topic is highly underrated, you know. Talk about climate, talk about spring. Get to know each other. Let it happen."

"Get to know each other, my ass. I just wanna jump her bones, that's all. Not like I wanna marry her."

"Actually, Frank, you do." Frank's dark eyes instantly narrowed. Deep, angry lines frowned across the bridge of his nose. Wilber lightly raised a hand in defense. "I didn't peek. It's just something I heard you think a while back. Sometimes I hear stuff without listening, just happens. Sorry."

Without listening in Wilber knew exactly what was going on with Frank. He felt caught, felt like he had just admitted a crime. The crime of an eighty-five year old man having feelings, thinking romance.

"I'm an eighty-five year old barely breathing fart-vessel in a wheelchair - there's no way in heaven or hell. Let's play another game," Frank, said, closing the Nurse Griffin subject. "I'm gonna beat your wrinkled butt this time." Frank moved his rook, waited. But Wilber kept looking at him and Frank got more and more uneasy. "Your move," Frank said gruffly.

But Wilber didn't move, and he didn't do Frank the pleasure of taking his eyes off him.

"You're worried about your age, Frank? I didn't hear you worry about your eighty-five years when it came to carnal pleasures on the couch. If you think you can handle that, then you can surely handle a little conversation with the lady." Wilber made his counter-move.

Frank moved his second rook, silently.

"Okay. What the hell ... Maybe I'll go up tomorrow," he finally grumbled. Wilber mirrored Frank's move.

"Why waste time? She'll be up there after dinner. End of the month paper work, I bet she would love a little distraction."

Frank's hand was hovering over the pieces ... He finally grabbed a knight and moved it into the open field.

"That's a bold move," Wilber said.

"Fuck you ... Champ."

They played on and Frank lost, nothing had changed and everything had changed. Routine or no routine, good time. Very good time, Frank thought and Wilber lightly nodded without realizing it.

FOOD

Nowadays he was mostly slurping his food, but sometimes Wilber didn't go for the soups. He couldn't stand leek and Thursday was leek. Wilber had taken the steak and should have known better. He looked around, his eyes wandering from one familiar face to the next, while his hands were absently working to cut the rock-solid mass they called 'steak' into tiny, baby-sized bites.

Chewing wasn't exactly his strong side anymore and Wilber decided that what he'd really like was astronaut food. He'd seen a documentary with John Glenn sucking on a tube once. Full meals in those tubes ... He'd love a juicy steak in a tube. NASA should start supplying homes, that'd be the smart thing to do.

Frank was sitting next to him, staring straight ahead but digging into his food. Frank didn't have Wilber problems. Frank still had a set of bright and strong teeth on him. Enviable. And not just the teeth. Most of Frank was still in amazing shape. Anybody guessing his age was always off by about twenty years. Just the legs. But he was still tall sitting in that chair, still broad in the chest, still full in his voice ...

Frank. Frank was a nervous wreck right now and it didn't take a mind reader to figure that much.

They were eating in silence. Frank didn't seem to remember Wilber's comment ... "About three months," Wilber had said. Then their whole conversation had ended up being about telepathy and Nurse Griffin.

Wilber's comment completely forgotten.

He could have given Frank a great deal more to chew on. It's wasn't 'about' three months - it was exactly three months, to the day. Three months from now Wilber was going to die. He knew this with perfect certainty. It was as certain as his name was Wilber Patorkin, it was as clear as the icy sky, it was as solid as the steak in front of him. Three more months worth, that was all that remained of Wilber's life.

Wilber knew a great many things. Simple facts he had learned. He wanted to share them with Frank, wanted to tell him about his answers to some of the big questions. The simplicity, the beauty of it all. The many lives, the learning stages, the final life. The chosen ones would reach that final life. But the many were bound to return and return and return... Wilber was one of these 'chosen few'.

The final life... "I'm happy, I'm wonderful, yeah, yeah, yeah," Wilber thought, continuing to cut the steak, ant-sized bites by now. "I know I've reached that point. I know the final place will be more beautiful than anything even I can imagine ... everything, perfection ... but I don't want to go."

Wilber stopped chewing. He was straining to hear, waiting for a reply, any reply, from the final place. From all those that had gone before him. But in truth he knew quite well that there wouldn't be a reply. Wilber's path was clear, nothing anybody could do about it. Three months. Then he would die, then he would move on.

He would tell Frank later. In time it would come back to Frank anyway. Right now the man had enough to deal with. Give him a break. Wilber crossed some mental fingers for Frank and Amanda.

Wilber proceeded to gulp down a bit of ridiculously overcooked meat. It got stuck and made him cough. Frank quickly wheeled around the table and slapped him on the back, hard.

"You okay, Champ?"

"I was, until you hit me." Frank grinned and continued chewing away. For a second Wilber was thinking about leaving the rest of his food ... just for a second, then he continued. He had eaten worse, a lot worse and a lot less.

The American Expeditionary Force, they had called it. Wilber remembered how awestruck he had been back then. Now it just sounded quaint. What did they think they were, a bunch of happy campers heading out for a weekend fishing trip? Wilber had signed up immediately, had felt it was his duty.

∞

World War I twisted Europe into a tight knot. Wilber and two million like him were sent in to stir up what had become a swamp of trampled dirt and dark blood. Private Wilber Patorkin was with the 167th, Infantry - the first Americans to engage the Germans. Battle of St. Mihiel, September 1918.

He was hugging trenches for most of the time. Life was expiring all around Wilber - Jack Henderson, 'French' Perrone, Charles 'Joker' Willis. They were outside Vigneulles, stuck in a trench, seven feet deep, three wide. Every wave going out dropped a stack of bodies back in. Wilber didn't even get a chance to crawl out, he kept getting buried under dead weight. Henderson stared at him with a gaping hole where his eye had been a moment ago. Joker, the guy from Coney, was up on the ridge, jerking back and forth like a marionette as bullets riddled his chest. The bullets kept on coming and Joker just kept on standing there, moving with them, hanging on invisible strings.

"Look at that, Joker's still funny," Wilber blankly said to himself. It was as if he were someplace else, someplace nice and quiet and peaceful. This wasn't happening. Then he threw up with nothing left to throw up. The Germans suddenly called for another halt, the gunfire died and Joker fell and landed next to Wilber. All wrong angles.

Four days later they had won the battle.

But Wilber never heard about it. He caught two bullets, one in the side, one in the arm, as soon as he finally made it onto the field. He started running and started killing.

Wilber jumped over the enemy trenches, and kept on running, and kept on killing. It was as if he, too, had strings that moved him. But these strings weren't holding him in place as they had held Joker Willis before, Wilber's strings were racing him forward. As if some higher force were propelling him past death, through madness and right into glory.

Troops saw him charge and followed Private Patorkin to resounding victory. But it took the Allied Forces three weeks to get to where Wilber had finally ended up.

The platoon that found Wilber reported him sitting peacefully outside a bombed-out chapel in an open field. According to the report he had been living off roots and grass and whatever else had been able to get his hands on. Apparently he hadn't been able to move anymore, had lost more blood than should have been possible. The medics took him back and declared him a miracle. Not only should he have been dead, his recovery was doubly remarkable. Just five days after they picked him up, Wilber was fine … just fine.

His wounds healed at an amazing pace … and there was not a scratch on his soul. Wilber Patorkin refused the trip home. So they made him Captain and pinned a few medals on him.

∞

Since then, Wilber had never missed another meal and had never left a crumb. Food. Three weeks of freezing and bleeding and starving. Wilber loved food, cherished it.

Wilber was still sitting in the dining hall when most of them had left. He hadn't even felt them go. Memories. Even Frank had gone, probably wheeling back and forth at the elevator, working up the courage to go up to the 7th floor. Wilber would probably join the gang for another exciting episode of 'Fierce Animals' on the Discovery Channel. But first he would sit here by himself and finish the rest of the cold steak.

LOVE

"Ridiculous, absolutely fuckin' ridiculous," Frank mumbled. He was pacing in his chair, back and forth, back and forth by the elevator. The vegetables were coming and going and they were giving him that look. 'What's wrong with you?' Frank was certain he could hear them thinking it, could hear one of them whispering it.

"Mind your own damn business," he spat. Frank glared and stared them down, all of them. He could kick their asses and he would. "What're you staring at," he exclaimed again.

He continued pacing and feeling plain stupid. Eighty-five years of living and he'd learned nothing. Nothing at all. Here he was, feeling like a damn kid. Feeling like watching Wilma Belle again, he twelve, she fourteen. He would never forget Wilma Belle.

Taking a bath back at the creek. She had been something and she would always be the one great first love for Frank. Wilma Belle. Damned if he wasn't sure, to this day, that she had planned the whole thing. That she had known about him walking by the bend of the creek on his way home. But she had pretended not to see him and Frank had felt hotter than he had ever felt in twelve years of life. She had known, absolutely. Young Frank had felt guilty for a month after, hadn't even been able to look at her anymore. But she'd smiled at him, every time she passed by the drugstore, smiling, always smiling. A hot summer, and every Friday she had gone for a swim in the creek. And of course Frank had returned and had watched her, hidden behind the bush, feeling that way again. Hoping, dreaming of something unknown, something more.

"Hey, Frank. You going up? I gotta go up." Jerome the orderly was patiently looking down at him.

Frank felt embarrassed, weak for a second. He had to get the damn thing over with. He simply had to or Wilber would nag him to death.

"Yeah, I'm going up."

OPEN

The elevator doors closed slowly, creaking, slowing down. The two sides strained and tried to touch like desperate lovers ... Then they stopped. Jerome was outside on the 4th now, Frank inside, frowning out at him. The young orderly had been walking away, but the creaking doors had stopped him.

"Close the damn thing, will you?" Frank said.

"Sure, Frank." The big man in the wheelchair looked rattled, nervous. Jerome couldn't help wondering. Frank would be loud, Frank would go nuts at times, but Frank was the man, Frank never opened his face like that. It was open now, like these doors, with a big sign on Frank's forehead reading, 'Scared Shitless'.

Jerome put his hands to the doors, stepped back, feet spread wide and his weight pushing the doors inwards and together. Jerome hated standing like this, reminded him of things he didn't want to be reminded of, but this was the trick Jerry the janitor had shown him. This was how the doors would, eventually, slide back into the groove. Jerome pushed hard. Kept on pushing, and kept on looking at Frank inside.

"You okay there, Frank?"

"Yeah I'm okay, sure I'm okay, I like sitting in here in this miserable box of doom old enough the wires are probably gonna snap any second. Yeah I love spending a little time in here, Jerome. I got nothing else to do. Now close the fuckin' door, you moron!"

Jerome could see how sorry the old man was, regretting the sudden outburst.

And Jerome was hit with the strangest sensation ... somehow he could feel, he could almost read what was going on inside Frank's head now.

∞

'Sorry about that, Jerome. It isn't you, it's me. I'm just so fuckin' nervous about talking up Nurse Griffin. I got the hots for the lady, you know.' ... Come on, Frank, say something to the kid. Strange kid, this Jerome. Look at him fighting the door, pushing, sweating. I call him a moron and he doesn't even blink, as if he hasn't heard.

∞

Jerome felt his arms beginning to tremble under the strain, sweat on his forehead now. He kept pushing against the doors, he liked the feeling. Now he lightly shook his head, as if trying to get rid of a bee buzzing near his ear. What he hell, Jerome thought. He had heard Frank's voice, hadn't he? Frank thinking about Nurse Griffin? Jerome shook his head again, shook himself free of the uneasy experience.

Bullshit, he hadn't heard a thing. It was just that he knew Frank Wilkinson, knew him without really knowing him. He knew that the old man didn't want to be seen like this, rattled, nervous. Frank needed to be strong and now he couldn't get away from Jerome's eyes, couldn't even turn away in the box. He was stuck in the elevator with

Jerome looking in. Jerome felt bad for Frank, but he couldn't stop now. He was where he needed to be, his hands in place, pushing still.

The left door gave way with a crunch as it snapped back into the groove, then the right door followed. Jerome could see Frank looking for words, trying for something. Jerome lifted his hand and smiled, then the doors touched. He stood there for another moment, watching the numbers go up and stop on 7th.

"Going up to see Nurse Griffin?" Jerome wondered.

Then he continued down the hallway, shit detail. He would be done by midnight, then catch a movie maybe. A movie, right. That would clear his head. He shook his head again and decided that he had definitely not experienced anything out of the ordinary just now.

He had not heard Frank Wilkinson think. No.

Shit like this didn't happen.

WAIT

Frank realized that he kept getting slower and slower the closer he got to her office. As if he were wheeling against the pull of a gigantic rubber band, slower and slower. Soon it would be extended to a tight line, soon the rubber band would propel him back down the hall with full force.

She was sixty-three, he knew. She was a goddamn spring chicken compared to him. He could still turn around, yes, he could still turn around. Let the rubber band of fear take him back to his room. Don't think about Amanda, think about something else.

How about Jerome? What the fuck had that smile been about? He had called Jerome a moron and got a smile and a wave for it. The kid was something, special. For just a fleeting moment Frank wondered about Jerome being a damn mind-reader like Wilber. "Nah, just a smart kid," he nodded to himself. Jerome had simply understood what was going on with Frank, just by looking at him. Wise for his age, wiser than Frank, that was for damn sure.

And then he came to a stop in front of Amanda Griffin's office. The door loomed like the gigantic fuckin' massive portals of Nôtre Dame. Paris, man, if this was then, WWII, he would stride right in there and ... but it wasn't. This was it, this was now. Frank, eighty-five, about to act like some lovesick puppy.

"Damn," he whispered, shaking his head.

It took a moment for her to open the door after Frank had knocked a shy one. He had waited, part of him fervently hoping she wouldn't hear. Hey, maybe she wasn't in. He could go away then, he could leave with an excuse then. But now here she was, looking at him, her eyes lighting up at the sight of him. Glorious Amanda. Frank's pump skipped a few beats.

"Oh, hi Frank. What's up?" Frank suddenly realized that she seemed in a hurry, that she seemed shaken ... and that she didn't open the door all the way. Looked like she wasn't going to let him in.

"Hiya, Nurse Griffin. Nothing, you know ... just came up for a chat. You know, weather and stuff." Ah, Christ. He was losing steam fast. The door still didn't open, she didn't want him here. Shit. Why had he come here in the first place? Fuckin' Wilber. Goddamn fuckin' Wilber.

"That's great, Frank, glad you found your way up here. Listen, I'm on the phone right now. But I won't be long so please wait right here, all right?" She was smiling, but the smile seemed just a paper-thin layer covering a rock of sadness. She labored to keep the light tone in her voice, she even managed to add a sly smile as she added "Then we'll talk. About the weather and stuff. You'll wait, right? Thank you, Frank."

Gone.

Frank was staring at the closed door.

This was good, right? This was a good thing, right? She asking him in, all happy to see him and all? But then she hadn't been happy, Frank had seen through that. She had been pleading for him to stay ... pleading ... what the hell was going on here. Still, she wanted him here. All he had to do was wait a little. Oh shit, would have been so much easier if she'd just brushed him off.

"Sorry Frank, no time for chatting, I'm a busy woman you know, gotta run this place." But she hadn't done him that favor. Frank sighed, parked his chair next to the door and waited.

SHIT

Some of them just couldn't get out of bed anymore. Shit and urine all over the sheets with them sleeping and never feeling a thing. Jerome didn't have the training to be a real nurse. But Nurse Griffin had given him a shot.

"Do this, do it well," she had said, "and I'll get you there. If you want to help people, if you really want to help people, then this a great place to be."

Jerome had woken Anton Tamo because Tamo was capable. So he had woken him and told him to go wipe his ass. Told him nicely, of course. Jerome never got mean, Jerome never got hot anymore.

Now he heard the old man singing in the bathroom.

The song was something Russian, something sweet. The old man always did that. It was Tamo's way of apologizing to Jerome. He would have told Tamo not to worry, not be embarrassed, but Jerome loved the melancholy melodies coming from the can. In that respect, Anton Tamo messing up the sheets was a good thing.

Every shitter dealt with it differently. Some of them cursed Jerome, others cried like babies. And then there were the pretenders, those who pretended to sleep and those who pretended that nothing had happened. Jerome shook his head and smiled at the thought of it. Guys staring at their own shit and saying, "What? What? I don't see nothing."

One time he'd gone with it and said, "Hey, what do you know. You're right, there's nothing there, my mistake.

Sorry about that." Then turned and made like he was leaving. It hadn't taken the old man a second to shriek and proclaim that his neighbor had shat in his bed out of pure malice.

The Russian voice was still going, unbelievably tender for a body as old and raw as Tamo's. He must have wiped his butt three times over by now. Now he was probably just sitting on the can, lid closed, singing, staying in there until Jerome said goodbye through the door and left.

Jerome dumped the soiled sheets in the cart, then pulled a fresh one over the plastic. He took pride in getting the bed nice and sharp just like Nurse Griffin had shown him. Crisp, straight folds. Clean.

Jerome was done. For a moment he just stood, staring at the white sheets, lost in the melody from a country he knew nothing about. Then again he knew Tamo ... that was something. After a beat he fished a candy in a red wrapper from his coat pocket, put it gently on Tamo's pillow. Like his mother had always done, working at the hotel. She had always brought him those special little pillow chocolates, well knowing they'd fire her if they caught her taking as much as a speck of dust from the place. She had done it anyway, for her baby, for her Jerome.

Jerome frowned and pushed that thought aside. Gotta go. No time to hang like this. More beds needed to be changed, more butts needed to be wiped. Gotta go. He almost left without giving Tamo his cue.

"You have a good evening, Mr. Tamo." Then closed the door loud enough for Tamo to hear.

∞

The singing continued as Anton Tamo opened the bathroom door. He was a haggard man, tall, all skin and bones. Still singing gently, he looked around the room and spotted the candy on the bed. Anton Tamo smiled. He hobbled to the pillow, took the candy and started unwrapping it carefully with his shaking fingers. And all the while he sang his song, soft, sweet and sad. It was a song from another time, another place he remembered so well. Odessa, sweet Odessa. And Tamo could feel the wind rolling in from the Black Sea. His tongue licked the imagined salt from his lips. Then, when he finished his song, he gingerly placed the candy behind his lower teeth. It would stay there and slowly disintegrate. Strawberry. Thank you, Jerome. Anton Tamo sat down on the bed, his hand feeling the comforting starch of the clean sheets, his eyes staring blankly into the trees outside his window. Strawberry. Lovely.

COLORS

It wasn't true anymore. Wilber was stretched out on his bed, fully dressed, eyes closed. It used to be just like he had told Frank. He'd hear thoughts sometimes, not precise, they would come and go. But not anymore. Now there were many. Now Wilber worked it his way, at his pace. It used to just happen, he'd hear thoughts, just like that. Now he could turn it on and off, like a radio.

It had knocked him flat the first time it had happened, literally. The rent had gone up and Wilber, unable to afford it, had ended up here. He'd been one hundred and five years old upon his arrival at the home and he had not been the Champ then. There had been no champ at that time, there had been Donnermann. Harold Donnermann, a grim looking, cantankerous Kraut - a man with nothing left going for himself other than his one hundred and six years. Wilber remembered him well.

∞

"One hundred and six."

Harold Donnermann told everybody close enough to hear. And he was prepared to make sure his record wasn't challenged. When Wilber Patorkin walked into the home that day, he was introduced to everybody. Among them a man with the red eyes of a white rat.

"And this, Wilber, this is Harold Donnermann. Hi, Harold!" the male nurse shouted with a fake smile. "This is Wilber Patorkin!"

"One hundred and six," Harold croaked.

"Harold is the oldest man in the State of New York, you know?" The nurse eagerly nodded to Wilber, wondering if the new guy had heard him since he didn't show much of a reaction.

"One hundred and six." Harold said again and looked Wilber up and down, red eyes glowing, menacing. "How old are you?"

"One hundred and five. Practically a baby compared to you." A bit of light conversation, Wilber thought. But Harold Donnermann didn't say a word. He just stared into Wilber's eyes with pure clean-as-a-bone white-hot hatred … and then it hit Wilber.

"You fucking bastard! You will not beat me. Never, you hear!? If it's the last thing I do I'll stick a needle in your neck. My record, mine, mine, mine. It's all I got, you understand?! It's all I'll ever be, my record, my name in the goddamn book. Mine, not yours. And look at how healthy you are - I won't have it, I can't have it. Don't you understand?! Don't be here, don't be alive!"

The fake-smile nurse next to Wilber was beginning to wonder about the silence, but kept the eager smile in place, well knowing Donnermann's temper. Harold Donnermann hadn't spoken a word, not a single word. And then Wilber fell flat on his butt, simply sagged and fell, like that. The nurse rushed to help him up again.

"Are you okay, Mr. Patorkin? Here, let me help you. Take my arm …"

Wilber didn't hear a word the nurse said, he just let it happen. He was helped up and walked away from rat-face. He did look back once or twice and saw the red eyes follow him all the way. Wilber had heard him speak. He had heard him speak! But nothing, not a sound had come from the man's mouth. And he wasn't a ventriloquist either, nobody else had heard the verbal assault on Wilber. It was as if it hadn't happened. But Wilber knew, he saw the unspoken words confirmed in those glowing crimson eyes. Donnermann had spoken all right, just not out loud. But the words were there and Wilber had heard the outcry of a lost soul.

Three months after that Wilber had already become comfortable with picking up bits and pieces of thoughts here and there. By then he had also learned how to best avoid Donnermann. The man hadn't lied, he truly did want to kill him. It drove Donnermann mad, nothing worked. Every time he picked up a needle, Patorkin had left the building. Every time he dumped rat poison on Patorkin's dessert, the guy said he wasn't hungry anymore. Nothing worked, like the man could read his mind. It didn't just drive Donnermann mad, it drove him straight to his final heart attack. Harold Donnermann never got past his one hundred and six. Wilber recalled not feeling all too bad about the news of his would-be killer's timely death.

∞

These days it was colors, words still, but all of them wrapped in colors, bright images in colors his eyes had never seen. Wilber soon realized that this could drive him around the bend, if he didn't get a handle on it. And he did. Like a radio.

Switch it on, and he'd hear the guys downstairs watching TV, zoning, their thoughts barely registering. On, and he'd hear a waiter cursing his customers, table seven, mushrooms, peppers and sausage, "Bitch with the Fawcett hair, changes her pea-brain mind every two seconds, next time I'll - ". Wilber could switch to different 'people stations' as easily as turning a dial. "I can't go on, I can't, please, please let it stop. I can't - ". Hurling thoughts with tremendous intensity, a woman giving birth, Wilber figured. And there was Anton Tamo dreaming about Odessa, his mind always back there. And Jerome trying to keep his mind a blank, and Jerry the janitor in the basement, thinking about another invention. Wilber could listen to a thousand voices at once, beautiful symphonies, like the ocean surf crashing against his mind. He could create almost unbearably brilliant canvasses of words that would have left Monet speechless. And, when he wished, Wilber could focus, zone in, concentrate, one voice, one mind.

Switch it off, and he'd hear nothing. Sometimes Wilber wondered how Frank and every other human being could live with that nothing, with that great desert of the mind. And sometimes he envied them. They were protected. Protected from hearing the other side. Because there was more than beauty. Wilber was constantly aware of unspeakable things, things more evil than most people could imagine. But that, too, was part of the symphonies of colors.

Enough. Wilber closed his eyes and within seconds was deep asleep.

WILMA

Frank had never seen her bathe again. The waiting, the hope against hope, had been sheer anguish for the boy - twelve years old, feeling like Greek tragedy. He found out a week later that she'd moved away, all the way to Biloxi and Biloxi might as well have been another planet. His heart broke to jagged little bits and pieces, he'd never be able to put it together again. No glue could fix it, no way.

Then Frank grew up and Alma Gordon's love made him whole again. They got married right after he graduated from the academy. Those blessed years with Alma and the two girls. They had loved moving to Frisco, Frank moving up the ladder, a big city cop now.

He should have never gone on that trip to Biloxi in the first place, just wanted to check out a lead. Overeager. Frank had nothing to do with the case. But the girl got raped on his beat, so he made it his case. He had beaten the crap out of Dinky and the little rat had squealed, with eyes darting, no way out. Frank got what he wanted, he got a name and a place. Nobody was gonna rape on his beat and get away with it.

He hooked up with a cop in Biloxi, Mike what's-his-name, hoping the guy would open a few doors. Now he was here, sitting in this fuckin' bar. Nothing happening, he wasn't even close to the perp. Mike had taken him to a bunch of bars. "Let's check on some leads," he'd said with a grin Frank would have loved to slap from his face. WW2 was over, everybody was busy feeling good. Nights on the town were happy jungles, were nobody killed nobody. Everybody was high and wild on victory. And the prick next to him was celebrating the fact that his wife was in the hospital with a severe concussion.

"She fell off the goddamn verandah, can you fuckin' believe it? See what I gotta put up with?" Mike looked up at the ceiling then. "Thank you Lord for taking her off my hands for a few. I promise to make the most of it."

Real funny - the guy had been plastered three shots back but kept going. Frank sighed and decided it was time to head back to Hammond. That was when she tapped Mike what's-his-name on the shoulder.

"Hiya doin', Sailor?" She didn't look at Frank, she didn't see him stare. She was busy spinning the drunk, getting him to make his move. She wouldn't have to wait long, Mike was drooling all over her. Wilma Belle didn't look fourteen anymore. She tried to look like Marlene Dietrich instead, acting all sultry like she had a thousand men waiting in line and didn't care about any one of them. But this Marlene Dietrich looked old beyond her years, make-up all over the place, dark rings under her eyes like lumps of coal pulling her face down. Frank couldn't help staring at Wilma Belle ... his Wilma Belle.

With terrified fascination he watched her work. He knew the standard plan. She looked bored and didn't even bother to hide it. She'd take her john out into the alley and blow him good. A drunk like this one would probably crumble right after the spill, his knees would give, he'd sag and sit against the wall. Wilma would wait a second or two, give him a shove, then roll him. Standard. Now she casually turned to Frank, to check this next potential maybe, another money bag.

∞

The drunk's buddy looked at Wilma as she turned - and she saw him stare as if she were a ghost or something. Then the guy snapped his head around, away from her, much too fast, and stared into the mirrors behind the bar. What was his problem? ... then the memory of the boy by the creek flooded her.

"Frank!" she wanted to yell but not a sound came out.

It was Frank. Oh dear God no. Frank from back then, little innocent Frank. He was a big man now, still those open eyes. That's how she'd suddenly recognized him. Frank was still looking away, like she didn't exist. And she didn't exist. Wilma Belle was dead. She was Kitty now, she was Whatever-you-want-Kitty, Kitty would take care of you.

Don't look away, Frank, please don't. I'm still here, I'm in here somewhere.

∞

Screaming inside. Frank stared good and hard at every customer through the mirror, tried hard to identify their drinks, guess their age, height, shoe-size. Still screaming inside, run, Frank, run, but his body was paralyzed. Just looking away, just pretending not to notice. He tried his hardest to convince himself that it couldn't be her, but he knew better. He wanted to look, wanted to speak.

"Hi Wilma, how you been? So, you're a hooker now. Good, good for you, good business. Don't look at me like that, I mean it. Me, I'm a cop so I know about these things. Jesus it's good to see you, remember the creek?" Not a word, couldn't even get his head to turn in her direction. His mind was still screaming. What happened, what the fuck could have happened between then and now?

Mike was staggering toward the back door now, pulling Wilma with him. She was just walking, no resistance, but she kept looking back, kept her eyes on Frank. Frank watched their reflection in the mirror behind the bar.

His shirt was drenched in sweat as Frank stepped into the alley a moment later. Mike was out there, leaning against the wall, eyes closed. And Wilma Belle was on her knees, about to go to work.

"Wilma Belle," Frank said quietly.

She slowly turned her head.

"Don't know nobody by that name."

Frank took a few steps into the alley, lit up a smoke. He forced himself into a mask of calm, but it was tearing him up inside. Mike was still leaning against the wall and Wilma wasn't making any attempt at getting off her knees. This was definitely Wilma Belle, not a doubt on Frank's mind.

"I thought I recognized you, sorry. You remind me of a girl I once knew back in Hammond. You ever been to Hammond?"

Wilma just stared at him. Mike opened his eyes and looked around blankly.

"Hey lady, you done? I didn't feel a damn thing. Hey, hiya Frankie, what the fuck you doing back here? You wanna piece of this?"

Frank slowly walked up to him, softly put his hand on the drunk's forehead, and then slammed it back against the wall. Mike didn't make a sound going down, he'd sleep it off in the alley. Frank held out his hand to help Wilma get up. She took a few bills from Mike's wallet, then got up on her own.

"I'm a cop, you know."

"So is he, so what." She dusted off her knees, straightened her clothes and headed toward the light of the street.

"Can I buy you a cup of coffee?"

"You don't know me," she simply said.

"Can I buy you a cup of coffee anyway?"

Wilma stopped at the corner, but she didn't turn.

"No."

Then she stepped into the light and Frank saw her profile, saw his Wilma Belle again, he twelve, she fourteen. Frank's heart in furious pain.

"Bye, Wilma Belle." She stood still for a moment.

"Bye, Frank."

She didn't look at him, didn't smile ... and then she was gone. Frank thought about running after her, but he knew it wasn't the right thing to do. Respect it, Frank. Leave it. Go catch that rapist. Wilma Belle was gone.

HOPE

Frank had found the perp. That night a vague tip had turned out to be gold. He had beaten the rapist's face into a bloody mess of skin and broken bones until they had pulled him off the limp body. Beating the crap out of that guy had meant beating the crap out of every John who ever laid hands on Wilma Belle. After that he had gone back home to Alma and the kids, got the collar and a few days off.

∞

What the fuck was Nurse Griffin doing on the phone for this long? How long had he been waiting here anyway, making a damn fool of himself. He suddenly got the image of a dog on a leash, the leash around a parking meter outside a Korean grocery place. The dog was waiting, patiently, wagging its tail at every friendly face.

"Fuck that," Frank muttered and wheeled off.

"Frank!" The door had opened and Amanda was running out. "I'm sorry, Frank. I'm sorry you had to wait. But I ... I ..." Frank had never seen her like this, she must have cried in there. She wiped another rolling tear from her cheek. Frank felt like an asshole again ... that seemed to happen a lot recently.

"What happened?"

"My dad just died, less than an hour ago. I've been talking to my mother all this time, just talking. I ..."

"I'm sorry."

"Thank you, Frank. So, how about our little talk?"

Frank looking up at her in disbelief.

"Now? We can do this some other time - "

"Frank. I'd love your company, especially now. You may have to keep me supplied with tissues, though." She started heading back to her office, turned and looked back at Frank, smiling, inviting. "Are you coming?"

Oh boy. Frank set his wheels in motion and caught up. Side by side they moved down the hall. Frank's mind was reeling. Talk, dummy, talk, be supportive, say something, come on. "What'd he die of? Your dad?" Frank slapped himself silly internally.

"Just old age. It was his time, that's all."

"So how old was he?"

"Eighty-four."

Frank fought with all his might not to get out of his chair and run like hell. He was pretty sure his legs would carry him right now. Eighty-five year old raisin chatting up lady who's eighty-four year old father had just died of old age. What the fuck was he thinking!? Nurse Griffin opened the door for him, smiling that smile.

"Come on in, Frank, make yourself at home."

Frank wheeled inside.

The door closed.

Oh boy.

NIGHT

Sharp. Razor sharp. The scream pierced his dreams. Wilber's eyes snapped open. Darkness, middle of the night, in his bed. Wilber couldn't feel his feet, couldn't feel his arms for a moment. At times his dreams took him right out of his body. He waited a moment, waited and listened. He kept staring at the dark ceiling, the crack in the right corner a comforting sight, reminding him that he was in his room. Safe and sound. But he was sure he hadn't imagined that scream, that scream bursting with boundless agony. He waited ... there. He could feel his feet again, his body was waking up, catching up with his mind now.

"No! Please stop. Please, please stop!"

Followed by another cry of sheer pain, yet Wilber's ears had heard nothing. It came from within his head, he knew. Wilber sat up carefully, let his legs dangle, let his feet look for the slippers. His brittle bones creaked louder than the old bedsprings when he rose to get his coat. The words kept coming, the screams descended into whispered moans, the cries were stifled now, but wouldn't be stopped. Wilber checked the clock as he shuffled to the door. The glowing numbers said 03:34. Who cares. He was wide awake now, wide awake. Another scream.

Wilber left his room on the fourth and followed the sounds. He'd be at the elevators in no time. Nurse Griffin had moved heaven and earth to get him a room right by the elevators. Good woman, and Wilber felt her grief, her father gone. He didn't notice the tear falling to the floor as he waited for the elevator.

A tear for Nurse Griffin.

He knew about her father, knew how close they had been, knew that he'd beaten his wife, knew that he'd been a drunk and a womanizer, a sales rep for orthopedic shoes. Wilber knew all about Alvin Griffin's love for his family.

∞

He had provided, Goddamnit. He'd done all he could, put the food on the table, made vacations possible. He was the first rep at his company who could afford to take his family to Hawaii. Vacation in Hawaii, that was something. Alvin Griffin surely deserved a little slack, didn't he? He worked his ass off for them. Did all he could and all he wanted back was a little slack. He was an alcoholic and he knew it. So what. That's how he sold his shoes. Invite the clients, get them a few beers, shots worked even better. Of course he'd have to drink with them, get close to them, get friendly.

"Hey, we're buddies, right? You and me, we're pals - now buy the fucking shoes." That's how he made a living, that's how he got them to Hawaii, that's how he put his kids through school. Amanda, his little angel, always his favorite. She played doctor even as a kid, always knew she'd want to help people. Perfect angel, his little Amanda.

She had forgiven him for all the times he had screwed around. She had always known. Man, he loved his family so much. Just never got to show it. Wasn't his thing, it stopped him cold every time. All the hugs and kisses and tender words that never made it. They stayed inside his body, inside his heart, until they finally finished him off. The heart couldn't take it anymore and Alvin Griffin didn't have the valve to take the pressure off.

Never told them how much he loved them, not once. But they knew, didn't they? Surely they knew.

∞

Wilber got in the elevator and didn't have to listen anymore. His fingers knew which button to press. Basement. Wilber saw Amanda's mother by her husband's bedside.

Wilber saw him trying to find the words.

∞

The words never came. But Martha Griffin knew, she'd always known. That's why she hadn't left him. Her husband had been a good man. Not a saint, but a real man with good and bad in equal measure. Martha Griffin gently kissed his cooling lips and cried for a while. Then she called Amanda and together they talked and talked and cried and laughed and cried again.

∞

Wilber thought of Nurse Griffin and Frank, made him smile. A smile that was forcefully slapped from his face when the elevator abruptly stopped.

BLOOD

Basement. Wilber got out, momentarily blinded by the darkness of the hallway. There were only two souls down here. Jerry the janitor and Jerome the nurse-to-be. The screams were Jerome's screams, the words Jerome's words, Wilber heard them clearly now. He continued to the room Nurse Griffin had given to the young man, little more than a storage space, really, right next to the heating units. It was noisy down here, the machines hissing, coughing and groaning sometimes, working to keep the place warm for brittle bones.

Wilber entered Jerome's room without knocking. He knew what to expect. The room was in the dark, and Jerome was asleep. He was not tossing, he was not turning. He was deep asleep. But what would have seemed a peacefully sleeping man to most, was something far different to Wilber. Jerome wasn't tossing and turning, wasn't even sweating, for one reason. He was frozen in terror, he couldn't move a muscle. Lying there in his sleep, Jerome was fighting death and was quickly drowning in a sea of black. Blackness was rushing into Jerome's mind from everywhere. Blackness was engulfing him and Jerome was struggling with all his might to keep afloat.

Wilber understood. He had known about Jerome from the beginning, Wilber knew about his past. Now the past was catching up, now that Jerome was asleep. Now that he didn't have the waking strength to wrestle his memories. Wilber took the one chair in the room and sat next to Jerome. He simply took the young man's hand, closed his eyes, and didn't move anymore.

YOUTH

"Motherfucker! I'm gonna fuckin' kill you! You see this, you see this, you stupid motherfuckin' asshole? You see this!?"

Jerome held an Uzi, gripped it tight, had it pointed right between the kid's terrified eyes. He was alone now, although his crew was watching from the other side of the parking lot. Jerome was hard. He was alone, he was the man and he had to do what had to be done. And Jerome was terrified, an eleven year old boy ready to blow a life away and no idea how he got there.

"Are you listening to me, motherfucker? I want the fuckin' money. I get the money, you live. I don't get the money, you die, right here, right now."

Nothing. The other kid was too scared to speak, looking into the black hole of the Uzi. Jerome rammed the barrel into the kid's forehead. Snap the fucker awake. The kid looked up at him now, tears streaming down his face, blood trickling down the bridge of his nose.

"I ... I don't know anything about any money. I don't know anything, you have to believe me."

Jerome barely knew the boy kneeling in front of him. He knew his name, that was about all. Hakim Washington. Hakim was two years older and about a head taller than Jerome. Didn't matter. Jerome was the man, Jerome was in charge, Jerome had what it took ... and Jerome had the Uzi. Hakim wasn't really black, not black like Jerome. His skin was light and now, staring death in the eye, he had gone pale enough to pass for white. It almost made Jerome laugh. He would have called the others, they would have laughed together at the crackhead in front of him now, gagging now, ready to heave. But this wasn't laughing time, this was serious, it was his ass if the money didn't show up soon. It would be his eyes staring at an Uzi if he didn't get the money back.

"You're dead," Jerome said, hoping he wouldn't have to do it. But he was with his back against the wall.

The boss was waiting for the cash, the crew was waiting on the other side, waiting for him to be weak. Hakim's body suddenly shook with violent tremors. He couldn't take the pressure anymore and threw up. Jerome jumped and just barely managed to save his Reeboks from getting splattered.

"You fuck! I'm gonna waste you right here and now!"

"No, please no!" Hakim was shrieking now, his body twitching like a fish on land.

"Where's the money!"

"Booker never gave me the money, I never got the money, I swear to God, I never got the money, I don't know, man! I don't know!"

∞

Hakim didn't fight the shivering anymore, his limbs gave way, he dropped to the cracked asphalt and cowered and whimpered and waited for the shot. It had to happen, the boy with the Uzi looking fierce, looking like a man, looking like a monster.

Hakim had never seen eyes like that, not clear, not stoned, not on anything. The eyes above him were liquid fury, ready to pour all over him.

Hakim didn't notice wetting himself, he just desperately tried to remember a good moment. One good moment, they seemed so far, so far. All he recalled was cold and hard and black. Goddamnit, he didn't want to go like that. No, not like that.

Think, Hakim, think!

His mind was spinning out of control, trying to grab a hold of a memory, a good memory, anything, a warm patch, maybe a walk with his dad. Yeah! Yeah that was it, yeah, yeah, he suddenly remembered the time when -

Bam!

GONE

Jerome saw his own life flashing by as he stared down at the dead body. He had only vaguely heard the voices from across the lot, calling him, urging, pushing. There had been no other option ... So easy, so fuckin' easy. Nothing to it. He had done what needed to be done. He was the man and there were no voices coming from across the lot now. He looked and didn't see them anymore. His chicken shit crew had scrambled for safety, running even before the sirens started. He was the man, he was standing, his first kill at his feet. Yeah.

"Yeah!" he suddenly yelled out loud.

He had killed the fucker, waste of fuckin' space, no loss. Jerome would get the money now. He'd always known this kid didn't have it, might have known something, but didn't have the cash. Now, whoever had taken the twenty-seven grand, now knew that Jerome took care of business. Tomorrow everybody would know. Hell, tonight everybody would know. He knew his crew would be all over the place, every corner, talking, talking. He could just hear them.

"Should have seen Jerome, man. He the man! Stone cold fuck didn't give an inch, didn't blink, took care of business. Jerome, my man. Yeah I'm with him. You with him or you dead, you understand. Man, you should have seen Jerome!"

The sirens came closer fast and Jerome walked away at a leisurely pace. They look for running, they look for scared, keep it slow. The cops flew by him now and one of them gave him the stare for a beat. But Jerome didn't blink, Uzi tucked away, he just kept on walking.

∞

The cop picked up the pace again, thinking to himself "Kid couldn't even pull his wiener, let alone a trigger."

∞

Jerome kept on walking and only once had to step into the shelter of shadows when unexpected tears streamed down his face. Innocence washed away, not in a trickle, but all going at once, in a flood. It took two minutes, then Jerome was washed clean of remorse. He felt fucking great now, nothing he couldn't do now.

Nothing.

PASSION

Frank was on his back, in his bed. Eyes open and thinking, "Oh boy ... oh boy." He smiled and couldn't believe his luck. Amanda Griffin, Headnurse Amanda Griffin, Amanda ...

They had talked for hours and every subject had been a luscious open meadow, free to roam. Frank had talked like he'd never even talked to his wife. This was different, this was new and infinitely better. She was something, Amanda.

She had told him stories of her dad, her face soft and warm when telling how the drunk would beat her mother and how she still loved him. She missed her father and cried on Frank's shoulder ... and they had laughed about the silliest things. She had even imitated the 'Wilber Shuffle', doing a perfect Wilber. Frank had just about fallen off his chair laughing.

Frank's smile grew wider, a big, happy grin. Old man getting it up after all those years. Yes indeed, Frank and Amanda had done the nasty. Ah shut up, Frank. Wasn't like that, admit it. What had happened up there in her office wasn't anything cheap, it had been simply beautiful. They had made love. Gentle love, patient love, passionate love. Of course Frank had always insisted that he still could, but until a few hours ago he had not really believed it anymore. Now he was truly back, alive, in love. Amanda. Frank's eyes closed with the face of Amanda burnt into his irises.

Somewhere in his head floated a few odd words. "About three months", someone had said. Frank couldn't place the words, meaningless words, probably. But somehow ... whatever. Once more thinking and dreaming about Amanda filled his every space and the three words were gone.

MARK

Wilber fought faces and names. Will Bennings, Jefferson Asuzu, Alyssa Grover, Al 'The Hawk' Greenfield, Hakim Washington, Kurt Vigger. Wilber warded off black faces and white faces. It took strength and concentration, but Wilber still found the time to count them. Six, six names and six faces ... and they kept coming and coming, reaching, tearing, trying to rip Jerome to shreds. Wilber was still just sitting there, holding the sleeping man's hand.

Wilber fought the faces because he knew Jerome was worth it. Despite everything Wilber saw, despite the horrors. Some people were worth it, and some people were lost. It was as simple as that, as simple and as terrifying as that.

People were marked for their worth.

Wilber hadn't been able to see it at the beginning, but the marks had become clear as Wilber had gotten a grip on his inner world. The marks were visible on everybody. Sometimes Wilber would sit at the stop, get a glance at a baby beaming at him as the stroller passed by. And there were the marks, on the child's forehead like a third eye. At that early age the marks were mostly faint, the paths still wide open. A circle and a line, nothing more. Circle above and line below, like the sun barely touching the horizon. Rarely would a path be clear at birth. Most of the times the choices made set the path for a life. Once the choices were made and the path was clear, the mark would reflect it clearly. Then the circle could glow a deep blue, with the line fading away. Or the line could shine with bright amber, leaving the circle barely visible.

Jerome's marks were fighting a war, the glimmer of the amber line trying to drown out the strong glow of the blue circle. Jerome was incredible and only Wilber knew it. Most people would make their choices in life and settle into their mark. Only the strongest of minds could even try to change the chosen mark. Until yesterday, Jerome had seemed to succeed on his own. When he had arrived at the home, when Nurse Griffin had taken him in, Jerome's amber line was still strong and beaming with that vicious power. Wilber had often stared at him in awe and wonder, as the line began to fade and the circle began to glow. What strength, what will. Great deeds in Jerome's future, no doubt about it. Wilber couldn't make them out yet, no choices had been made and Jerome's years to come were still a blur. But one thing was clear. Jerome was worth it.

Wilber felt Jerome's hand gripping his now, the first movement since he had arrived. And a first glimmer of sweat appeared on Jerome's forehead, lending his marks even brighter glows. The young man was fighting, fighting as hard as he could. Yes, Jerome was definitely worth it.

FEAR

He got the money back and didn't have to lift a finger or ask another question. Nothing to it. Somebody had paid a cabdriver to deliver the package. Macy's shopping bag stuffed with twenty-seven grand. Everybody happy, bosses impressed, crew acting like he was a king or something. It felt good. And the cops never pinned him, never even put him in the closer circle. Jerome's life went on, pushing big now. And he was given more and more of the hounding jobs. Jerome's reputation grew quickly and his boyish face put fear in the eyes of men.

He didn't go home anymore. Why should he ... and how could he? And even if he wanted to, he couldn't go back. Back to his mother, back to the little chocolates on his pillow. Never. His mother knew, she had always known. She had tried to steer him clear of his current path ... all the greater her disappointment. She had always had her ears close to the pulse of the hood ... Yes, she knew about her little boy. She never let him see her tears. One day Jerome, about a month after killing Hakim Washington, found himself faced with a locked door. His mother had changed the locks.

Jerome played it cool for a while. Walked away, came back hours later. She still didn't let him in. That night Jerome started talking through the door, started yelling and finally kicked and pounded the massive door with angry fists until the knuckles bled. His mother was behind that door, and his mother did not speak one single word to her only son. Jerome finally sat down against the door, exhausted and lost. That was when the piece of paper slid out under the door. He wearily looked at it, gingerly picked it up. Jerome could hear his mother's voice saying the words as he read them in silence.

"My heart is dead. Go away and never come back."

Jerome stared at the words for a long time. He sucked in all his grief and buried it deep inside. Then he got up and left. Seven months later and he hadn't seen her face again. After blowing Hakim's brains into the pavement, Jerome's life had taken a whole new direction. He was the man, he got the jobs and he got them done. He got respect from up above.

"Look at them," he'd say to his own image in the mirror. "These guys three times as old as me. Whatever they got, I can take." The big guys got him more jobs, bloody jobs. Jerome, the man, taking care of business. When he was twelve, the first glimmer of a mustache appeared and a funny thing happened. The big guys had always looked at him with a hint of hidden amusement. Now Jerome began to detect a glimpse of something else behind those respectful eyes ... fear. Big fuckers were scared of little Jerome. They knew he had what it took, they knew he had everything and one more thing: Jerome had youth, Jerome had time. Only twelve and moving up fast.

Jefferson Asuzu was twenty-three and had climbed the ladder similar to Jerome. He simply didn't have Jerome's drive, the drive that would lead Jerome to his goals like a bullet to the center of the target. Dead center. Pretty soon

Asuzu got worried about his position, with Jerome possibly moving into his spot. So Jefferson Asuzu snitched around a few corners and tried to cancel Jerome to the cops. But when he left the Blue Star whorehouse on Green and 7th a few nights later, he never made it to his Caddy. A bullet in the back of his head ended his career and he was dead before his bitch started screaming for help. Jerome dropped her, too. It didn't make a difference anymore, Jerome was moving up. Asuzu's place needed taking, and nobody put up a hand when Jerome claimed it.

There was blood on his path, but he had two cars, a driver, bitches and more money than he could spend. Soon Jerome killed again, for no reason now. It had happened simply because the fucker had looked at his woman. Wasn't right, don't look at Jerome's stuff, not if you wanna live. Then it happened. An unknown face up top, a rich white face probably, gave him up to the law. Out of nowhere a swarm of cops descended on his life and Jerome was taken down hard for his first murder, for Hakim Washington. Turned out Hakim Washington didn't get him made, Hakim Washington got him done. They never pinned any of the other murders on him. Just the one. Cops standing around him, pounding him with their boots, laughing now, because 'the crazy little fuck got what he deserved'.

The pounding during the arrest was nothing compared to the nine years that followed. Youth home, gang wars and single detention for endless periods of time. He was the man, he was still the man. When a knife in the back almost left him paralyzed, something snapped and Jerome saw for the first time who he had become. He got to thinking, he got to crying and he got to realizing his path. After youth home a few years in the psychiatric ward ... Then he was free.

∞

Jerome was pouring sweat now, tossing, turning, his back arching. Wilber opened his eyes and let go of Jerome's hand. His work was done. Jerome wasn't frozen anymore, he could handle it now. The glowing circle on Jerome's forehead was winning over the line.

Wilber stretched his legs for a moment and a cramp slowly disappeared like a poisonous snake in a desert dune. The he got up and shuffled from the room, closing the door silently.

BRAIN

They had never understood him. But that hadn't bothered Jerry Newell, not when he was a kid, not now. Nobody got him, ever. Nobody understood his ways, nobody saw his genius. Jerry had spent a lot of his youth thinking about that. Not worrying about it, just thinking about it. Trying to understand why he wasn't hurt, wasn't bothered. Most people needed to feel understood, needed to belong, needed to be liked. Not Jerry. There was probably a gene missing somewhere and that was just fine with Jerry.

Missing a gene was nothing compared to what his brain gave him. Jerry was a genius, he just didn't have the credits. He had never gone to school, not for one single day in his life. Jerry had slipped right through the cracks of the system. Wasn't hard going unnoticed on his uncle's farm in nowhere Nebraska. His mother had died giving birth to him. Meant nothing to Jerry. He still didn't feel either way about that, after all he'd never even known the woman. His father had died the following year in a hunting accident, a tragic death, apparently. Some said Jerry's uncle had shot him for a woman. But nobody ever found out what exactly happened and Jerry never felt like listening to the rumors. Whatever. He'd always been busy with other, more interesting things.

Numbers. Numbers were where the passion was. Some people had it and most people didn't. Forget about school. Jerry's brain was beyond brilliant from the get-go. He had never bothered to announce it, though. He just helped people fix things. Cars, tractors, harvesters, calculators, whatever they set in front of him, Jerry could fix it. He read every written word he could get his hands on, thanks to his killer uncle. It was the one good thing he had done for Jerry, gave him the old dust-covered books. Two years old, little Jerry looked at the pictures in those books and started reading at the same time. Nobody taught him, and nobody noticed. There was just the farm, no people anywhere near, no schools, nothing.

When he was nineteen he sent a detailed layout for a spaceship rocket booster to NASA. The scope of the booster was enormous, but Jerry figured they'd need not one, but two. Jerry was certain they'd need special fuel for the engines and came up with liquid hydrogen and liquid oxygen. He had never read about those words, he just knew. The knowledge was planted in him, no studies required. He never heard back from NASA, not a letter, not even a free visitor's pass to visit the Center. Then, on the twelfth of April 1981, Jerry watched on television as his very own boosters carried the first space shuttle, the 'Colombia', into orbit. Jerry remembered just sitting there on the ground in front of the television.

"Look at that," he had said to the TV. "They're working just as I've planned it." Jerry didn't harbor any bad feelings, he had not even been particularly excited. Just content to see that his work had paid off. Jerry had, however, that same day, packed his bags and left the farm.

At the age of forty-six the place in nowhere Nebraska had become too small for Jerry Newell.

WARM

He gripped the monkey wrench with both hands, let his muscles tighten, then pulled with one fluid move. There. The bolt gave way. Jerry continued on the Iron Fireman, the G-120 heater they finally got two years ago after Nurse Griffin had pestered that congressman long enough. She had a gift with people, no doubt. Nurse Griffin always knew what to say and it was only thanks to her that the home was still on its feet. The old Fireman boiler, WW2 model, had given up during that summer. Good timing. It had given Nurse Griffin two more warm months to work on the congressman. Incredibly, she actually managed to get the politician, a weasel who had never followed up on even one of his campaign promises, to find and cough up thirty-nine thousand dollars. Jerry had not been happy to see the old metal go, the nuts and bolts he'd pampered for twelve years. But the new Fireman was worth the scrapping. No more problems, working with this bright red monster was a joy.

Jerry replaced the bolt that had been badly disfigured by the plumber this morning. Jerry hadn't been able to stop the man in time. The ignorant taking the wrong size and yanking. He had scratched the bolt and scraped his knuckles. Jerry, a skinny little man and not prone to violence had lost it then. He had taken the plumber by the collar, pulled the stunned man to the door and had sent him off with a powerful kick. Slammed the door shut before the man's curses had had a chance to reach him.

Jerry ended up fixing the boiler himself, just as he had wanted to do in the first place.

"Warranty," Nurse Griffin had said. "It's their job to fix it. They are required to send a specialist within twenty-four hours. I know you can probably fix it, Jerry, but it's their job. Let them do it."

Yeah, right. Specialist. Jerry shook his head, determined to never again let another 'specialist' near his baby.

There was a knock on the door, firm but patient.

"You okay in there?" Jerry recognized Jerome's voice.

He unlocked and allowed the young man free passage into his sanctum. Jerome surely knew what had happened, but it didn't show. No smile, nothing, he looked preoccupied. The young man went straight to the corner, where his cleaning supplies were stacked and shelved.

"How's it going?" Jerry asked, just making conversation. He continued on the boiler, pulled the last bolt back into position.

"Okay."

"You get any sleep last night?"

"Yeah."

"Nice talking to you."

Frankly, Jerry didn't care much either way. Jerome was a nice enough kid, but conversations were, for the most part, waste of time. He decided to concentrate on his next invention. A few ideas on distant space exploration, a few ideas that just might - then, from the corner, Jerome's voice interrupted.

"Sorry, Jerry. You know, I ... I slept like shit, but, I mean ... I don't know. It kind of feels like it's been a rough night, like I been working, but I feel good now. Inside, real good." He quizzically, timidly, looked at Jerry. "You know?"

Jerry took off his steamed glasses, wiped them carefully with a clean handkerchief. He looked up at Jerome, the boy looking seven feet tall compared to his own four feet eleven frame.

"Take any drugs recently?" Jerry said with a light smile. Couldn't help it, because the usually tough and monosyllabic Jerome had never poured out that many words all at once. Sounded like a kid, confused somehow. Jerome shot him a hard glance that Jerry didn't understand. But he understood that he must have touched a bad spot. "I'm just kidding, Jerome."

"Yeah." Jerome cleaned out the closet, old rags and bottles were forcefully tossed into the bin in the corner. Then he started looking for today's supplies.

∞

He needed two gallons for the kitchen floor, at least. Jerome cursed himself, a little remark like that making him cringe. After all this time. He wasn't that Jerome anymore, he was different now. He desperately wanted to tell Jerry about last night, wanted to tell someone.

He had woken up soaked, puddles of sweat below his back. Must have had nightmares but he couldn't remember a thing. He just ... felt good. And it was the strangest thing because, because he felt like somebody had been there with him, like somebody had been holding his hand. The moment he had woken he had looked around the room, expecting to see someone. But he had been alone. Of course he'd been alone. Then, on a hunch, he had touched his right hand, right was warm, left was cold. Right hand was warm ... Somehow that raisin's face had popped in his head then, Wilber Patorkin, the Champ ...

He must have stared at Patorkin this morning, watched him shuffle off to the bus stop as usual. Jerome must have stared, because the old man had turned his head, nodded and smiled at him. That knowing look again.

Jerome shrugged it off, these thoughts not getting him anywhere. He grabbed two large jugs from the back of the shelf and made for the door. There he remembered something and turned.

"Hey, Jerry."

"What?" Jerry was kneeling by the boiler again, half hidden under it.

"About the plumber ... Nice kicking." Jerome dug up a smile and left, closing the door behind him.

∞

Jerry liked Jerome, a good kid, a lot of potential. Not a brain like Jerry was, but still, he was going to make something of himself. As he went back to the boiler, Jerry muttered to himself "You have a nice day, Jerome."

NOISE

Wilber wasn't happy, he was not happy at all. His world was about to be taken apart. He hadn't bothered to read the piece of paper that had been stuck to the advertising boards for two months now. It seemed the community had decided to move the bus stop up by about two hundred feet. People had apparently been complaining for a long time, and with a stop closer to the school entrance, closer to church and community center, everybody would be served much better.

Everybody, except for Wilber.

Two big men in orange overalls had arrived in the early afternoon and had begun to remove the stop. They had allowed Wilber to stay on his bench, while they were taking down everything around him. The roof had come off already, good thing it wasn't raining today. Now they were dismantling the sideboards. Next they would unscrew the newspaper vending machines, the trash bin, the stop's sign ... then the bench.

Leaning forward, Wilber could see some more men in orange. They were busy preparing that new stop up ahead. Jackhammers were drowning out every other sound, ripping open the sidewalk. Wilber could imagine the gaping holes to anchor the stop over there. The new stop would be identical to the old stop. Everything would stay the same. Except for the location. What were two hundred feet anyway - nothing much for most people. But two hundred feet were a rough twenty minute walk through uncharted territory for Wilber Patorkin. No, Wilber wasn't happy as the man with the bull neck and the bear paws ripped the advertising board from its sockets.

Everything changed.

"Yeah, yeah, yeah," Wilber grumbled. Everything always changed. But he didn't always have to like it. Odd. It made him sad, this change made him sad. And it made him cranky ... and that made Wilber smile. Cranky old man defending his bench from the evil men in orange. Ha, what a sight. He should have accepted the walking stick today, he would have made Nurse Griffin happy. And with the cane he could have beaten the crap out of these guys. Well, maybe not. But it felt good thinking it, anyway.

A man walked by, a young man in Wilber's ancient eyes. Wilber saw him daily and the man would always say hello with a quick smile.

"Hello," the man said in passing.

They always locked eyes for an instant, with Wilber mumbling his own hello then. This little routine never took more than a few seconds, from the moment the man walked into Wilber's sight to the moment he vanished again. Wilber could lean forward, watch him go for another while, but he never did. The few seconds were gold enough from just one person. More would be nice, but Wilber had never been a greedy man and had always cherished moments like these.

In those seconds Wilber got to feel pure love radiating from Duncan Grey, the passing man. Same thing, every day. Wilber knew Duncan's life, knew of the job he muddled through day in day out. Wilber knew what Duncan's wife looked like, her long dark hair, her shining eyes. She would be there now, waiting for Duncan's return home, waiting for his smile, just as he was aching for hers.

And Wilber knew the faces of Duncan's three children, two boys and a princess. Nicky and Milo, six and four, Superboy and Spider-Man. And there was Supergirl, two-year old Ellie. Wilber smiled. Bliss. Wilber could see with Duncan's eyes and heart. And so he knew that those four souls waiting at home were what put the bounce in Duncan Grey's steps. Wilber could hear their laughter, could feel their kisses. Wilber saw little Ellie more stumbling than running into her father's arms. Wilber saw their living room strewn with toys, saw them play and draw and listen and tickle and toss and fly. Five souls, five circles. Wilber had never actually seen those children, yet he deeply loved them with all his heart. Wilber had never actually seen Duncan's wife Nathalie, yet he wished for nothing more than to embrace her as a proud father would. Wilber's heart ached with glorious pain.

"Hey, you crying down there?" Mr. Orange stood on the bench right next to him, looking down. A nice man, genuinely worried, Wilber realized. He wiped the tears from his cheeks and smiled up.

"I'm fine, my friend. I'm just fine."

"What'd you say?" the man asked.

Wilber just smiled and left it at that. Why bother the man. How to explain that he was crying for his unborn child. How to explain that in crying he was deliciously happy just the same. Crying, laughing, feeling. Felt good being alive, it still felt good to be alive. The two overalls each grabbed ends of the advertising boards.

"Yeah well, you need anything, Pop, you just let me know, 'kay?"

"'Kay." Wilber watched them walk off with the boards. Now he didn't have to lean forward anymore. The view was unobstructed all of a sudden, the walls gone, everything but the bench gone. Wilber knew the one with the bear paws and the gentle heart had taken the other one aside earlier. Had whispered to leave the old fart on the bench for another while.

"I don't know, Joey, kinda seems important to the guy. We'll just move all the other shit first, alright?" Joey had nodded his okay.

They were almost at the new stop now. Two hundred and seven feet, Wilber figured. He felt old ... Wondering if he could add a new routine after all these years. He felt really old.

"Sorry, Pop, it's time to go." Seemingly out of nowhere Mr. Orange was standing next to him again. Mr. Paws had his hands already on the bench, but was waiting patiently. Surprised, Wilber looked to the new stop. Must have dozed off for a few. There it stood, almost ready. Only the bench was missing now. Wilber got to his feet and Mr. Orange helped him up. Wilber nodded, smiled and shuffled off without another word or glance.

∞

"Sorry," said Mr. Orange to Wilber's back, feeling like he'd just single-handedly destroyed the old man's planet or something.

GOAL

Amanda was watching Wilber shuffle toward the home. She had been horrified when she had seen the construction workers take the stop apart, she had completely forgotten about that. For weeks she had been thinking about it, worrying about it. For weeks she had been reminding herself.

"Don't forget to tell Wilber. Tell him gently, somehow. But not today, just let him enjoy his days at the bus stop for another while."

There was no way he'd be able to continue his routine from now on. The new stop was too far away, an easy walk for her own healthy feet, but at heart-wrenching, body-tearing world away for the Wilber-Shuffle. He would have to find something else to do now. Unbearable sadness filled Amanda Griffin's heart, her eyes welling up, tears looming heavy. Look at him go. Look at the old man shuffle toward the home. Look at the frail body, struggling to keep moving, struggling to stay tall. Looking as if he would break any second now

He would have to take a walking stick ... Amanda felt powerfully guilty. She could have told him, should have told him. She had had it in her hand to break it to him gently. But it had just plain slipped her mind - so many other things to think about, the leak on the roof, her father, the boiler, Jerome, the fichus, Frank, the budget, the two deaths on the third, Frank, the plumber complaining, Frank. Frank. A smile broke through her sadness as she continued watching Wilber approach the building.

And then, somehow, she just felt better. All gone, no guilt, no tears, no sadness anymore, she realized with amazement. It was as if a strong, fresh breeze had cleared her heart. Wilber's face was in her mind for some reason, a smiling Wilber nodding at her, saying it was okay. She kept looking down at Wilber and felt him looking at her, although he had his eyes glued to the sidewalk, as always. Wilber Patorkin never looked around, always concentrated on the ground, always planned that next little step. Still, it felt as if he were looking at her ... and it felt good, reassuring.

∞

Bonebreakers, that's what Wilber called them. Everything from pebbles to cracks, leaves, twigs and cans - they all had the power. The power to kill. It was simple enough: Contact with any of the above could mean stumbling and stumbling meant falling. Make contact with the asphalt, you find yourself in the hospital. Find yourself in the hospital, you're as good as dead. A fall, any fall, would break his bones. Wilber was well aware of it and always concentrated accordingly. He had no plans of spending the remainder of his days in a hospital gown, his flabby butt hanging out in the open. Nope, he had no plans of giving some medical genius the opportunity to examine this ancient hull.

"Damn," he suddenly muttered. He would have to start using a cane, not the walker, but there'd be no way around the cane if he wanted to even consider making a daily trip to the new stop. So far away ... so far away.

Wilber stopped and didn't move anymore.

He sent Nurse Griffin a few good thoughts. The woman was worrying too much. Wilber was just standing there now, not listening anymore, just there. People walked by, sending him frowning glances now and then, but mostly just ignoring the old man standing there, staring down at the rust-red leaf by his feet.

"Can I help you?" a woman's voice asked.

Ann Riker uncomfortably looked at the little old man. He had seemed so lost, so utterly lost. She'd been walking on the other side of the street and somehow, like a magnet, it had pulled her over here. Now he was staring at her with those glistening eyes, incredible eyes for anybody, but on him they seemed unreal. She had seen this old man ever since she had taken on the stupid job six months ago, ever since she took the 93 to work. Ann had never said a word to him, not a hello, nothing. She had simply ignored him all this time. How strange, he was probably the one person she saw on a daily basis who did not piss her off. And yet, not a word. Then again what would she have said, made stupid conversation, talk about the weather, have a nice day and all that crap? She got enough of that shit at work. Always polite and always with a nice, huge and obviously fake smile. She hated her job at the bank, hated everything about it but the check at the end of the month. She hated the other tellers and their backstabbing, gossiping ways, she hated her slimy boss and most of all she hated Jeff. The bastard of an investment manager on the second floor had gotten her pregnant. She had just been plain stupid, so incredibly plain stupid she still kicked herself about it.

The fetus was gone, of course.

She'd taken care of that immediately, four months ago, four months and seventeen days ago. Just a fetus. She couldn't raise a kid, not with the way things were, not with a prick like that for a father. It hadn't been the time, everything had been wrong about it. The abortion had been the perfectly right thing to do. All taken care off in less than an hour ... she would be six months pregnant now. Her belly would be rounding now, motherhood, her child. Her child.

∞

Ann Riker, Wilber thought, what do you know. She was thinking too many things, people and places at once, no focus, no peace in there. The child, her child ... Wilber took her arm with a warm smile.

"Would you accompany me to the entrance?"

∞

"Excuse me?" Ann frowned at Wilber as he took out his dentures without hesitation. "What are you doing?" She took a step back as he unwrapped a chewing gum, chewed it vigorously, then stuck his dentures back in place.

"Would you accompany me to the entrance?" Wilber repeated, this time sounding clear, presenting vowels and consonants in a fairly acceptable fashion for a change. Ann was clearly startled by his dentures, but that was just what Wilber had wanted. To get her mind off the race track for a while.

"Oh, of course," she said.

Wilber took her arm again, held on and off they went. The woman practically flew and Wilber had to grip her arm tight to slow her down to his speed. She needed slowing down.

"Thank you," Wilber said.

"You're welcome." Her simple reply was meaningless. She wasn't listening, she wasn't here. Wilber knew that her mind was going again. Going fast. There wasn't just the child, there was more. Wilber felt the hard walls around Ann, walls of defiance and hatred and anger keeping her cries buried deep down. Slow down, Ann. Wilber's mind raced with her. He saw the horrors of her childhood now, saw the pain and terror in the little girl's eyes. He saw the child lashing out at every open hand, never trusting anymore. They were all the same. Her mother's boyfriend showing her what he had learned in Nam. Showing her how they had pulled out his fingernails. Showing her exactly how that worked on the little girl's left pinky. Just one moment. There were more images, horrifying, unspeakable. She had put a lid on it, on everything. She was all strength now, grown up hard and tough, on her own. She was independent ... and alone. Never close, never anybody close, until Jeff Berger got to her that night. It hadn't been the first time she'd slept with men, she'd had her share. But this one had really gotten to Ann Riker, through her defenses and into her heart.

If the man had pierced her heart, the child had cracked it. And it was this crack she couldn't seal anymore. She tried to glue it, tape it, nail it shut with great boards of fright - nothing worked. All the horrors were coming back up now. She wouldn't be able to keep them in check much longer. Soon they would grip her throat and strangle her to death ... she was close to losing it, she was close to reaching the place where nothing mattered anymore. Not her independence, not the payments, not the money, not the life. Suicide wasn't just a distant thought anymore, an option, it was quickly becoming her goal, her final aim.

"Your child will be born," Wilber said as clearly as possible.

The woman continued walking for a beat, as if she hadn't heard. Then she stopped. Wilber looked into her terrified eyes and could see that her mind was desperately trying to find words, words that wouldn't come.

"This is not the time for questions, Ann. Just let me tell you a few things I've learned. You know, we tend to consider ourselves too important. We think we can take a life." Wilber gently shook his head. "Well, we can't."

He didn't wait for a dialog to start, knew that she would stay silent and solid as a statue. He also knew that she was listening.

"People kill shells, not lives. We kill bodies, not souls. Your child's soul was ready to be born. You chose not to let it, Ann. But that was all, just a choice. That soul will find another time to be born. The only soul you ever hurt, Ann Riker, was your own."

∞

Ann was reeling. He knew. The old man knew, knew about her, knew about her child. Impossible. It was simply impossible. She felt faint. The cold breeze chilled her skin ... until a sensational warmth started spreading inside her. She hadn't felt warm like this for ... longer than she could remember. This wasn't just warmth, this was heat. Glowing heat, a bright fire was lighting her up now. She was standing here on the sidewalk with the old man, staring into his glistening eyes. And yet she could see herself strolling through a flower-covered meadow, flooded in sunlight. And the old man was walking next to her, holding her hand, smiling.

A moment ago she had been lending her arm to help him to the home, now he was guiding her. So much warmth, such love.

∞

"Breathe, you have to breathe," Wilber said calmly.

She had completely forgotten about that. And with his words she suddenly sucked in fresh air. The sudden burst made her cough, the sudden cough made her laugh ... the sudden laugh made her cry. And a flood of pain washed from her soul.

"How?" She gasped in between sobs, staring at him as if he were the Messiah in person.

It made Wilber smile, she was actually thinking God-thoughts, trying to fit him into a frame with Jesus, apostles and prophets. Wilber gently patted Ann's hand, brushed a strand of hair from her eyes, made firm eye contact again.

Her sobbing was receding and so was the line on her forehead. It would take a while for the circle to find its color again ... but it would happen now.

"How do you ... I mean ... how ..."

"Ann. You should go home now."

Wilber kept looking into her eyes. Her tears were gone and she was just aching for words and explanations.

Wilber knew better.

It wouldn't explain a thing, whatever he told her.

All she needed to know, she knew now.
All she needed to feel, she felt now.
All she needed to be, she was now.

∞

Ann was lost in his eyes, felt dizzy, as if she'd been spinning a child's wildest circles. And yet she was standing, solid, looking at him. And suddenly she knew that it was fine. She suddenly understood that she had found herself and that she was standing in the middle of herself. Almost unbearable, this happiness bouncing inside her like a crazed pinball.

∞

"Thank you," she said simply and quietly. "Thank you." She turned at started walking off, suddenly turned again. "Oh, I almost forgot - "

Wilber lightly raised a hand and that stopped her from taking his arm again.

"I'm just fine. You go home now."

"You're sure you can make it?"

Wilber didn't look to the nearby entrance of the home. His eyes were fixed on the new bus stop, in the distance. He slowly lifted his spine, pulled his shoulders back, raised his head a little.

"Yes. Yes, I'm sure I can make it."

Ann beamed at him and walked off, feeling like the happy child she had never been. Feeling new. Wilber watched her go and a part of him accompanied her for another while.

No cane, ever. The new stop wasn't going to finish him off, wasn't going to win. Wilber would make that distant place part of his world. He would make his world bigger once more.

"You're alive, Wilber. As long as you're alive, you set your goals. Places to go, things to achieve. Conquer that stop. That's your next goal." He shuffled on with a determined smile, his gleaming eyes challenging the tiny obstacles at his feet now. For a moment he considered kicking the squashed beer that lay close to his right shoe. But he came to his senses just in time. 'Let it be', those boys had sung back then, let it be.

Wilber continued his high-speed adventure home.

ROOF

"And then she just bounced off. I've never seen anything like it, Frank." Frank and Nurse Griffin were up on the roof of the home. Getting Frank up the final set of stairs hadn't been easy, but Jerome had volunteered to carry him up.

Now Frank was comfortably sitting in a faded-pink plastic beach chair, Amanda next to him. It was late night and the clear sky froze their breaths. A beautiful night,

Frank thought, stars out, really fuckin' romantic, when you thought about it. Amanda filled his glass again. She'd gotten a bottle of champagne, Spanish stuff actually, something called 'Cava'. Amanda knew a lot about a lot of things. But right now she didn't have a clue and there was nothing Frank could tell her.

"That's something," he simply said.

"That's something? Frank, you should have seen it. First he took her arm, let her help him. I got worried right then and there. Wilber never lets anybody help him. Then the woman suddenly stops and stares at him as if he were an alien, I swear Frank, I've never seen anything like it. And when she started crying I almost ran down to see what the heck was going on. I have no idea what happened. But Wilber must have said something, done something, I don't know. You could see the change. I saw it with all that distance from the seventh floor. It was as if a light inside that woman had been switched on. I'm telling you, the woman that stopped to help Wilber wasn't the same woman that happily walked away just a few minutes later."

She downed her glass in one, filled up both their glasses again. Frank wasn't that crazy about this sweet stuff, but hell, it made her happy. He leaned over and gave her a kiss. She beamed and instantly forgot about Wilber.

"Who would have thought," Amanda said.

"Thought what?" Frank knew what she was talking about. But he kept a straight face and played stupid for her enjoyment.

"You know, you and me."

"Oh, that."

"Yeah, that." She playfully smacked his shoulder, laughed and sat over onto his chair. Cuddle up, baby.

"Don't get any ideas, Amanda. I ain't takin' off my clothes out here in the fuckin' cold."

"You watch your language."

"Sorry." He didn't mind saying sorry, since he knew his language didn't bother her in the least. She liked it colorful. She was a colorful kinda woman. Man she was something. He couldn't help taking her face into his hands, pulling her close and planting a big wet one. What a woman. Who would have thought, indeed. He took another sip from his glass, pinky out, high class style. He did it with flourish and it made her crack up again. What a laugh.

"So what do you think happened?"

"I'm irresistible, Amanda. You didn't have a chance."

"I'm talking about Wilber and the woman."

"Oh, that."

"Yeah, that," she said, cracking up again. "Come on, Frank, you know Wilber better than anybody. What do you think?"

Frank looked up at the stars. Tell her about Wilber? Tell her about Wilber reading people's minds just like that? Tell her that, for Wilber, people's brains were like watching TV? Tell her about all the things Wilber had told him? Yeah, good idea, Frank. Amanda would definitely understand that. Right.

"I have no idea," he finally said.

"You know, there's something about Wilber. About the way he makes people feel, the way he looks at people, too. Sometimes I could swear the man can read minds."

Frank couldn't avoid staring at her.

"What? What did I say?"

Frank was still staring, staring hard now, as if caught in Medusa's eyes and turned to stone. Frank staring through Amanda, staring into the night. Frank suddenly remembered.

"About three months", Wilber had said.

About three months. Oh my God. How could he have missed that, how could he have forgotten about that? Frank had been thinking about Wilber dying, thinking "How much longer, Wilber? How much longer you gonna live?" And then Wilber had answered his thoughts and said "About three months". Just like that. How could he have missed it? Jesus fuckin' Christ, Wilber was about to die! Wilber was going to - Something tugged at his galloping thoughts, something was reaching in, something was trying to break through. Something that was scared.

"What, Frank? Frank, talk to me! Frank!"

Frank snapped back when he heard Amanda's frightened voice. He took a deep breath, looked at her with wide eyes.

"Wilber is going to die, Amanda."

"What? How do you know? What are you saying, Frank? Is he sick? Did he say anything? Frank. What's wrong with Wilber?"

"He's going to die three months from now."

"I don't understand, Frank. What? How can you ...? How do you know?"

"I don't know. He ... he just told me."

Headnurse Amanda Griffin stared at him. She was smart, she made sense of things, everything. Not this, not Wilber. Please, not Wilber. Frank suddenly realized that Amanda was in worse shape than he was.

His arms pulled her into a tight embrace.

MORE

Wilber could see Frank and Amanda on the roof. Frank's introduction into Wilber's world had been more than clumsy and Wilber now shook his head at the way he'd done it. But he had wanted to tell Frank for a long time, had so much wanted to let his best friend in on his secret. And then it had just happened, carelessly, the three words, his impending death.

Bam.

Stupid.

Of course he had wanted to tell Frank everything, well, a lot of things, anyway. And of course he would have told him eventually. And so now Frank was up there on the roof, finally remembering the three words. Wilber could hear Nurse Griffin's disbelieving sobs on the roof. He could hear Frank's consoling whispers ... He would talk to them.

But first he needed to settle again. He had almost given up today, given up because of something as meaningless as a few hundred feet. He was weakening. He couldn't let it happen yet. Too much thinking, he had done too much of that, trying to make the most of his gift. Or whatever it was.

Wilber sat in his chair in the darkness of the hall, the chess board neatly arranged in front of him, the black and white pieces waiting to be played again. Wilber had thought of letting Frank win this afternoon. Couldn't do it. It would have been dishonest. Then again Frank wouldn't even have noticed a win - his thoughts somewhere else, somewhere upstairs, somewhere with a woman.

Would they have ever been together if it hadn't been for Wilber rattling Frank? No, probably not. Would Ann Riker have killed herself tonight in her bathtub? Yes, probably. Definitely. Wilber had seen shades of oozing red darkening the water around her. Yes, she'd be dead now.

The gift, Wilber, the power of the gift.

White pieces in front of him. Wilber blankly stared at them. White, black, it was all the same. So much sorrow. What a waste of passions and lives. What a terrible waste, it seemed. Wilber rose from the chair, wobbly legs, legs that wanted to sleep. But his mind kept him up, his mind wasn't ready to go. Somehow Wilber had known about the date. It had been there, just there.

09 December 2001.

That would be his departing date. That would be his body saying farewell, farewell to all things known. Onward.

But he wasn't ready to go. Wilber knew he wouldn't be ready for a while. So much more to do, so much more to learn in this life. Wilber shuffled around the narrow table, sat down on the opposite side, Frank's side.

Black pieces ... all the same.

∞

Back when the voices were new to him he had heard Clarissa Severance. Just the distant voice of a shrieking woman at first. Wilber had been in his bed, listening to his 'radio'. The shouts had shaken him and he had instantly tried to focus. He remembered sitting up straight, concentrating, listening to the details. He had reached into her mind and had suddenly known her name, her address, her life. Through her mind he had also heard her husband, Henry. Henry the lawyer.

"You fucking cunt, no, you hear me? No!" Henry's shirt was ripped open, stained with spilled Dewars. His T-shirt underneath was half torn by sharp fingernails, streaks of red shining through now. There was a bottle in his hand, a broken bottle, a jagged half of the bottle. "I won't let you. Ever."

Clarissa sat on the floor like a frightened mouse staring into the eyes of the snake. She was silent and scared, looking up at the strange face, the face she had married eleven years ago. She didn't know this face, this roaring face of hate. With a chance to look in a mirror Clarissa wouldn't have recognized her own face, a face swollen out of shape in places, a nose broken to a pulp. She tried to move back, slowly, stay down Clarissa, stay down. Don't make him angrier than he is, don't give him a chance to strike out again. She forced herself to keep looking into his eyes, trying to hold them in place, trying to keep him from looking at her moving hands and feet. Get away from him, get to the bathroom.

The kitchen knives? Are you crazy, Clarissa? You won't do it, you can't do that. You're not like ... him. He will do it, get away, Clarissa, get away now. The upstairs bedroom, the balcony, get out that way. But it's freezing outside. Better freeze than stay in here, Clarissa. Just grab a few clothes and jump down into the snow. You can do it, Clarissa, you can do it. But he has the keys, all the keys, no car, the distance to the next house immense in the dark and frozen night. You should have never let him do it. She had never wanted to move out here in the first place. It was too far away from people, too alone with him. Up the stairs, Clarissa. You can do it. Do it now.

Freeze or die.

Wilber could see Clarissa inching her way up the stairs, her voice trying to soothe and calm, her husband always right there. Following her, the bottle glaring at her, the jagged edges calling for her blood. And Wilber suddenly realized that Henry Severance was listening. Not to his wife, not to Clarissa. Henry was listening to a jabbing voice inside his head.

"Kill her, Henry, kill the bitch. She's got the money, she got all the fuckin' money you slaved so hard for. She'll never give you any credit, all the fucking work, it'll never be good enough for her. Kill her, kill the no-good barren cunt. Get a new one, Henry. You can do better, you can ..."

Wilber listened, horrified. A voice was speaking to Henry, a voice not Henry's own! And then suddenly the voice turned to Wilber, sensing the presence of the listener.

"Hey Wilber. Yeah you. Wilber Patorkin."

"Who ... who are you?" Wilber muttered inside his head. His thoughts were reeling, there was someone else out there. Somebody else with the gift.

"What did you think? Wilber Patorkin, the cosmos' gift to humankind? What did you think? That you're unique? Come on Wilber! When will you learn? There's never, ever, just the one. There's you and there's me, Pal. And there's others."

The voice was making pleasant conversation, as if nothing was going on, as if he hadn't just been urging Henry Severance to kill his wife.

Clarissa was at the landing and Henry was still following her. He seemed distant. Clarissa was beginning to hope.

"Why are you doing this?" Wilber asked.

"Why are you trying to help people?" the voice countered.

"Because it's the right thing to do."

"Says who?"

"Says ... God."

It took Wilber an instant to realize that the voice's following onslaught wasn't directed at him, but straight into the conscience of Henry Severance again.

"Hey! You're beginning to disappoint me. Get it over with! Henry, wake up! Don't you see what she's doing!? Do it - Do it or she'll make you suffer for the rest of your life. Take the bottle, ram it into her ugly mug and twist it a few times. Come on, now, what's it gonna be? Where's your spine?? You can have her grin at you all the way through the divorce or you can rip her heart out right now. It's in your hands, Henry. It's in your hands."

With this Henry lurched forward and pushed the tearing glass into his wife's underbelly before she could yell out in terror. As Henry sat down next to the limp mass that had been his forever-after until a moment ago, his mind faded from Wilber's grasp.

∞

Then Wilber was alone in his room again. Alone with the knowledge of the murder of Clarissa Severance. He felt completely helpless, nothing he could have done. That voice had been too strong in its hatred. Then that voice came back, loud and clear in Wilber's head, loud and clear and maddeningly pleasant.

"And that, my friend, was that. I know, I know. You'll want to ask that 'why' question again. Don't bother. There ain't no decent explanation, Pal. Nothing that would make you happy, anyway. I do what I do, because it's ... fun! And I suppose you try to help people because that works for you. Boring as that sounds to me."

Wilber tried to block his sudden hatred, his disgust, his horror. It wouldn't get him anywhere. Clarissa Severance was gone, that moment had passed. The best thing Wilber could think of doing was to try to make sense of the big questions.

"Who are ... we?"

"Okay, Wilber. Let me give you a quick rundown on the goods here. You and I, we got the gift. There's a few of us out there. We get the gift for different reasons. Some of us are born with it, some get it with an accident, a tumor, that sort of thing. Some just fall out of bed and have it. And some break the mold, as you call it, by simply holding on to dear life. What's our mission, you're dying to ask? Nada, Pal, niente, zip, zilch, nix, absolutely nothing. We don't have to do a damn thing. There ain't no master plan. Life is what we make it. You wanna be a nice guy, that makes you happy? Good. Wanna slice some loser's wife, that makes you happy? Good. Me, I love making messes, big fuckin' ugly messes. Makes me happy, see? In the big picture, it doesn't mean a fuckin' thing."

Wilber stared at the sink in the corner, with the moonlight lending it an unpleasant pale glow. Wilber's eyes hurt, he hadn't blinked in the last ten minutes. Then he suddenly rubbed his eyes, rubbed them with angry force.

"I can't believe that," Wilber said.

"Why not? The picture doesn't fit with God and destiny and all that crap? Well, Wilber, that's just too bad. Here's the gospel truth according to Al, that's me: You have a life, live it, be happy. If you're happy, you win the jackpot."

"What's the jackpot?"

"Look, Champ," Al continued impatiently. "That's what I'm sayin'. There ain't no jackpot, it's just a figure of speech. There ain't no big mystery. We come, we live, we go."

"Go where?"

"Fuck you, Wilber, you're getting on my nerves and I feel a nice little car crash coming on. Gotta go."

"No wait!"

But there was no more. Wilber waited in silence, for what seemed like an endless time.

"What?" Al asked suddenly, indignant.

Wilber carefully looked for the words. Not to let Al off the hook before he had a chance to get some more answers.

"So you're saying you and I, we're no different than everybody else. That our gift is nothing more than a difference, some people are tall, some are short."

"That's a grade A 'Bingo'. We, my friend, are just a little 'taller' than the rest of them."

"So everything we can accomplish is for nothing."

Wilber could almost see Al furiously shaking head.

"No!" Al yelled. "What are you, a moron? Of course not! We can accomplish anything, everything we want. Just like the tall man gets to slam-dunk, the short man gets to fly planes. You and me, we accomplish by thinking. That's our thing. What you do with it, is your business."

"No master plan?"

"Nope."

"You are lying, Al."

"Be my guest and fuck off."

Wilber tried to get Al back then. He screamed into a void. He screamed out loud until Nurse Griffin and a night watchman rushed into his room. Wilber hadn't realized his own agony, his own terrifying shouts. Nurse Griffin spoke in a soothing voice. She tucked him in, stayed with him for over an hour, at some point even sang a lullaby. Wilber finally closed his eyes, pretending to sleep to make her leave. Alone again, his eyes snapped open once more.

Al might have been listening the whole time, might have been laughing. The nurse singing to the old fart as if he were her baby. But nothing. Al didn't speak anymore. If he was still out there, he didn't let Wilber know.

Wilber was lost after that, lost and despairing - and then bitter for a long time. Bitter about the gift, the curse of the gift. The glorious accomplishments he had dreamed off.

He had thought of world peace. He had thought of spending time with leaders' minds, had thought of helping them, guiding them, showing them a glimpse of the universe he now knew. The world would have been a better place. Wilber had hoped of making everything better.

The depression that followed Al's explanations would have driven most people mad with glistening coal-black agony. And it had hurt Wilber, hurt him deeply ... until finally, he understood.

∞

Wilber was still sitting at the chessboard, the hall still dark and empty. He smiled now, thinking of Al, thinking of his own beginnings and all and everything he had learned since.

Yes, Al had been right, of course. It was all the same. All the same, all just pictures of the same object, different angles. Some of them stunning, some of the frightening, some of them shiny, some of them dull, some of them fascinating, some of the mundane, some of them lovely, some of them deadly ... always the same object.

Wilber gently took the black king between his fingers, then pushed the piece forward. It fell with a soft thud that nonetheless echoed through the hall. Yes, he could topple governments, this frail little man could incite wars, could cause the destruction of this planet.

All the same.

Things would be different for a few million years, but in the larger sense of the object, nothing would have changed. Al was right, and yet ...

Wilber just as gently put the black king back in place, then carefully slid king and queen closer together until they touched. Instantly Wilber could see the invisible glow pulse lightly around the two figures. Wilber knew so much more now. Al had frightened him back then, but Al was a frightened soul himself. For whatever reason Al was one of the chosen few, a soul with enormous power ... and yet he didn't have the gift of light, of experiencing pure joy. The sight of a new born butterfly, the sound of a simple drop of water, the scent of a yearning rose, were things meaningless to Al.

It had taken Wilber a few years after that encounter to hope and dream again. And with that he had moved on, he had learned more. Now Wilber could hear the others, knew of them. He could listen to Al when he felt like it. Al was still out there, killing, causing pain and destruction across the planet, happy in the creation of his own miseries. Pretending to be happy.

Good and bad, circle and line ... choices. Al had chosen the line, and Al was going to fade into nothing exactly as he had chosen for himself. His power, his choice, his destiny, nothing. In Wilber's eight years of mind reading experience infinite knowledge had filtered through and found fertile ground. He had been willing to learn, aching to learn.

And a future there was, a destiny there was.

Choice was everything.

Same object, different angles ... it wasn't about that.

"It's not about that, Al," Wilber spoke clearly in his mind now. "I know you're listening. I know you're scared. You can cause World War III, it won't matter. I can stop chaos, killings, even natural disasters as much as I want - it won't matter either. It's not about the big picture, Al, it has never been about the big picture. You were right there. But it's not about nothing either. It is about us. That's what it is about. Me, myself, I. Selfishness, Al, you should like that, shouldn't you? We all are our own universe. We choose. If we choose to fade away like the horizon at the end of the day, then that's what we get. But if we choose the never-ending rise and fall of the circle - "

"Great," Al suddenly cut in. "An eternity's worth of the same shit over and over again. Big fucking whoop-di-doo."

"Al," Wilber smiled with hope as Al spoke to him for the first time since their first encounter years back. "Do you want to know more?"

"I know more than you ever will. I know everything there is, Pal. I know what you're doing and so do you. You're a scared old man, scared of dying, scared because you really don't know what comes next. Your desperate attempts at making something bigger, something more meaningful out of what we have are plain pathetic."

"Then why are you talking to me now?"

"You have wasted my time for the last time and you're wasting it now. I'm outta here."

Silence. This time Wilber didn't scream, didn't force Al to stay. Wilber knew that Al was still listening.

"Do you want to know more?" No reply.

"Do you want to see?" Nothing.

"Do you want to be?" Silence.

Oh, well.

WORK

Duncan Grey sat down and let a broad smile spread across his face. This was the best moment of his entire working day. He always reached the subway in time, always hoping for the seat. The one in the rear, the one with the heater unit stuck right below, blasting hot air.

"Yeehaa," he softly muttered to himself as he removed hat, shawl and gloves. A tiny moment of perfect bliss, his frozen butt connecting with the hot seat. What joy. The rest of his day would be miserable as always, but this, this alone was worth quite a bit of crap.

Dostoevsky. The paperback was in bad shape, the front page missing and the corners looking as if they'd been chewed by a Doberman. Duncan liked his books in pristine condition, never bent their spines out of shape and read them with care. And yet he let his fingers gently slide across the mangled pages. Smiled again. This Doberman's name was Ellie. The little princess had somehow managed to empty his coat, had hidden the keys in his boots, eaten a pack of Wrigley's including the wrappers, and attempted to digest 'The Brothers Karamazov' for desert. Duncan removed the bookmark.

' ... what followed was almost an orgy, a feast to which all were welcome. Grushenka was the first to call for wine. "I want to drink. I want to be quite drunk, as we were before. Do you remember, Mitya, do you remember how we made friends here last time!" Mitya himself was almost delirious, feeling that his happiness was at hand. But Grushenka was continually ...'

Duncan frowned and softly closed the book. Nothing, not a word. He couldn't remember a single word of what he had just read. His mind was suddenly back home, leaving for work. Something had been wrong, something he couldn't put his finger on. Five in the morning, church bells across the street had announced it loud and clear. He had left the house on tiptoes, as always. He had slowly turned the keys, Nicky was a light sleeper and once up, the little play-o-maniac wouldn't hit the sack again. Duncan had looked up at the streetlight, tiny little specs of snowflakes hanging suspended in the air. No wind and the air too cold for real snow. Time was in slow-motion this early. He had turned the corner a little behind schedule. He liked to be past the bus stop by the time the church bells rang out ...

"The stop. They've moved the stop!" Duncan suddenly exclaimed and the old woman next to him gave him the evil eye. Duncan looked at his reflection in the window opposite him. He hadn't even noticed, hadn't noticed a thing when he had rushed by the stop yesterday and this morning. The stop meant two things to Duncan. One, the stop was part of his routine, pass the stop when the bells strike five times. Two, the stop was the old man. Duncan knew every line in the old man's face. A fascinating face, so old, beyond old. That face was luminous somehow, those eyes unbelievably clear like that lake in the Rockies he had once seen as a kid. He'd almost died there, almost drowned in that icy lake. Drowning in the old man's eyes wouldn't be bad, Duncan had always thought, drowning in those eyes would be a marvel, a new place somehow.

He loved his moments with the old man. Only a few seconds. And on the days the old man wasn't on the bench, Duncan would worry about him as if the man were his grandfather. Where was he? Sick? Dead? But then the old man would always be there again. Looking at him with those eyes. In those few seconds Duncan always felt a connection ... as if the man could see right into him. And yet that didn't feel intrusive, didn't feel as if someone was spying on him, quite the contrary. It felt warm, gentle. Duncan often felt his thoughts floating to the old man on the bench, wondering. There was something about him. Something so special.

He had been thinking about stopping on the way home. Just suddenly stop and stand. Look down at the old man, really say hello, find out about his name. Talk to him, maybe just sit next to him for a while. That would be brilliant. But every day was the same, he had to hurry home. His job drove him to the brink of insanity, no challenge, no brain required. But there was simply no way he could afford to let it go, pay was too good, benefits out of this world. The job was trying to punch holes into his soul, but he had five superheroes to fight that evil. Himself, Batman. His wife, Robin. Nicky, Superboy, Milo, Spider-Man and Ellie Supergirl. Nicky had given them all their hero's names. And Duncan smiled as he remembered how his heart had surged with love and pride when he had been officially named Batman by his son.

The family. As long as he managed to get home to his family in time, he could keep the monster at bay.

He picked up Dostoevsky again. He tried to read on but his thoughts stayed with the old man for a long time. He had seen him walk once. Not a walk, really, more like a shuffle. How could he possibly make that longer distance? It would take him forever. Duncan was worried - and suddenly felt guilty. Purely selfish thoughts, realizing that he was worried about those few seconds. That he might never have those moments with the old man again.

Then the subway stopped. Duncan Grey left in a hurry, squeezing his way past the crowd, the old woman's evil eye following him all the way.

NEW

A long vacated bird nest up in the branches of the tree, blackbird, from the looks of it. A giant crack in the sidewalk, must have happened when they had drilled to anchor the new stop. A lovely Italian lady, probably about three hundred and eighty pounds, spending most of her time at that third floor window across the street. She hated winter, Wilber knew. She couldn't find clothes her size and couldn't hang the laundry out the window to dry anymore. The picture-perfect Italian Mamma. She was sixty-seven, all her five children long gone and scattered across the States and her husband disappeared one day thirteen years ago. Nobody knew what had happened to Antonio Palocelli. Wilber knew.

∞

Francesca Palocelli always followed her daily routine. It was what allowed her to get up every morning, the routine allowed her to keep going. She got up at six o'clock sharp, never rolled out of bed, but sat up straight and swung her legs out onto the cold linoleum floor. Her children had given hear a nice little rug once, for Christmas, a few years back. They had put it right there by the bed. "To keep your feet warm, Mamma," they had said. Ever since the last one of them, Tino, had left the apartment, the rug was living out its life in the back of the closet. She had never liked it in the first place and she much preferred feeling the cold on the soles of her feet. The cold reminded her.

She never looked to the right side of the bed, the empty side, Antonio's side. The pillow was always fluffed, ready. But for thirteen years no head had rested there ... the sonofabitch had gone and left her, just like that. She knew she would cry when looking at the pillow, so she never looked. Instead she ground her teeth and clenched her jaw. The man didn't deserve her tears. Five children she had given him, and her youth, her body and her trusting love. He had even slept with the neighbor, hadn't even had the decency to try and hide it from her. Sonofabitch. Her cold feet walked her to the bathroom where she soaked her face in freezing water, rubbed her cheeks until they were a deep purple. She'd always done that. None of those expensive creams she'd heard off. Her face was still smooth, round, but smooth. Not the face of a sixty-seven year old woman. She had done all she could to keep Antonio, God knew. Breakfast, laundry, cleaning the apartment, checking for fresh roaches, shopping ... the routine wasn't easy to keep up anymore.

There was an old man sitting across the street at the new stop. Every day he was there now, just sitting there. He was interrupting her routine by his very presence. Whenever she passed the window she found herself stopping and staring down at him. Once in a while he would even look back up at her and smile. It was the strangest thing, sometimes she felt as if that guy was sitting there because of her. Just because of her. One of these days she'd go down to set him straight. Pervert, that's probably what he was, a dirty old man ... She stopped ironing, found herself glancing down at him again. No, that wasn't it. The old man was there to ... help her? Somehow that thought didn't let go of her. She shook her head and forced herself to focus on the old blouse again. She should have thrown it away ages ago ... but Antonio had always liked it.

∞

The Italian lady moved in and out of sight. Wilber didn't acknowledge her this time. It would just make her even more nervous. It was two weeks since they had moved the stop. Wilber loved it here. He would have shaken the orange men's hands now, plus a pat on their massive shoulders for moving the stop. This was better than good, this was great.

A new world.

He saw some of the same faces at the stop, same times. Not Ann, though. She had called in sick the day after her conversation with Wilber. She had simply taken off and gone to visit Devil's Peak, a place she had wanted to see ever since she'd seen 'Close Encounters Of The Third Kind'. Nature showing off, Wilber thought with a smile. He had accompanied Ann for a while. Had been with her yesterday when she had stared up in awe at the magnificent rock. Ann was fine. Just fine. Duncan still hurried by every evening. And, Wilber smiled to himself at the thought, he had noticed that Duncan had almost stopped that first day at the new stop. He would, eventually.

Wilber welcomed every new face. Smiled at them. Most ignored him at the beginning. But now the first ones were already settling in, getting used to Wilber, getting used to the ancient face with the shining eyes. Getting used to him tilting his head at the sound of the approaching bus. Even at this increased distance, he could still hear the bus before anyone could see it.

The new stop was full of wonders, full of presents, for Wilber. It felt just like Christmas ... his last Christmas. In these last two weeks Frank and Nurse Griffin had made no mention of their knowledge. Wilber could see their glances and Wilber knew of their sadness. He didn't visit their minds and gave them their space and time. In fact, Wilber was glad they didn't confront him with it. All of a sudden, Wilber wasn't that clear about his departure date anymore. Less than two and a half months now? It seemed impossible. He felt great, too good to leave. He had been given the chance to see another world with the move of the stop and he fully intended to explore this one, just as he had the last one. No, he couldn't die yet, absolutely not ...

... and yet he knew he'd never see blackbirds feeding their young in that nest.

KICK

He had been waiting outside Headnurse Griffin's office for what seemed like a long time now. No idea what this was about. But her voice hadn't been smiling when she'd called him on the intercom.

"I need to see you in my office, Jerry." That was all. No "Hi Jerry, how are you today?", no "Good morning, Jerry. Any good dreams to tell?" Nothing, her voice set, firm, official. She loved hearing about his dreams, usually. Not today. The door opened abruptly and a tall stick in a dark suit strode out briskly, a hint of an icy glance down at Jerry. Jerry watched him heading for the elevators. Headnurse Griffin was standing at the door, stern faced.

"Come in, Jerry."

With another glance at the man by the elevators, Jerry entered her office. She closed the door, went to her desk and sat. Then she just looked at him silently. Jerry didn't feel uncomfortable, not really, just wondering.

"Who was that?"

"That, Jerry, was Mr. Bachmann of Sutter, Henderson, Wingham and Bachmann. That fine gentleman is representing a certain plumber, Jerry." Jerry wasn't often surprised, now his mouth dropped open.

"The plumber?"

"The man you apparently crippled for life."

"Excuse me? I ...," Jerry's mind was racing back to sending that ignorant off with a shove and a beautiful kick. Jerry almost smiled at his rare meeting with physical violence, but smiling was out of the question now. Unless he wanted Nurse Griffin to do some kicking on his own butt.

"Just shut up and listen. Mr. Bachmann claims that you assailed his client who now lies at home with concussions, a shifted disk and lest I forget, severe mental trauma."

Jerry just stared at Nurse Griffin. Her face was practically set in stone, her face was ... not like her, he suddenly realized. She wasn't like that, her animated features were never frozen like that. She seemed to be fighting movement, her jaws working overtime. And then suddenly she burst out laughing. Laughing loud and contagiously. A startled Jerry missed a few beats, then added his own, confused laughter.

"It's not funny!" she yelled in between roaring laughter. But the more she tried to stop, the more the stormy waves of laughter shook her body.

"I'm sorry!" Jerry managed to shout in between his own high-pitched giggles. "I'm really sorry!"

"Oh just shut up for a minute!" They were still laughing uncontrollably when Frank wheeled into the room.

∞

"What the hell is going on?" With a flash Frank recalled watching Laurel and Hardy as a young man. Watching those two laugh had been the single most contagious thing on the planet, no virus could work his magic as fast as those. Frank had had some of his all-time best laughs with Stanley and Ollie. Now these two here didn't exactly look like a comedy team, but their laughter sure as hell ran a close second to the masters of slapstick. Frank joined in, he simply couldn't help it. His wheelchair started shaking, he was laughing so hard.

"What the fuck is going on here!?" he asked again, this time roaring with uncontrollable laughter. Amanda tried her best to speak and finally managed to spit out a few words.

"They're going to sue the home for two million dollars!"

Jerry's laughter died on the spot and that broke the spell for the others, too.

"What?" Frank asked as if he hadn't heard.

"Our friend Jerry here kicked the plumber." Jerry immediately tried to rise to his own defense, but her raised hand cut him off. "I know it's a bunch of bullshit, Jerry.

But I wouldn't have to deal with this bullshit if you hadn't kicked him in the first place."

"Two million dollars for a kick?" Frank tried to sound casual, at ease. But he could read Amanda, knew her laughter had come out of something else. "Hey Jerry, it's okay."

"But I - "

"Just go back to work, Jerry." Frank had his eyes fixed on Jerry, telling him to get out of here. Jerry hesitated for a second, then left quietly.

Frank wheeled closer to Amanda. She had stared down at her desk. Now, hearing him come, she got up and walked to the window. She kept her eyes away from him, kept the desk in between them, kept him at a nice and safe distance.

"Can't be that bad, Amanda."

"Do you have two million dollars?"

"They can't be serious."

"They are." She didn't look at him.

"Two million, huh?" Frank said.

"Yes."

" ... You wanna be alone, right?"

" ... Yes."

Give the lady some space, Frank. You can hug her some other time, she's a big girl, she knows what she's doing.

Come on, Frank. Get out of here.

He forced his hands to the wheels, gave them a sudden spin and did a one-eighty.

He left the room without another word.

∞

"Thank you, Frank," Amanda thought. She couldn't have looked at Frank. Frank, the best thing that had happened to her in decades. Wonderful Frank. She wasn't going to break down now. She wasn't going to break, period. She had brought this place back, she had fought every crack in this building, she would fight this, too. Amanda ground her teeth.

She stayed by the window, looking down. She planned on staying in this position until Wilber's return. She would wait right here, wait for him to shuffle into view. Wait for him to make her feel better. Whatever it was that Wilber did for her ... she needed some of that now.

Come on, Wilber, come on home.

The trees had lost most of their leaves by now. Merely a few faded yellow specs sprinkled across the branches. Fall ... Fall was okay. But fall was turning into winter, cold and snow looming daily. Right now Amanda needed some glistening sun shining into healthy greens, she needed happy birds singing and dancing across blue skies. Amanda let go of her jaw, felt her face sag.

Not a good moment, not a happy one, Amanda.

GO

Something was going to happen. Just a thing, a freak thing, nothing Wilber could put his finger on. He just had to wait and see. But something was definitely going to happen.

Anyway, time to go. Wilber had spent the afternoon in place, his bench as comfortable as ever. Tomorrow he'd tackle the mamma across the street. He would tell her about Antonio, her missing husband. Enough for one day. Time to head back, time for a bit of chess. Wilber got up and began his long shuffle home. He felt Francesca Palocelli's eyes on his back. She'd be there tomorrow, she'd probably put on her black Sunday clothes and actually come down and visit him tomorrow. No way Wilber could know that, but he felt it, just as she felt it. There was a powerful volcano bubbling within her and without knowing it, she was looking for a safety valve named 'Wilber Patorkin'. Tomorrow.

What a day this had been. Glorious. As he gingerly walked back, Wilber let the day's images march parade, let their colors and their flavors once more shine on his mind. A bird he'd never seen before, hints of blue and green under those wings, marvelous. A glowing boy smiling at him with intense joy - he was probably going to be like Wilber some day, not knowing yet, but feeling something. The sound of the church bells, closer now, he could hear the creaking metal, an odd twang in between high and low, like a voice pleading for a little oil. Francesca Palocelli, of course, and dozens of other faces he had never met before. The black priest, for one, seeing him when he had opened the portals, not smiling. Not much faith left in that man, should have never become a priest in the first place probably, but ... Frank?

∞

Frank saw Wilber stop and look up, still fifty feet away. Wilber raised his hand and smiled. How the fuck'd he know? Wilber never looked up from the ground, afraid of missing a step, afraid of the 'bonebreakers', as he called them. Frank figured it might have something to do with Wilber's thing, that mind reading stuff. He wheeled closer and was soon next to Wilber.

"You been reading my mind again?" Frank asked casually.

"Told you I wouldn't." Frank nodded as he spun the wheels and turned on the spot. As Wilber continued the shuffle, Frank joined him. Snail pace is good, Frank thought. Gives us time to talk, get a few things out in the open.

"Wilber Patorkin. The Champ. You doin' okay?"

"Yep."

"Before I go telling you a lot of shit ... could it be you already know about Jerry and the two million the fuckers want?"

"I know."

Frank just accepted it, no point in asking how. "Well good. So, any ideas?"

"About what?" Frank was getting aggravated. Stupid question.

"About what to do. About how we're gonna save the home. About how we're gonna scrape up not the two million but the cash for a lawyer. The home is in serious trouble, Wilber. And don't tell me you don't know that."

"It'll be okay."

∞

No need to make a big deal, Wilber thought, no need to explain a lot of it. No need for Frank to know about the plumber, a decent man named Alvin Powder. Alvin had made the simple mistake of telling his cousin about the incident. A cousin who was working as a legal assistant for Bachmann, a cousin who was now trying to grease his way into the firm. But this lovely relative of Alvin Powder's wasn't going to make any money off Jerry's kick. Wilber had talked to Alvin this morning, a casual little conversation inside Alvin's head. After that Alvin had locked himself in the toilet of the 'Olympic', the diner on the corner of seventeen and Worth. All the banging and hollering hadn't made him open that door for the next three hours. Alvin Powder would swear for the rest of his life that the voice of an angel had spoken to him that day. That voice had showed him the path of sweet honesty. Wilber knew that Alvin would call his cousin later today and tell him to forget about the whole deal. He wasn't going to rip off anybody. Actually, at the moment Alvin Powder was considering passing Jerry's kick right onto his cousin's scheming behind. Wilber smiled at the thought.

∞

"It'll be okay?" Frank had waited for more. But nothing. Wilber had spoken his cryptic fuckin' line and that was that. Frank was torn in between shrugging and yelling. Jesus Christ, Wilber, who are you?

"Yep."

" ... Okay." Frank slowly exhaled. He didn't have a clue how he was supposed to break the happy news to Amanda, but what the fuck. Wilber said it would be okay, good enough for Frank. Frank suddenly realized that Wilber could be telling him about a chicken giving birth to a cow and he would believe it. He had absolute faith in Wilber, simply because ... it felt right. If he'd be asked to choose between God and Wilber at this moment, he'd pick Wilber in a flash. God, he didn't know. Wilber, he knew. Besides, Wilber had not royally fucked with his life like that other guy ... if there was such a thing as God in the first place. What if there was no God? What if, Frank pondered, there was no such thing as a supreme being, watching, protecting, caring. What if there were only people like Wilber? People with ... a little something extra?

Wilber stopped and looked down at Frank.

"Frank, you make not listening kinda hard." Frank just looked back up at him. It didn't bother him now, Wilber could listen in all he wanted. Looking at ancient Wilber Patorkin, he suddenly decided to drop the crap. He knew he wasn't here because of Amanda, Jerry or the two million. He had come out here, because he wanted to get to Wilber, because he was afraid. Frank was scared to death. Death, shit. Wilber's death.

"You really gonna die?"

"We all die." Frank frowned at Wilber and Wilber quickly added, "Stupid line, I know. I'm sorry Frank ... Yes, I am going to die in two weeks and three days. Don't ask me how I know, because I don't know. There's nothing wrong with me, no cancer gnawing on my prostate, no tumor spreading in my brain, nothing like that. I'm just going to leave. That's all."

" ... Shit." Sudden tears were streaming down Frank's cheeks. Shit, shit, shit. And Wilber looking at him with that face, that wonderful angelic smile of his. As if he knew the world inside out, as if he knew Frank's soul. Wilber reached down, wiping Frank's tears with a lemony-fresh handkerchief.

"I'm not exactly happy about it myself, Frank. I would love to stick around for another while."

Frank just nodded, sniveling into Wilber's handkerchief, feeling like a little kid, feeling like that kid yelling, 'Shane! Come back, Shane!'

∞

Wilber looked up ahead. The street was busy. Children were running home from school, their high-pitched screams reverberating everywhere. The grocery store across the street was doing good business, people coming and going. It looked like it would be raining in a while ...

Something was going to happen.

... Not tomorrow, not far in the future, soon. Something is going to happen, Wilber. What are you going to do? A chill made Wilber shiver, he pulled the scarf tight, closed the top button of his coat. Nothing he could do now. Just be there when it happens, Wilber, just be there.

"Let's go home." Wilber lowered his eyes again, fixed to the ground. And off he shuffled.

∞

Frank watched him inch forward for a moment, the frail shell that held Wilber Patorkin. Then he set his chair in motion. With one flick of the wrist, one turn of the wheels, he had caught up with Wilber.

Wilber-time. Enjoy it, Frank. Enjoy it while it lasts.

KIDS

How the hell did it ever get this way, he wondered. Jesus. It wasn't what they all said, not that they were screwing like bunnies day in, day out. As a matter of fact, they were more careful than most married couples. But God had apparently decided to keep them coming. It was ridiculous. Pretty close to immaculate conception, Walt thought.

The lights changed and Walt Wirowsky yanked into first. The bus surged forward like a mad bull. Walt wasn't in the mood. He didn't purposely take it out on either the bus or the passengers, it just came out that way. He didn't feel like smiling much today. Normally he liked to drop a line, lay a joke on a sad face, help a little old lady up the steps, holler something funny back at his passengers. Not today. Today he was preoccupied with something else. He loved children.

One, two, three, perfect.

But they'd kept on coming. Walt had gone through every imaginable rubber he could get his hands on. He had bought the whole assortment at the drugstore, Ramses, Sheik, Trojan, you name them. He bought so many condoms that the ladies behind the counter started whispering every time he showed up. He swore he had heard the word 'pervert' several times. It got so bad he couldn't go there anymore. He tried stores across town, he tried the 'specialty' places. Places that made him look left and right before walking in, places that made this grown man blush. He tried more brands, tried the extra-ribbed, extra-strength, ultra-safe and he found some more unusual ones on the shelves between alien-looking dildoes and black and metal things that were painful just to look at. Didn't do any good, the babies just kept on coming.

Four, five, six, no problem.

But still it continued. Of course there was a certain pride that had gone with it. His friends making cracks, 'Walt the Wonderschlong', that sort of thing. Yep, no question about his reproductive powers. And his dick wasn't even that extraordinary. Solid average, but he managed to break the damn rubbers most of the time just the same. Of course his wife was on the pill on top of that. Double protection, right. Walt suddenly and furiously banged his fist onto the horn in the center of the steering wheel. He kept his fist there for too long and the roaring horn turned a few heads and frightened a mother with her children on the corner. Look at her, three kids, heaven. He slammed to a halt at the next stop. More people than usual left the bus, Walt didn't notice any of the frowning glances. He'd have to do the route nine more times today. Then back home to Gertrud and the kids.

Seven ... and eight.

Jesus, number eight on the way. Unbe-fuckin-lievable. He shifted, popped the clutch. The wheels of the bus screamed, planted black rubber and propelled the bus forward once again.

Gertrud. She was amazing. They deeply loved each other and he had never, not once, worried about her faithfulness. Besides, with all those kids on her like fleas all day long, even if she'd wanted to, she wouldn't find the time to screw around. Until a few kids back they had still found the time to love them all with equal measure. Now there were seven and seven and a half months from now there'd be eight. Eight children.

"Thank you God, thank you so very much," Walt grumbled. What the hell were they supposed to do, not have sex anymore? They did all they could, double, even triple protection sometimes. But every now and then one of those little suckers got by them. Fate, that's what it was. God was testing them and Walt could just hear him.

∞

"Hey, Pete, whaddaya think? Walt got enough? Think he can handle another one?" God leaning back on his throne, Saint Peter on his back, floating on a cloud.

"I don't know, God, maybe we should leave well enough alone. One more and he won't be able to fit them in that tiny apartment anymore. One more and he won't be able to feed them anymore. Of course, we could organize a nice big house in Jersey, get him a raise. Maybe let him win the lottery, how about that?"

"You kiddin' me, right? Where would be the fun in that? I mean, seriously, what would be the point if he could afford three nannies? Nope, buddy, Walt gets to suffer a little more. I mean really, it ain't exactly like I'm giving him the 'Job' treatment. He's still got his health, the love of his wife and seven, soon eight - hehe, wonderful children who will all grow up to be kind and prosperous."

"With another kid he may not live to see them get rich."

"Well, that'll be up to me now, won't it?"

"So what's it gonna be?"

"Haven't decided yet."

"Oh come on."

"We'll see."

Saint Pete frowns and rolls over on the cloud. Sticks his head right through, watches the planet below. Sees Walt in the bus, unhappy Walt. Saint Pete exhales. "Sometimes, God, sometimes you really ... ah, what the hell."

"Hey. Watch your mouth, will ya?"

"Sorry."

∞

Walt Wirowsky nailed the gas pedal to the floor, let the engine roar, the way he always did before the tunnel. Get through the black hole, there's the old man on the other side, maybe he's still at the stop, still sitting there. Walt checked his clock on the dash and realized that he was ahead of schedule. He suddenly knew what he was going to do. He was going to stop today, spend a few moments at the stop, talk to the old man. Yeah, that was exactly what he needed right now.

Walt almost smiled.

LIGHT

The moment Amanda left the building, the clouds parted and bright sunlight startled and delighted her. The oddest sensations struck her. She felt welcome heat despite the breezy cold. She felt the scent of spring flowers all around her when there was only damp grass and slush from last night's light snowfall. Sunshine, incredible how a simple ray of light could brighten a soul.

Moments ago she had suddenly decided to abandon her routine. All this pressure weighing her down required a little change, a little something extra. She'd still be in her office, considering her options, but then she had spotted Wilber and Frank on their way back home. Wilber and Frank, Frank and Wilber. What a couple. And then she had suddenly known, down there, with those two, that's where she needed to be right now.

FART

Henry 'The Fart' Barnum was racing, not home, not anywhere, he was just racing for his life. He couldn't go home, even though the sight of his parents would have probably scared the crap out of Tommy and his gang. When 'Mommy' and 'Daddy' were awake, they could frighten just about anybody. But right now they'd most likely be sleeping and so he couldn't make for home.

Go, Henry, go!

His senses were screaming for him to go faster. He couldn't feel his legs anymore, just kept running, faster, faster. Couldn't slow down. Mommy, and Daddy. Henry didn't usually say the M and the D words. When he did, he'd spit them out, with actual spit flying, but of course only when they couldn't hear him. "Moooo-spit-mmmy", which didn't work so well, and "Spit-daaaaady", which was kinda funny. Spit, trying to cast them out, spit, spit, spit. But his wish hadn't come true yet. Every time he reluctantly got home after school, there they were.

There had always been the cracked bottles on the floor, broken glass that had taught little Henry to dance at an early age. There had always been billowing clouds of burning smoke, responsible for giving little Henry the gift of coke-bottle glasses at age three. There had always been rotting fast-food, resulting in little Henry's gut, a gut fit for a fifty year old trucker. And there had always been the random needles on the carpet, death pointing up at little Henry. Surprisingly, one of those syringes had given little Henry something useful - it had given him the will to live.

"Mommy's gonna knit you a nice sweater with those," she had once announced with honest intention. His mother had actually tried to do it, but had never managed beyond the first line with that purple yarn. She had ended up cursing and letting the syringes fly. One of them had zoomed by Henry's head, little Henry trying to lose himself in 'Goodnight Moon' at the time. Henry had seen something out of the corner of his eye. He had turned then, very carefully, and had found the syringe stuck in the wall right next to his head. His mother had laughed hysterically. Syringe number two had ended up buried deep in the ceiling and there it still was, eight years later.

Henry, now eleven, had made that syringe his promise to the world. He knew that one day that syringe would fall ... and then his parents would fall, too ... one way or another.

Tommy and the gang were catching up.

Go, Henry, go, go, go!

Tom Moorer was a mere inch from grabbing Henry's jacket when Henry's fear let another screaming fart rush to his defense. Henry's version of an octopus shrouding itself in a cloud of black ink saved him. Tommy gagged, as if hit in the throat with a rock, and stumbled back. Best thing fast-food had ever done for Henry ... gas. Endless amounts of noxious gas.

"Get the Fart!" Tommy screeched as the rest of the pursuers rushed on. Down the street, past the church, past that staring black priest, just staring, not even trying to help. Henry would have loved to stop, would have loved to hide behind tall legs, but his feet kept pounding ahead. Fierce terror had become his 12 cylinder red-hot Corvette engine now.

Go, Henry, go! Go, Henry, go, go, go!

Just a little longer - then he would zigzag and cut across. There, on other side of the street, the old man from the stop with a guy in the wheelchair. Nah, no good, they wouldn't be able to help. They could barely move. No, he had to lose Tommy and his pals, he somehow had to get away from the gang. Same old crap, every place they had ever moved to. There were always the bullies, and there was always some gang taking offense at Henry's presence. Henry was fat, Henry was ugly, Henry 'regular Henry' smelled ... and Henry 'The Fart Henry' stank. Thanks, Mom, thanks, Dad. They sure had done their best to mess up even the slightest chance of him having a normal childhood. But nobody had figured on Henry's will, Henry's will to be.

Go, Henry, Gooooooooooooo!

NOW

Wilber shuffled on in silence and only after a moment noticed that Frank was falling behind. Falling behind? Wilber had actually taken the lead! He stopped and looked back. Frank was staring at something across the street, and Frank looked positively pissed.

"You leave that kid alone!" Frank roared. "You get the fuck home, you vicious little shitbags!"

Wilber followed Frank's gaze and saw five boys racing after a chubby kid. He knew of him, naturally, Henry Barnum, they called him 'The Fart'. You keep running, Henry, Wilber thought, you keep running because your time will come.

"You fuckin' bums! Leave him alone!" Frank continued. He wheeled past Wilber in a futile attempt at keeping up with them. "I'm gonna shove a fuckin' tripod up your - "

"There's Nurse Griffin," Wilber called out loud, almost losing his dentures. Frank looked up and saw Amanda heading toward them, less than a hundred feet down the sidewalk. Frank slowed, let the children rush on and Wilber could feel how Frank tried to let himself simmer down a bit. Frank waved to Amanda. Amanda raised her hand as well.

Wilber's head tilted to the side.

Bus coming, he thought. A second later the 93 bolted from the black hole of the tunnel. Too fast, Wilber thought, always too fast. Someday something would happen ... Wilber suddenly stared and realized, his jaw slack, there it was. 'Someday something' was now ... and Wilber watched uncertain future come into focus.

Amanda was closer now, smiling at Frank. The bus less than thirty feet behind her. Henry was shaking off a hand that had grabbed hold of his jacket, his arms flailing wildly. Then the frightened wide-eyed boy cut across, completely unaware of the bus.

Wilber raised his hands, palms toward the bus, as if he could block it from his view. He shouted, "No! Watch out!" ... Not a sound came from Wilber's wide open mouth. Just his dentures loosening, slipping.

For an instant, the world seemed to stand still. Wilber calmly looked around. Headnurse Griffin had stopped, the bus just behind her. Her eyes were now registering the imminent disaster, her mouth open in surprise. Frank's wheels were motionless, a smile still on his face, his arm still raised in a greeting. Wilber saw Walt the bus driver staring helplessly down at the boy who was below the windshield, barely ten feet from his bus' bumper. The boy was gonna die and there was nothing Wilber could do about it.

∞

Henry's head was twisted, his pounding feet hanging in mid-air. He had suddenly felt the bus, and now it was coming for him. Too late. Dead, no more Mommy and Daddy. In that split-second Henry settled into his destiny - dead, now … Could be worse. Henry's heart cried out loud even as it smiled with immense relief.

∞

Gotta yank the handbrakes, the steering wheel, gotta yank something! Walt Wirowsky stared through the windshield, down at the boy in front of the bus. Squashed like a bug, splattered like a fly across the bumper … Complete horror and complete acceptance. There was nothing Walt could do, too late … the kid was as good as dead.

Then he suddenly felt the bus, the entire bus, yank sideways. Walt was thrown from his seat and violently hurled against the passenger door.

∞

Wilber's hands were still raised ... Ten feet, eight, six. His silent scream grew louder and wilder than anything he had ever heard in his life. His dentures dropped and clattered off the sidewalk and into a sewer hole. Wilber watched in awe as the entire bus shook with sheer force. The direction of the 93 suddenly and powerfully shifted, as if King Kong's invisible hand had given the bus a sudden shove to the right. The bus missed Henry by mere inches and that was the last thing Wilber saw.

Then he gently faded into unconsciousness.

CHAPTER TWO

HOSPITAL

WHITE

I can't feel a thing, she thought. Take your time, Amanda. Take your time. She had woken to a strange sensation, something she couldn't place. It hadn't frightened her, but she did sense a glimpse of some unpleasant truth heading her way. She didn't open her eyes. Where was she? The place smelled white and clean, and the bed, not hers, felt crisp and fresh under her.

Then she remembered.

"Amanda?" Frank's voice, wonderful Frank. She still didn't open her eyes but her fingers gladly clasped his hand. "Everything's gonna be fine, Amanda. You're going to be just fine, you hear me?" Picking up the lie was easy with closed eyes. Frank's face might have been able to fool her, but his voice gave him away. Frank was hurting, his voice fighting for steadiness.

Amanda opened her eyes and smiled at Frank.

Hospital. Fuck. Jesus fuckin' Christ this couldn't be happening, this couldn't be real. But here he was, with her. Frank had been in the hospital for all of the last seven days. It had taken him a few curses, a few tears and a sucker-punch until they had decided to let the old maniac stay day and night. No fucking way he'd have gone home.

Amanda in 317, Wilber two floors up in 531.

All Frank had was in this whitewash of a building and Frank would have slaughtered half the hospital staff had they tried to remove him from here. There had been only one orderly with a heightened sense for rules and regulations. Frank had tried to reason with him for about a second, then the asshole's condescension had rubbed him the wrong way. Frank had simply grabbed hold of the white cloth, then pulled the man close and let his other fist rush up to connect with the man's chin. Frank had not felt that powerful in years as the instant the orderly slammed back into the wall and sank to the floor, eyes rolling like a cartoon character.

"Fuck every single one of you!" Frank's voice echoing through the hallways, heads turning, everybody keeping a safe distance now. "I am eighty-five years old and I got two reasons left to live for. Both reasons are here in this hospital so I ain't going home! You get Superman to try and kick me outta here and I'm gonna kryptonite his ass, you hear me?! I will not leave this hospital until I leave together with my friends. Now I want a bed in Wilber Patorkin's room."

Nobody had moved, neither for nor against him, faces closed. But then an old guy had approached, looking like some fairy tale wizard with his full white beard and his flowing white outfit like a cloak on him. He had talked to Frank like a man, not down, straight on. Explained that he was the head surgeon around here, first name Frank, too. Frank Jew-something. And Frank the Jew was all right. He arranged for the bed and everything and said not to worry about any charges. Frank the Jew had simply swung his magic wand at a few underlings and with that Frank got set up with a separate room, three meals a day, plus his private TV, VCR and phone. Frank was grateful, but seven days later he still hadn't seen the inside of his own room. He spent practically all his time with Amanda and wheeled up to see Wilber in between.

"Hi Frank," she said simply.

Amanda's face was swollen, large bruises visible in between bandages. And still she was beautiful, her smile beaming at Frank. Amanda. First time she'd opened her eyes in seven days and now Frank simply lost it. He couldn't hold back the tears, she was awake, she was awake. And seven days of working on strength and lies evaporated into nothing. He couldn't pretend in front of her, he couldn't lie to her ... and he couldn't tell her. And so he just cried.

∞

Amanda looked at Frank, his head pressed against her hand, his face turned away. She could feel his hot tears drenching the back of her hand ... she could feel ... that was something.

TEETH

Okay. Wilber opened his eyes when Amanda Griffin did, same exact time. They had both been in a coma. Wilber probably could have gotten himself out of it earlier, but what the heck. Amanda had needed company in limbo, it might have sucked her away otherwise. And so Wilber had stayed with her, had talked to her - nothing she would remember now.

The bus had shifted direction against the laws of physics. It should have been impossible for the bus to move the way it did. The 93 had literally been slapped off its regular route, thus saving Henry the fart's life. Unfortunately Headnurse Amanda Griffin had not been equally lucky. Henry's good fortune was to be her misery. The bus had plowed right into her.

Good thing the hot dog vendor had set up his stand right there.

For an instant Amanda was carried by the bus, like a hood ornament. Then the brakes gripped and Headnurse Griffin continued traveling on her own. As if catapulted she flew toward the hot dogs where Bekim Jussuffi had just opened the umbrella a few minutes earlier. It looked like rain and Bekim liked his customers happy and dry. He heard the brakes screech behind him. By the time Bekim turned, Amanda plunged head-on into the umbrella, toppling both the stand and Bekim. He managed to scramble aside just as the bus bulldozed into the stand, sending hot dogs and onions flying.

Shaken, Bekim thanked Allah for his life, then cursed the moron of a bus driver and moments later told the ambulance driver that he thought he'd heard a snapping sound when the lady had landed.

∞

"Whaddaya know," Wilber mumbled to himself in wonder.

No other explanation but the impossible. Wilber hadn't had a problem with 'impossible' for years now. There were simply new experiences once in a while, things that hadn't been seen, things that hadn't been thought of. But impossible? Nothing was. He himself had obviously shifted the bus, had saved little Henry and in the process had just about killed his best friend's love. Well done, Wilber. There was nothing he could have done differently, though, Wilber realized that with utter calm. It had happened the way it had been supposed to happen.

Something new. Another step into a foggy destiny. Mind reading was pretty much mastered. Now this. And obviously this wasn't the Uri-Geller-garden-variety spoon wiggling, this was large, 'this' could move entire fast-moving buses. Wilber wondered, for just an instant, what else he would be able to do. What would this be good for? Then a voice butted in.

"Nice going, buddy."

Wilber didn't have to open his eyes. He knew there was nobody in his room. And he knew the voice.

"Hello, Al."

"Wilber, my poor misguided fuck-up of a pal, you did well there. There's hope for you yet. Almost snuffed her out. Congratulations."

"You know it was an accident." Wilber regretted it the moment he said it.

"Of course it was," Al said sweetly. "Tell me, friend Wilber, having fun crippling old ladies?"

"She'll be fine."

"Not in this life."

"You don't know that."

"Don't feel bad, Wilber. It's a waste of time, that feeling miserable bit. Learn to enjoy the disasters you cause. Trust me, it's a hell of a lot of fun."

Wilber took a deep breath, then gingerly sat up. He felt fine, no bones broken despite his fall. He consciously kept his mind blank for a few beats, pulled on his robe, walked to the window. It was snowing quarter-sized snowflakes, roofs and trees all white. Beautiful. Stark and cold, but beautiful.

"Pal, don't think I'm waiting around. While you're ignoring me I'm sending a forty-seven passenger bus down a cliff in India. I'm telling you, that place is so fuckin' overpopulated, I just can't win! However many I stamp out down there, double and triple grow back, worse than fuckin' mushrooms. Oops, forty-nine passengers. Didn't see the babies in the back. Ah, do you hear them scream, Wilber? What a feeling, being with them as the bus sails through the air. Suspended, forty-nine people living at their most passionate and ... Boom! Nice crash, that's the way - ah shit! I can't believe it, all forty-nine of them dead even before they flames hit. Oh man, this could have been a truly great one ... still. Guess we'll just have to keep on trying, right Wilber?"

The snowflakes were sailing, swirling, playing in the wind. Gusts sent them up again, up along the walls of the hospital. Both ways, flakes going down, flakes going up at the same time. Anything is possible. Wilber suddenly willed snowflakes in all directions. He had moved a ten ton bus, he could surely move snowflakes. And he could. Flakes started dancing the wildest formations in front of his hospital window. Then Wilber turned to his room, looked around and let his mind grab hold of the furniture. A chair moved across the floor, the bed slid up the wall and the table flew a perfect circle around the bed. It was so easy. Wilber kept his deeper mind to himself and wondered about Al. Who was he? Where was he? And why was he?

"I wasn't ignoring you, Al, I was just enjoying the view."

"Did you like my little India story, Wilber? Did you hear them all scream?"

"Yes, I've heard them."

"And?"

"What do you expect me to say, Al?"

"Oh I don't know, 'You're disgusting', maybe. 'You're a sick fuck, Al', maybe. You know why I canceled that bus,

Wilber? I'll tell you why. Thought it might get to you. After all, you seem to have a thing with buses, don't you? A bus kills your wife, then you waste your years watching buses go by ... and now you use a bus to get the nurse. What's with that, Wilber? What is it with you and buses?"

Wilber sighed softly. There was no point in continuing this. Time to go, or Al would really piss him off. One last question, though.

"Where are you, Al?"

"St. Petersburg." Al's reply had come just a little too fast, too quick to carry the ring of truth with it.

"St. Petersburg, really? ... I don't think so, Al. I think you're here. I think you're here in Brooklyn. And I think you're here because I am here."

"Look who knows so much."

Wilber knew he was right. Al was near, somewhere in the same city. "And I know why you're here."

"There is nothing you can tell me."

"You would love to do more than just manipulate people's minds, wouldn't you? I bet you would love to move entire buses." Silence. "It's so easy, Al. I can move anything I want." Nothing from Al, static. "I can probably move buildings now. No limits. Tell you what, Al. Meet me at the hospital cafeteria, noon tomorrow, and I'll tell you everything I know."

But there was only silence.

Wilber got back into bed and closed his eyes moments before a young orderly named Gregor Sutter walked in, checked the sheets and took Wilber's pulse.

∞

Gregor smiled when he noticed the change. Wilber Patorkin was getting better, pulse clean and strong again. Incredible. Here was the oldest man in the United States of America, one hundred and fifteen years of age and he was getting stronger! The young orderly felt something like awe. A guy like this one, a guy this old had to have something special, wisdom, maybe, health, definitely. He turned around to make sure he was alone. Foolish, but still, he didn't want to look stupid in front of others. Because he was about to do something he wouldn't be able to explain. He gently placed his hands on both sides of Wilber's sleeping face, closed his eyes and stopped breathing.

∞

Wilber kept the smile on the inside. The young man hovering over him was attempting meditation. Gregor Sutter, a roaming soul looking for a direction. Wilber could see the young man's apartment, cramped full with a thousand books. Everything from Celtic beliefs to the power of Buddhism, from Egyptian gods to the harmony of Feng Shui. Lots of useful directions, but Gregor had simply read a lot and understood nothing. It was obvious that the young man had no idea what he was doing. Gregor had simply felt the urge to somehow absorb a little of whatever it was he thought Wilber possessed. Wilber sort of enjoyed the young man's enthusiasm for something he had no knowledge of. Give the man a present, he thought to himself. Wilber sent a little jolt into those two young hands, kept on sleeping though, not a move.

∞

Lightning bolts, that's how Gregor Sutter would describe this moment to friends and family until his dying day. He felt two solid lightning bolts surge through his hands, up both arms, whirl through his brain and finally unite in his heart with a white-hot flash.

Gregor came to, sitting on the floor. He checked his watch. Jesus, he must have been sitting here like this for more than fifteen minutes. He scrambled to his feet, felt woozy. Everything around him seemed kind of ... strange. Not out of focus. Quite the opposite, everything around him seemed perfectly clear and positively glowing. Every object, every line, seemed to have its own life.

And every now and then throughout Gregor Sutter's life, he would swear he could read other people's minds.

∞

It was a while after Gregor had rushed off to continue his rounds, when Al's voice came back.

"Noon's not good."

"How about one, then?"

"How about three?"

"You're on."

Wilber smiled and didn't smile at the prospect of actually meeting the infamous Al. "Out of curiosity, what's so important you can't make it earlier?"

"Ain't me, Pal, it's you. You got a visitor coming."

"Tomorrow, really? Who?" Just two buddies talking.

"Wouldn't want to spoil the surprise. See ya tomorrow."

Wilber nodded, just accepting it and knowing that Al had gone. Gone to burn and kill no doubt. This time, though, Wilber was mistaken, because Al suddenly popped back on.

"Oh yeah. And do yourself a favor ... get a set of teeth, buddy. You may wanna look halfway decent."

And with Al's parting words, Wilber remembered the fate of his dentures. Down the sewer. Right ... Lovely. He moved his lazy tongue around the empty cavity. No teeth, hmn.

SCAM

"Piss off." Frank called it loud enough for the guy to hear. The Transport Authority inspector had been here four times already, and there he came, ambling around the corner, for an encore. To Frank, 'piss off' seemed like the only possible greeting at this point. What was he supposed to tell him? So he was a witness to the accident. So what. He told the story ten times over and he had better things to do. Wasn't his problem that the driver of the „bus of doom" was suspended. He had told Mr. Inspector all he knew, all he had seen. So it didn't make sense, so a bus couldn't move like that, not Frank's problem. He had his friends to take care of. As the guy came closer, flashing a tired yet professional smile, Frank said it again with great clarity.

"Piss off".

It was easy staying calm. Paul Wenderwiler heard worse day in day out. Nobody liked him because nobody liked questions. Even the ones who pretended. Paul knew, for a fact, nobody liked questions.

Especially when they figured out that Paul could get past the bullshit in a heartbeat. He didn't look like it, a fact that had him nicknamed the Transit Authority 'Colombo'. Made him proud and he spent extra time each morning perfecting his unkempt hair, his weary slouch, his droopy eyes and, of course, his just-past-acceptable wrinkled clothes.

No bullshit. Buses did cause accidents from time to time, naturally. There were legitimate claims, of course. But there also were those trying to make a buck off the company. And that's where Paul Wenderwiler came in. He had the great ability to ferret out the phonies. He alone had saved the Transit Authority seventy-two million in bogus claims. So 'piss off' didn't bother him, if anything, 'piss off' gave him just the right fuel to try to crack that nut this time.

Paul clicked on his smile as he approached the wheelchair man, Frank Wilkinson. The guy was definitely loony, a white man acting and talking black for no apparent reason. During his first visit six days ago, Paul had noticed that Wilkinson's wheelchair was spray-painted black. What a nut. Not his problem, his problem was the accident. His problem was the claim that would, without a doubt, be brought against them any day now. His problem was figuring out just what had happened. The little boy had been too scared to have seen anything. The lady was still in a coma, as far as he knew, same as that other guy that had fainted at the sight of the accident. So Paul had just two sources, Walt Wirowsky, the driver, and Frank Wilkinson, the guy trying to wheel away from him now. He'd catch up with him at the elevators. The odd thing was that their stories matched. Their bullshit stories of the suddenly shifting bus matched perfectly.

"Hi there, Mr. Wilkinson."

"You got a hearing problem?" Frank said, waiting grimly and obviously frustrated at the elevator.

"Sometimes. You know, it seems to help me filter out the unpleasant stuff. So, how are you to - "

"I said, piss off."

"Good to hear. Me, I'm not that good today. Slept uneasy. Guess this case has got me rattled. Special cases keep me up all night. Look at my gut. TV dinners, sometimes three a night. What am I supposed to do, right? Wife left me eleven years ago and I don't blame her. Who could take a nut like me? When a case bugs me, I just forget about everything else."

Paul could see the wheelchair-man grit his teeth. Good. He liked to lay it on a little, spread some of his own bullshit, get them unnerved, get them boiling, spitting, talking. The bullshit story about his wife leaving just fit his image. It seemed to make him more real. Fact was, Marjorie was home, their three kids were in college, and his gut was due to his wife's excellent Mediterranean cooking. The only truth was the late nights. And this case did keep him up. Come on, a bus shifting directions like that ... it just wasn't possible.

"You don't mind if I tag along, do you?"

Frank didn't open his mouth, got in the elevator, pushed the button for Wilber's floor and resigned himself to another mind-numbing monolog by the guy. Mr. Inspector leaned against the wall, next to him. They had the ride to themselves.

"How're the patients doing today? No wait, don't bother telling me, I'll check the charts. You know, Mr. Wilkinson, I do understand. I'd probably be pissed off, too.

Some idiot keeps coming by, asking the same stupid questions over and over. But hey, that's my job. I hear accident, I start looking for the scam. It's what they pay me for. And yes, it is what I love to do. Nothing like breaking a good scam. Now this one, I just can't figure it. Yet."

Fifth floor, Frank got out and wheeled toward Wilber's room. The guy tailing him. Damned if I let the fucker near Wilber, Frank thought. Frank started considering different moves. If they guy tried to get into Wilber's room, he would have to stop him somehow. Check your own fuckin' chart, asshole. Frank considered hurting the man ... but he decided to simply stop for now. So did Mr. Inspector.

"I have to figure, who's trying to sue the company on this one, right? Who's in for the cash? The old lady? Nope, her part's straight forward. She's just the innocent bystander. So where's the scam? I got two witnesses, right? You and the driver. You both tell the same story, the bullshit story. Now I have to ask myself, why would Frank Wilkinson tell Walt Wirowsky's story? Where's the scam? Then I'm thinking, could the driver himself try to sue the company, blame faulty equipment? Sounds stupid enough, so I check it out, right?"

Frank was not ready to take any more of this. He set the wheels in motion and headed for room 531. Just try getting in there with me, fucker, just you try. The inspector, too, moved again and followed Frank like a puppy.

"So I check around. Turns out Walt Wirowsky, 'The Wonderschlong', as they call him at the depot, has been at it again. They already have seven children, now number eight is on the way. Walt won't be able to make his payments anymore. Good old Walt needs a little help ... so he figures he takes the money from the company. He arranges the accident. However the hell he did it, I don't know yet. But don't you worry, I always get the details. Then he lays on the bullshit story, a bullshit story nobody would believe ... unless he had a second witness. You."

Frank couldn't believe his ears. He turned the right wheel hard, spun around. And slammed the metal footrest into Paul Wenderwiler's shin. The man yelped, cupped the pulsing spot with both hands and hopped on one leg. Frank noted with quiet satisfaction that the idiot did have a pulse after all.

"Get to the fucking point."

"I needed ... a connection. And that, surprisingly ... wasn't all that hard to find. Walt Wirowsky's father went to Hammond High. You know the place, don't you? After all, you grew up in that place, too. After all you went to the same school. And the funny thing is, you and Wirowsky's father attended the same years. You knew him, knew him well. Just as you know his son."

Frank was perplexed. He caught on quickly, but was nonetheless stunned. What the fuck kind of a coincidence is that, he thought. Wirowsky? Hank Wirowsky, the skinny little kid he used to defend against the Barker boys? That Hank Wirowsky?

"Hank Wirowsky?"

"Great. We're talking again. Yes, Hank Wirowsky. You know? I like you, Mr. Wilkinson, you got talent. You play stunned like a pro. As if you didn't know a thing ... but you knew. Look, I'm just guessing here, but I'd say Walt probably came to you, maybe somehow you even came up with that plan together. So here's what I think. I think you and Walt planned the whole thing. You just didn't figure on the boy and the lady."

"The bus driver is Hank Wirowsky's son?" Frank asked, still stunned at the incredible connection this moron had discovered.

"Alright, alright, Mr. Wilkinson. You can come off it now. I said I liked your act, but please don't overdo it. So why don't you tell me what really happened?"

Frank swallowed a heavy dose of anger. Fuck it, why get aggravated. I have more important things to do, Wilber is waiting in there and I'm talking to wannabe-cop-face out here. Guy thinks I'm a good actor ... Frank suddenly frowned, put his hand above his eyes. Alright, Frank thought, give the man a little grieving, a little 'caught-in-the-act' guilt. Frank's chest heaved once, twice, not too much.

∞

Bingo, Wenderwiler thought. The wheelchair man was stifling a sob behind his hands, he was ripe and ready to spill. Paul Wenderwiler bent toward him, put a hand on Frank's shoulder. Give the man a little buddy-buddy stuff, I know where you're at. Frank Wilkinson was a tough old man, but Paul had him now. He put his face close to Frank's ear.

"I know how you feel. You feel terrible about that lady, you feel guilty as hell. But that wasn't your fault, Frank. Nothing you could have done. Walt Wirowsky suckered you into this, he made you part of the scam. It's him I want. Come on now, Frank, you can tell me, take the pressure off."

"Okay." Frank Wilkinson looked at him, deeply frowning, sniveling. Then he flashed the wildest grin and rammed his forehead into Mr. Inspector's paralyzed face. Paul Wenderwiler reached for his bleeding and broken nose as he fell. "You don't know much, do you, Pal."

"You're crazy." Paul Wenderwiler stared up in disbelief. He had a handle on most things, physical violence was not one of them. He had never been able to take it, never been able to dish it either. That was why he had flunked police academy. That was why he was here now, pretending to be happy in his fucked-up job. Now the maniac in the chair obviously didn't have a problem with physical violence. Paul hated his job, especially right now. He felt like letting it all go. Maybe start something new, gardening maybe. He'd always loved flowers. Yes, why not. Forget about the scams, forget about saving the company's ass. What had they ever done for him? Pay was solid, pension guaranteed. But where was he after all these years, and more importantly, who was he? He needed a change, a new direction, and at this instant he saw his path clearly.

Landscape Artist. Yes, that was it. Use the savings, learn the trade, open a business upstate someplace.

Landscape artist, yes indeed. Paul Wenderwiler smiled.

∞

"You oughta take care of that nose. Five floors down is emergency, they'll set it before you can sneeze."

"Okay," Wenderwiler said with a vacant smile. One hand was holding his nose in place, the other leaving red streaks on the wall as he struggled to his feet.

"And you leave me alone from now on, you understand?"

"Okay." The inspector was absently dusting off his pants, leaving more red streaks. He kept on smiling and turned to leave.

"And the same goes for Amanda Griffin and Wilber Patorkin, you hear me?"

"Okay."

"Okay?"

Frank began to worry. Maybe he had hit him a bit too hard. He had just wanted to startle his ass a little, not permanently scramble his brain.

"Okay." Paul Wenderwiler nodded again, lifted his bloody hand in a friendly wave and walked off.

Frank was tempted to follow the man, make sure he got to emergency alright.

But then Paul Wenderwiler entered the elevator, waved a last time like a happily spaced-out flower child and was gone.

Frank shrugged and headed for Wilber's room.

PEE

He had to pee. Urgently. But now was not the time - he needed to take care of Rosenberg first.

Clarence Wainright was Chief Administrator at Brooklyn Medical Center and he couldn't remember a more exciting day than the present. This was good, this was amazing - if only Rosenberg wouldn't screw it up. Clarence was standing outside Chief Surgeon Franklin Rosenberg's office, breathing deeply, trying to get a grip on his excitement. He would have to manage the man behind this door somehow.

Franklin Rosenberg was the best there was. He had been the youngest to graduate, top of his class, top of any class, any year, for that matter. The man had been promoted chief surgeon when most others were still digging their way through anatomy books. His career curve had risen sharply, meteoric, as everyone had predicted. Rosenberg had gone on to head some of the most prestigious units across the United States. And then, after twenty-two years at the very top, Franklin Rosenberg had taken the job at Brooklyn Medical Center. Clarence was proud of BMC, but he was well aware that the place was a clearly visible dead end for a man of Rosenberg's brilliance.

Clarence didn't know all the details - after all he himself had come to BMC only four years ago - whereas Rosenberg had been here for the last seventeen years. Incredible, Clarence thought, as he absently nodded to passing nurses. He couldn't be bothered with their barely hidden grins right now. Everybody knew that he was scared of Franklin Rosenberg - hell, as a matter of fact he didn't know a single person not scared of the man. You'd better fear a man like Franklin Rosenberg. Clarence couldn't get himself to grab the door knob just yet - relax, Clarence. Compose yourself ... he detested the man inside that room as much as he admired him. What guts to come here.

Clarence knew that the bold move had cost Rosenberg his family. His overpriced wife had left him, his two grown sons didn't speak to him anymore. Now Rosenberg lived in a rusty semi-detached in Rego Park, alone. After seventeen years at BMC Rosenberg was still brilliant ... he just didn't stand on ceremony anymore. And that was exactly Clarence Wainright's current problem. Where others were diplomatic, Rosenberg was straight-forward. Where others were polite, he was scathing. Where others pretended, he simply left. Rosenberg didn't get invitations from the medical community anymore, he was considered an embarrassment. With a sigh, Clarence Wainright walked into the lion's den.

BEARD

Clarence strode in with practiced firmness, swift and wide movements - nothing hesitant about his movement. Leadership courses had taught him that ... but Franklin Rosenberg had probably not taken that course, he did not even look up from his paperwork. Clarence stood there like a school boy, waiting for his punishment. Nothing to do but wait - he knew Rosenberg wouldn't acknowledge him until he felt like it. Nothing to do but wait - and look around.

Window was open, the snowflakes were playing odd games outside. Clarence' glance wandered across the diplomas and certificates on the wall. He smiled at them for they meant one victory for Clarence Wainright. He had fought so hard to get Rosenberg to put them up again. Unbelievable, Rosenberg had dumped all this 'trophies' in the cellar storage years ago. The man had more diplomas than any other doctor in the country. As new Chief Administrator Clarence had instantly seen the missed potential. These diplomas impressed clients, these diplomas made money for the hospital. And so Clarence had fought with all his might for Rosenberg to put them back up.

Rosenberg still didn't look at him. He was signing papers while at the same time reading the Medical Weekly. Franklin Rosenberg's beard was long and white and always brought on wizard references. There was something to that, Clarence thought. There certainly was something special about Rosenberg, not exactly Gandalf, but still, impressive ... and now Gandalf looked at Clarence.

"What's up, Clarence?"

"Wilber Patorkin. He's awake, he's out of his coma and feeling just splendid." Clarence was desperately trying not to jump up and down. He knew he'd look like a kid in desperate need of a restroom.

"That's good news. Now Clarence, why don't you go take a piss and come back when you're calm." Sigh. Clarence tried to ignore the unpleasant comment, the way he always did. This was, after all, Franklin Rosenberg's way of talking to people, all people. Always saying the first thing that came to his sharp mind, which was often highly inappropriate. Rosenberg's comments were unfortunately also correct pretty much all the time. It was a plain fact that Clarence had resigned himself to years ago. Even now - of course he had to pee. Not now. Rosenberg was too much for everybody's good. Clarence would have to make sure to keep him away tomorrow, somehow. Tomorrow would be one of the greatest days in the history of Brooklyn Medical Center, and he, Clarence Wainright, would be the one who made it happen.

"Guess who's in town tomorrow," Clarence asked.

"Clarence, tell me or get the fuck out. I'm busy."

"Melvin Taylor." Clarence couldn't help grinning. Rosenberg on the other hand didn't show the slightest bit of interest.

"I'm still busy."

"He's coming here."

"Why?"

"Because Wilber Patorkin is here."

Rosenberg's eyes were seemingly piercing holes into Clarence and Clarence fought the urge to rub his forehead. Don't be afraid, Clarence, you can do it. He just had to get Rosenberg to stay away tomorrow, somehow. He rarely got Franklin Rosenberg's full attention. He seemed to have it now, Rosenberg was still looking at him, silent, clearly waiting for more. Clarence swallowed hard and continued.

"He's the oldest man in the entire United States. Taylor's people thought a visit might make a great photo op for his re-election campaign."

"What if I don't allow visits?"

Clarence turned an instant crimson red and started puffing.

"He's fine! I read the charts myself, I've even - "

"Lighten up, Clarence. If the President of the United States wants to visit our special guest, why the hell not."

"I've already sent out a press release," Wainright pressed on. Things were going well so far. "The hospital will be packed tomorrow. I've also gone through a program with the President's people, it'll include a lunch with staff and patients, then a private visit with Wilber Patorkin and then you know, well, I - "

"Clarence, give yourself a rest. I will not attend."

Clarence Wainright could barely hide his immense relief, giving Rosenberg his best professional sincerity look.

"Are you sure, Franklin? I'm certain the President would love to shake your - but I mean if you're sure, I don't want to be the one forcing you to do anything you don't want to do, you know. You certainly don't have to - "

"That's kind of you."

"Hey, anything I can - "

"I'm still busy." Rosenberg sunk his head again, focused on the work in front of him. Nothing left to say, Clarence thought happily - it had worked.

Tomorrow would be a success. He left as quietly as he could, leadership courses forgotten.

MONEY

Franklin Rosenberg kept looking out the window. The snowflakes. Wainright. Money. Easy enough to see through the guy. Get the cameras in here, show off as much as possible. Get a few sound bites on the news. With a little luck there wouldn't be any cop killings to snatch the city papers' headlines tomorrow. Yes, Clarence Wainright would probably manage to have the picture of the President and the name of 'his' hospital on the cover of the 'Times', the 'News' and, with the oldest man alive headline, even on the cover of the 'Post'. All that publicity would translate into money, fresh funds, new donors. Yep, it always came down to money.

He looked around the room and didn't see framed diplomas. He only saw bare walls.

He leaned far back in his high-backed chair, put his feet on the table and onto a stack of still unsigned papers ... and lost himself in the snowflakes.

SLEEP

Every time the doctors and nurses came to check on her, she pretended to be asleep. She didn't want them to tell her anything. She didn't need to hear the truth from strangers and she definitely didn't need to see their eyes looking down at her with pity. She was sure she wouldn't be able to handle that.

Somebody tried to wake her now, touched her arm, nudged her lightly, one set of fingers even pricked her. She didn't budge. She had woken from her coma hours ago, but nobody other than Frank had seen the white of her eyes yet. They stayed on, performing their duties with hushed voices. One took her pulse, another gently dabbed her forehead. Then her gown was opened and efficient hands moved all over her. Two tempered washcloths worked in almost perfect synchronicity. The washcloth on her right was slightly ahead when it was her armpits' turn. Then the left one pulled even again. Both washed her hands, palms, fingers, thumb first, then moved up again in one swift move.

"Where is he?" It was the uneasy voice of a young woman. Amanda could just imagine her, skinny, glasses, short hair. Trying to hold her own next to the older voice, undoubtedly a senior nurse.

"He's up in 531."

"How long has he been there?" Both washcloths were rubbing across Amanda's breasts now, hands lifted the generous sizes, cleaned under them, moved on again. Not what Amanda would have thought of as an erotic moment, yet it still made her think of Frank.

"About an hour, I guess."

"We should really move it."

"We are doing our job, Elizabeth. Nothing to worry about."

"I'd still rather be done before he gets back. He has a terrible temper. Yesterday he growled at me like a mad dog. All I was trying to do was replace the old tube. That man is scary, and he is dangerous. I cannot understand why Doctor Rosenberg lets him stay here."

As their hushed conversation continued, they started washing down, turned Amanda to her left side, cleaned her up. Amanda was startled to find that she must have soiled herself without realizing. She kept her eyes shut. It wasn't unpleasant. These people were doing their job, solid professionals. And somewhere Amanda actually welcomed this as a first-hand learning experience. She now knew exactly what Anton Tamo and the others at the home felt on a daily basis.

"Bad enough when he battered that temp a week ago," the young voice continued. "Did you hear about today?"

"I passed emergency, yes."

"He broke the man's nose! An innocent man asking him a few questions about the accident and he broke his nose!"

"Shh." The senior voice let the sound float with pure authority. Not a word, not even a harsh sound. But it silenced the young one. Amanda was rolled back. They quickly moved down her legs, or so Amanda assumed. Amanda listened hard to their conversation about Frank. They had to have been talking about Frank. Maybe somewhere she took in the fact that she wasn't feeling them washing her legs, that she couldn't feel them cleaning between her toes, something that would have driven her mad with uncontrollable laughter normally. Maybe she knew what had happened. But she pushed it aside, just concentrated on their voices. Tell me more about Frank, tell me of his daring deeds. My Frank. My Frank. He will be the one. He will tell me everything there is to know.

"The man didn't even seem upset." The older nurse chipped in after a long silence.

"Of course not. He was completely traumatized."

"He did have an odd smile on him."

"I'm telling you, wheelchair or no wheelchair, that man is crazy and shouldn't be allowed to freely move about the hospital."

"Now stop it. We have no idea what that was about. None of our business. Besides, I heard he isn't even going to press charges. Maybe he just slipped, who knows."

"Yes, sure. Do you really - "

"I said, stop it." The authority voice again. Amanda couldn't wait to ask Frank about all of this. They dressed her in a fresh gown, tucked her back in and left the room with the silence of ghosts.

Amanda opened her eyes, wondering what the older nurse looked like. She had seemed very much like herself. Amanda liked her without ever having seen her face. She imagined inviting the lady for a cup of coffee, maybe a stroll in the park. Get to know each other better ... stroll in the park ... stroll in the ... walk ... Then, without struggle, she sank into dark pools of sleep again.

PAIR

Jerry and Jerome sat next to each other on the A train. Jerry was staring out the window - trips away from the home were anything but ordinary for him. Both men were dressed up, clean pants and jackets under their windbreakers. Jerry was even wearing a tie. A black tie. It was the only one in Jerry's possession, dating back to the funeral of one of his uncles. Jerome had shaken his head at the black tie, but hadn't been able to help out. Ties had never been part of his wardrobe.

This morning Jerome had put a piece of chocolate in a purple wrapper on Jerry's pillow. It had always made Jerome feel better as a kid. And Jerry, Jerome understood clearly, needed all the encouragement he could get. The chocolates. Incredible stuff. His mother had always brought those little chocolates home from work. She had worked at the Waldorf Astoria as a cleaning lady, late shift. One time she had taken him along, had to because she hadn't been able to find a sitter. He had been only six then. What a place! Jerome had run around the floors, slalomed around the people, his mother forgotten. A tiny little black kid giggling, racing down the halls, having the time of his life. It wasn't until later that he found out that his mom almost got fired because of him.

That night the fun had ended abruptly with hotel security showing up on the scene. A ten foot black guy had come by, on request of some very unhappy guests. What kind of a hotel was this anyway, where a kid like that could just run around any which way it pleased. The giant had grabbed Jerome's shoulder, pulled him close, lifted him up and had tucked him under his arm like a weightless package. Then he had carried Jerome to the employee entrance in the back where his mother had waited. The giant had set him down gently, with a smile for his mom and a pat for Jerome's head. Then he had left again without a word.

No chocolate on the pillow for little Jerome that night.

Jerome glanced at Jerry. Jerry's ten fingers were folded into a tight knot. Jerry's neck and jaw muscles were in the middle of an extensive workout. And Jerry's eyes were glued to the winter sky outside, glued to anything outside.

"You okay?"

"Absolutely." Jerry didn't look at Jerome.

"Good. We should be there in about ten minutes." Jerome shot the janitor another glance. No reaction, jaw still tight as a high-wire.

How things had changed since the accident. Gone from usual to strange, from ordinary to frightening, from distant to close as could be. Jerry hadn't been himself since the accident. Had barely said a word since, and Jerome had been worried. But it wasn't his place to tell a grown man what to do.

∞

For the first two nights there was silence. On the third night after the accident it started. The walls between their rooms in the basement were not much more than cardboard, so picking up on it was unavoidable. Jerry crying, stifled most of the times, but once or twice every night a wail would escape. Jerome couldn't sleep anymore after that. It wasn't the noise that bothered him, but Jerry. The strange little man had become something approaching a father figure for him. Nothing that had been said, nothing that had been done. Jerome just felt close to the weirdo. They got along, without ever really talking, without knowing the first thing about the other. They didn't need words.

Then yesterday, Jerome was in line to pick up his lunch at the cafeteria, Jerry arrived and got in line behind him. Jerome was well aware that Jerry had been avoiding him all week. There they were, just two guys waiting in line, chow time, "Hi, how'ya doin'?" back and forth. The usual. But their eyes were all different. Jerome knowing about the crying and Jerry knowing about the thin walls. Jerome probably looked at Jerry for a little too long - because suddenly Jerry's welled up. He turned on his heels, dropped his tray back on the stack and left the hall. Not hungry anymore, Jerome followed him out.

By the time Jerome caught up with Jerry, the janitor was busy fixing the rear door, trying to replace the rusted hinges. Jerry had the door unhinged and the power drill ready to pull out the worn screws. Jerome said nothing, just stood there, for an eternity, waiting ... until Jerry's hand let go of the drill. It hit to the concrete ground with a loud thud, breaking the casing and sending some more pieces flying. Not acknowledging the broken tool, Jerry looked straight up at Jerome, his eyes wide.

"I'm sorry. This ... is new to me."

"What is?"

"Emotions."

"Feelings?"

Sitting down on the ground, absently taking the broken pieces of the drill and reassembling them, Jerry tried to explain.

"Do you love your mother, Jerome?"

"What?" Jerome felt his voice getting edgy.

"Bare with me, please."

"She's dead," replied Jerome, then sat down next to Jerry.

"I'm sorry to hear that, Jerome. But what I meant ... let me rephrase this. Did you love your mother?"

" ... Of course."

"Do you cry at movies?"

"Shit, man, what are - "

"Just answer me," Jerry said firmly. Staring at Jerome, his eyes almost pleading for an answer.

"Yeah, I guess I cried at some movies."

"Would you be you happy if you won the lottery?"

"Sure."

"You see ... not me. I've never felt much at all. Don't misunderstand me, I mean I feel some things. I enjoy a good meal, a good laugh or a good movie. Just different. Everything I've always felt was sort of ... neutral. Simply put, no highs, no lows," Jerry had continued. "It never bothered me, you see, I never minded being different. My mother dead, just a fact. My father dead, same thing. My life spent in nowhere, no problem. No schooling, whatever. Being ridiculed, so what. My inventions stolen, who cares ... Things have just ... never meant much to me. But since the accident ..."

Jerome watched helplessly as a volcano erupted from within Jerry. Jerry curled up, cried again, his whole body heaving violently.

"Jerry ... Hey, Jerry ..."

Two J's freezing their asses off, Jerome thought.

Two grown men sitting on the frozen ground, one of them crying like a baby. Jerome knew about crying, Jerome knew all about ups and downs.

And Jerome knew then that the situation was about to get a definite shade weirder.

He lightly shrugged to himself and took the little man into his powerful arms.

Wrapped him up.

Kept him there.

MAGIC

He was heading for the hospital with Jerome. This last week had been the worst of Jerry's entire life ... and the best. There had been no way to stop all the crying and sobbing ... and no way would he have even tried to stop it. Incredible. Jerry felt alive, suddenly so alive since the accident.

He had started crying for one reason. He had felt guilty, guilty because of his kicking the plumber. It was clear to Jerry, the fault was his and his alone. It had all happened that same morning, the morning the lawyer with the two million dollar case had appeared. That same morning Nurse Griffin had laughed hysterically, clearly on the verge of a breakdown. Jerry knew with absolute certainty that Amanda Griffin had walked out of the home because of that looming disaster. She never left the home during the day, she never took time out of her schedule. She had only done it that one time, walked out to meet Frank Wilkinson and Wilber Patorkin. She must have needed fresh air, must have needed get out of her office, away from those two million dollars threatening to destroy the home.

Two people, two comatose people, in the hospital because of him. Nurse Griffin, the kindest woman on the planet, the warmest human being he had ever met. She had given him his life at the home, she had given him trust, honesty, family. All those things had just been there, until the accident, understood but emotionally meaningless. Now, though, now they carried weight for Jerry, tremendous weight. Same with Wilber Patorkin, in a coma because the old man had been there and had seen it happen. Wonderful Wilber Patorkin. Until the accident Jerry had never realized just how much that old guy meant to him.

That man was like a sun one didn't even acknowledge until clouds broke the light and the warmth. That was it, exactly. Wilber Patorkin was the home's very own sun. And, walking through the home since the accident, it had become painfully obvious that a lot of the others were missing their sun as well.

Magic. No other way to describe it. Because, as miserable as the guilt-riddled crying had been, it had also been an absolutely amazing experience. It had been a low, and not just any low, but a seemingly bottomless low. A sensation of great magnitude. Crying night after night, Jerry had found himself actually getting addicted to it. He had wanted for it to continue. Jerry's heart had seemed to burst with pure misery and Jerry's heart had kept on begging him to feed it with more of the same.

In this last week Jerry had come to a simple and logical realization. How odd that something as clear as this had eluded his superior brain all these years.

Life equaled emotion.

Good or bad, happy or sad, no matter.

Highs or lows, you were alive.

It was as simple as that.

And that meant that his entire life leading up to the accident had been flat, neutral, and therefore dead. That realization had made him cry even more. He had found himself in a cycle of tears - the more he had loved the crying, the guiltier he had felt, the more he had cried.

∞

"They're awake," Jerome suddenly said.

Jerry looked at him and Jerome saw the tears in the little man's eyes again.

"Who's awake?"

"Nurse Griffin and Mr. Patorkin. Don't ask. I just got this feeling. I think they're out of the coma."

"That's great ... You know more about this feeling stuff - I'm sure you are correct."

Jerome noticed that Jerry pulled out his handkerchief and started sobbing once again. Jerome didn't look at any of the other passengers on the train. Out of the corner of his eye he saw Jerry's shoulder jerking up and down. Strangers didn't matter, Jerry did. Jerome put his arm around the little guy's shoulder, nothing more. Once more they didn't need words, not after spilling their entire lives to each other yesterday. He had been stunned to hear about Jerry. He had been even more amazed when Jerry didn't spit at him after he had finished his own story.

Jerry's sobbing was softening again. Good. Jerome kept his arm around him. He continued looking out the window.

From here Brooklyn looked bleak, cold, a miserable place to live.

Jerome knew better, he loved Brooklyn.

SIMPLE

Wilber woke from ocean-deep sleep when he felt a hand on his wrist. Frank. Frank sitting in his wheelchair at Wilber's bedside, a canyon of misery and a mountain of joy. The Transit Authority Inspector forgotten.

"Hiya, Champ," Frank said.

"Frank." Wilber looked at him with a heavy heart. Nothing he could have done different, he had been telling himself. True. Still, that knowledge didn't change the fact that he felt like crap.

"Look at you. Seven fuckin' days in a coma and then you just pop right back to normal. Good to have you back, Champ. Good to have you back." He gripped Wilber's hand, shaking it firmly, tears welling up, working a happy smile. "Do you have any idea what's been going on? Jesus, Wilber, you should have ... man it's good to have you back."

"I'm sorry, Frank."

"About what?" Frank said, frowning at Wilber.

"About Amanda." Still no dentures in his face. Wilber heard himself mumbling, incomprehensible to others. He did his best to make up for the missing teeth by working his tongue double-time. As it seemed, though, Frank didn't have any problems understanding him. A mixed blessing at this point.

"She'll be fine," Frank suddenly said, and Wilber felt Frank's guard go up, saw Frank's fists in fierce knots. The heavy heart. Wilber softly shook his head and Frank's eyes widened in angry disbelief.

"She'll be fine, damn you," Frank repeated. It sounded more like a prayer, a fervent wish.

"That's not what I meant, Frank. I ..." It's so easy, Wilber. Just spit it out, just be honest. Never mind the inconceivability of it. Just tell your friend Frank what happened. Just tell him that your thoughts moved the bus and crippled his newfound love.

"I moved the bus," Wilber said.

"Huh?"

"What I said, Frank. I saw the boy in front of the bus and simply wished the bus out of the way."

"Huh?"

"Frank." Wilber looked into Frank's lost eyes. Frank was trying hard to understand. Wilber continued looking at him ... then the furniture started moving. It took Frank a moment to realize that the chairs and the table were floating in the air, he stared at them, still lost.

"Wilber? Are you doin' that?"

"Yep."

"Then stop it."

Wilber let the furniture float back into place. As if nothing had happened.

"Champ. It's been kinda busy for me, the last week or so, you know. I haven't slept all that much. And I'm eighty-five years old. Try to remember that, will ya? People my age get heart attacks like other people get a cold. So please, stop pulling shit like that on me."

"Of course. Sorry, Frank. I just thought showing you would explain much - " Frank wearily lifted his hand.

"Nah, just tell me. Don't impress this here sorry ass. I don't think I can take much more."

"But you understand?"

"What?"

"That I moved the bus, Frank. That it was my fault. An accident, yes. But still my fault." Frank stared at him, his eyes slowly narrowing, his lips tightening into a barely visible line. "I had no idea I could move objects, Frank. I just saw the bus heading for the boy. I wished it wouldn't happen, wished for the bus to move. And it happened."

"Amanda is ... because of you?"

"Yes."

Frank seemed still as a statue for a while. Then he turned his chair and headed for the door. There he suddenly turned again and fixed his glare on Wilber.

"Then make her whole again."

"I can't."

"You can read minds, you can move buses and didn't even know you could. Now heal Amanda," Frank spat, despair just below the anger of his voice.

"I can't, Frank. Once in a while I try to help a little, let people know things they already know. Like that Inspector, Mr. Wenderwiler. I just made him see his life, opened up a few possibilities."

"You were there?" Wilber just nodded and continued.

"But there is nothing anybody can do for Nurse Griffin."

"Don't say that. You have no right to say that. You don't have a fuckin' clue what you can do. So try it."

Even if ... Wilber didn't continue the thought. Instead of answering Frank, he simply nodded. He would try. But her body could wait, first her soul needed attention.

"You have to tell her," Wilber calmly said to his friend. Frank looked as if he'd just been slapped in the face.

"I ... how can I ... who the fuck are you telling me what I have to do? Besides, she just woke up, give me a fuckin' break."

"I'm just saying, Frank. You are the one. Not the doctors. You have to tell her." Frank gave Wilber a look.

"How would you know? What's the good of me blabbing and stuttering and crying like a baby? What can I tell her that a professional can't explain much better?"

"She doesn't need explanations. She just needs truth. And she won't take that truth from anyone but you."

"Ah, fuck."

"... Yep."

Frank sank back deep into his chair and Wilber's mind sank back with him. Wilber didn't think of restraining himself, it just happened. Frank rubbed his face, his eyes, with both hands.

"So what's gonna happen? Come on, Champ. You know so fuckin' much, you tell me. What's gonna happen? What about Amanda, what about me, what about you?"

"Can't help you there."

"But you will try to help her, right?"

Wilber nodded again, his face somehow pained, his eyes glazed over, his cheeks white as the linen.

"Wilber, you okay? Wilber."

Wilber snapped back, looked at Frank. He gently took Frank's hand in his and spoke softly.

"Frank. I will try to help ... but I know that I shouldn't. Had I known I could move that bus, Frank, I would not have done it."

Frank looking at him, blank again.

Wilber knew that Frank was seven nights beyond dead tired, but Frank needed to understand this.

Or Wilber needed Frank to understand for his own sake.

"Frank. Listen to me. This is very important. If I had known about this new gift, I wouldn't have used it. The boy would be dead now. I would have stood there, I would have watched it happen. I wouldn't have done a thing about it. I have no right to take people's lives into my own hands. The boy was meant to die. Now, because of me, he lives. I have changed his destiny, and with that, the destiny of many. It is never just the one. One action, one ripple, causes a wave somewhere else. It's the old dilemma, Frank. If I save a woman ... she may well live on to give birth to the next Adolf Hitler. If I kill a - "

The door opened abruptly, so fast the air was sucked out into the hallway with a noisy 'whoosh'.

∞

Three men and a woman entered with crisp steps, crisp haircuts and crisp suits. The first man, trim and grey, planted himself at the foot of the bed, the others instantly got busy around the room.

"What's going on?" Frank was intrigued, but didn't seem the least bit intimidated.

"FBI," the guy at the footrest announced in a grave voice. "I am Agent Hutchinson, these are agents Harris, Frome and Wenker. We will now sweep this room."

"That's Wenker with an e." The young suit smiled in the corner smiled as he took a gleaming gadget from a briefcase. After clarifying the spelling of his name, and after weathering a brutal stare from his superior, Agent Wenker started in on his task.

"FBI? What's Wilber done this time? Hey Wilber, you made the White House disappear or something? Guys - can we see some ID here?" Frank's frown increased when the four agents all flashed their ID's in one fluid motion, held them in plain view for two seconds sharp, then folded them back into their suits with equal flourish.

"Can I help you?" Wilber, preoccupied with giving Frank a clearer picture of his own do's and don'ts, hadn't thought of reading their minds yet. He looked at Agent Hutchinson with openly puzzled eyes.

"Excuse me?" Agent Hutchinson was leaning forward, trying to understand mumbled words.

"Forget it, Pal. Wilber's lost his dentures when the accident happened. Without his teeth, you won't understand a word he says," Frank said earnestly.

"What is your name, Sir?"

"Frank Wilkinson. I'm his translator."

"What did Mr. Patorkin say?"

"He asked if he could help you."

Agent Hutchinson looked at Wilber for a long moment, as if he were trying to connect distant dots in his head.

"You haven't been informed?" He shot his three partners a glance as they continued to sweep the room. They were in the midst of checking every corner, every piece of furniture, waving their expensive looking instruments along the walls, the floor, even the ceiling. Agent Hutchinson received an absent look from Wilber. He raised his hand to cover his ear-piece and spoke softly but firmly into his wrist.

"Subject hasn't been informed of the Don's visit."

∞

At that moment Wilber was listening to the woman, Agent Frome. She was excited to be here. Her first advance detail with 'The Don'. The President of the United States, born and raised in one of Brooklyn's toughest neighborhoods, half Irish, half Italian. He liked being thought of as a tough guy, a street kid, all truth, all straight on, gloves off. The Don. The code name had nothing to do with some romanticized image of goodfella godfather stuff, and the President knew that full well. Still, he had laughed his presidential butt off when he first heard the FBI given name.

'The Don' was obviously short for Don Juan, an clear reference to the President's womanizing. As Agent Frome patted down the curtains, she mused about her recent assignments. President Taylor made no secret of it. He loved women, lots of them, whenever possible. He always said it kept him going, said that making love gave him the juice of life. Agent Frome smirked.

Taylor wasn't the loftiest of men, but then he had never pretended to be in the first place. She had, by now, spent countless weeks on crap detail, watching doors, clocking mistresses, filtering out potentials. Not that the Don was in any way particular about women, he liked them in all shapes and sizes. And why the hell not.

He was a single guy and his love for women had been an open fact during the campaign. She had voted for him just like everybody else.

He was a marvel, clearly destined to become one of the greatest presidents in American history.

And Agent Frome was absolutely certain on one issue: Should Taylor ever ask her ... she would. No hesitation.

∞

"Oh, the President's visit," Wilber suddenly exclaimed. "I completely forgot." Agent Hutchinson looked to Frank, his chiseled face motionless, but his eyes impatiently waiting for the translation.

"President? The President?" Frank was looking back and forth between the FBI and Wilber.

"What did Mr. Patorkin say, Sir?"

"Oh. He said that he completely forgot about the President's visit. The President is coming here? I mean, here? To Wilber?"

"You forgot the President of the United States of America was paying you a visit?" Hutchinson had his eyes firmly locked with Wilber's. Wilber couldn't help smiling. The man was used to staring people down. Had done so all his life, even as a little boy. So Wilber stared back ... and after a moment, after exactly four seconds, Agent Hutchinson looked away. Wilber knew just how unnerving that was to him.

"No shit, the President is coming here?" Frank asked again.

"Yes," Hutchinson answered abruptly. He was glaring through Frank.

"Clear," Agent Frome called. Hutchinson looked at her and just blankly nodded.

"Clear," Agent Harris called. Hutchinson whirled around to Harris and acknowledged him with a dismissive wave. Agent Wenker was still checking along the floor, under the patient's bed.

"When? Today?" Frank continued. "When's he coming ... and why? What the fuck, Wilber? The President of the entire fuckin' country is showing up and you don't tell me shit about it?" Frank was visibly miffed and Wilber shrugged.

"Noon tomorrow, right?" Wilber said, looking at Hutchinson.

"What did he say?" Agent Hutchinson practically spat the words at Frank. Frank frowned at the large man who seemed pretty upset for getting asked a few simple questions.

"Wilber thinks the visit's at noon tomorrow."

"The President's meeting with Mr. Patorkin is scheduled for fourteen hundred hours," Hutchinson corrected.

"Tomorrow?"

"Yes tomorrow! Wenker, Goddamnit. Are you finished?"

Agent Wenker popped out from under the bed.

"Yes, Sir. All clear."

∞

Wenker got up and joined his colleagues at the door. The three agents all watched their boss. Hutchinson was famous for his calm, Wenker knew. Academy rumors had it that Hutchinson's pulse had never risen above sixty, regardless of psychological exams, physical tests, extreme stress situations including torture simulations and sleep deprivation exercises. Hutchinson was a block of ice ... and Hutchinson had just lost his temper to the oldest man in America.

"Are you okay, Sir?" Agent Frome asked. Hutchinson was staring holes in the floor and it was becoming embarrassing. Wenker watched as the boss shot Frome an icy stare, then addressed Frank Wilkinson once more.

"Agent Wenker will be posted outside this door until after the President's visit. Access to this location will be restricted to essential personnel."

"How about me?" The old man Wilkinson asked the question as if it were a threat, glaring at all four agents at once. Wenker liked him instantly.

"Essential personnel only, Sir. Code One security procedures. Access will be granted to hospital staff. There will be no excep- " Agent Hutchinson stopped in mid-sentence. His mouth remained open. He seemed in a place far away, totally absent, yet completely concentrated. Then his voice clicked in again, slightly mechanic, as if he were reading the words off some inner script.

"Of course, any and all friends of Mr. Patorkin are also welcome."

Wenker couldn't believe his ears.

"Thank you, Agent Hutchinson," Wilber Patorkin said and Frank translated the mumble before anyone could ask him to do so. Wenker and his colleagues had to practically shove Hutchinson out of the room.

OUT

Agent Hutchinson had left room 531 without another glance at the patient. He was out, thank God he was out of the damn room. What the hell had just happened in there!? Why had he looked away, he had never lost - never! All his confidence gone in there, everything he'd worked for all his life. His towering strength, his aura of power and pure authority - gone with a simple look from the old man. Wilber Patorkin, who the hell was he? ... But he was fine again, in charge, in control. Standing outside Room 531, his team planted before him, waiting for orders. Did he see questions in their eyes? They wouldn't dare. Agent Hutchinson was back, his great calm was back, the famed Hutchinson calm.

"Any questions?"

"No, Sir," Harris answered, a bit too fast. Hutchinson glared him down, then focused on Wenker.

"Do you have anything to say, Wenker?"

"No, Sir."

"Good. Agent Frome, did anything happen in there?"

"What are you referring to, Sir?"

Hutchinson took a long beat, then continued with a deliberately quiet voice.

"Should I, at any time in the future, hear anything about what did-not-happen in there, you may rest assured that I will make it my life's goal to destroy your careers. Do you understand?"

"Yes, Sir," his team replied in unison. Wenker took up position at the door as the others walked off down the hallway.

"What about his teeth?" Frome asked.

"He doesn't have any." Harris grinned and froze when Hutchinson sent him one of his deadly glares.

"Good thinking, Agent Frome. The Don may want to actually hold a conversation with Mr. Patorkin. Find Wainright or Rosenberg and have them arrange for a decent set of teeth."

Wilber Patorkin, Hutchinson thought.

He kept on seeing Wilber Patorkin's eyes, staring at him. Damn.

IN

Frank grinned at Wilber.

"What?" Wilber asked innocently.

"You talked to Agent Hutchinson, didn't you?" Frank tapped his forehead with the index finger. "In there, right?"

"Just a little."

"He's an arrogant sonofabitch."

"Not anymore he isn't."

"The President of the United States of America. Whaddaya know." Frank wheeled over to the window.

It wasn't snowing anymore, the sky still white, though. It could start again any second.

"Why's he coming, anyway?"

"Just to say hello," Wilber answered.

"Yeah, right. Well, this may be small potatoes in Wilber World, but I for one wanna see what's up. I'll be here."

"Of course you will ... Frank?"

"What?"

"Go tell her."

Frank didn't turn to look at Wilber. His head slumped forward a inch. Then he picked himself up, turned the chair, wheeled past Wilber. He nodded lightly and waved.

"See ya later, Champ."

The door swung closed behind Frank. Wilber sent his thoughts along and muttered softly, "You need me, Frank, I'll be there with you." As for right now, though, Wilber had to try a little something.

He closed his eyes and focused on a place not far away.

FLOAT

The street cop took a leave of absence. Hell, he was close to retirement, anyway. The Hungarian bag lady left town in a hurry. She had a thing about that kind of stuff, made her toes itch like crazy, no good. The young woman in the dark suit didn't continue her shopping. She went straight to her therapist and analyzed for three straight sessions. The Korean grocer barely blinked, he had seen stranger things. Besides, it wasn't his business if somebody let his dentures fly.

The dentures had been lodged in a crack right below the entrance of the sewer hole. Other than a bit of grime and a few cockroaches, nothing had touched Wilber's teeth. Then they had risen, a little while back, freed themselves and levitated to about five feet above ground.

An old set of teeth floating in the air.

Most people didn't even notice, most people were too busy running through their lives. Some did see the flying object, but their minds immediately rationalized the sight away. Impossible ... and forgotten. Few people actually saw the dentures float past the home, past buses and cabs, always above the sidewalk. And even fewer saw the initial passenger. A medium-sized cockroach was riding the dentures, feelers twitching nervously.

The dentures gathered speed and flew parallel to the A, as if racing the train. The roach held on for dear life. When the conductor glanced from his little frosted window, he did a double-take. There was a set of teeth flying right outside the window. He rubbed the frost off and was almost certain he saw a cockroach losing its grip and sailing back into nothing. The teeth suddenly seemed to buck like a wild horse, then veered off at a sharp angle in the direction of Brooklyn Medical Center. Brooklyn Medical Center ... ?

"Shit!" he yelled out loud. The conductor had already overshot the stop at full speed, hadn't even thought of stopping.

After getting severely reprimanded by his usually pleasant boss that evening, the A train conductor would stop off for a few, stagger home, plastered to his eyelids, and end up sleeping on the couch. Bedroom door locked, food cold on the table. Fuck it. What did she know, anyway. She hadn't seen the teeth, man. She hadn't seen shit.

Couch felt good.

He dreamed of flying dentists that night.

GREAT

The President was pissed off as he looked from the windows of his suite at the Waldorf. Park Avenue down below, heavy traffic rushing in both directions. Manhattan ... yuppie town.

"So ... you made up your mind yet?" Al asked.

President Melvin Taylor, knowing full well he was alone in his suite, still did a slow scan of the room. Yes, alone. All alone except for the voice in your head. Deal with it.

"My mind's been made up long before I ever heard your voice," he answered with restraint.

"Looks like you ain't as smart as they say." Al seemed pleasant, he actually seemed concerned. "Look, Pal. I'm just trying to save your life."

"I will go."

"Well, you go, you die."

"You cannot know that."

"Buddy, go to the fuckin' place tomorrow and you sure as hell will find out."

Taylor casually walked to the bar, got himself a twenty year old McCallan, poured a double, no ice. Then he returned to the window, drank a little, let the taste melt around his tongue, let it flow to the back where it brought on that singularly sweet sting.

Voice talking in his head.

Jesus H. Christ. Other men would have gone crazy by now. Not Melvin Taylor. Some voice suddenly coming on, talking as if it were a goddamn phone call. It had started yesterday. He'd been in the middle of a fund-raiser, listening to mind-numbing speeches of people trying to cash in on his presence. Hell, it was all part of the deal. There were many necessary evils, fund-raisers being among the least of them. Still, they could seem deadly. Whenever possible, Taylor would, on such occasions, put on the thoughtful face. He had the great ability of not missing a single thing, even when his mind was working more important issues.

∞

He mentally flipped through his international agenda. Russia, could wait. France, fuck the stuck-up bastards, he'd call them in a week. NATO needed attention, Germans getting cocky again. A summit, yes, he would set up something soon. India, Pakistan - priority, their feud over Kashmir always on the verge of escalating into full-blown war. Mindless idiots. Taylor was certain that they'd end up using their nuclear -

"So fuckin' what," a voice said.

Taylor frowned, casually glanced left and right. He even managed to look behind him without seeming distracted. Nobody had spoken to him. The Democratic speaker was rambling on. Nothing had happened. Taylor continued assessing the situation. At this point Pakistan was far more probl -

"So they nuke the shit out of each other. Contaminate a few surrounding countries. So fuckin' what, is what I say. No harm done. Hey Mel, I'm talking to you."

The President kept the thoughtful face in place, his mind racing. A voice talking to me, in my head. Impossible. Man if ... probably reads my thoughts. I have to ...

"Pal, easy, don't go nuts on me. Of course I can read your thoughts. And you, Mr. President, Sir, can speak to me by simply using your mind. They say you're one of the best, Mel. You oughta be able to handle this, right?"

"Who ... who are you?" the President's mind stuttered.

"That ain't the question. The question is, 'What do you want?' Ask me that one and you might get an answer out of me."

Incredible. Taylor was looking around again. Nobody, not the crowd, not the selected few along the podium, seemed to be aware of what was happening.

"Okay. What do you want?" Seemed easy enough, talking with his mind.

"I want to warn you."

"About what?"

"Your visit to the hospital tomorrow. Don't go."

"Why shouldn't I?"

"Because you'll die."

"How would you, whoever you are, know that?"

"Take my word for it. Hey, you know, maybe I'm God, maybe I'm your guardian angel."

"If ... the situation were reversed, if some unknown voice were telepathically warning you ... would you believe it? Wouldn't you rather think you were hallucinating?"

"Hey, it's your life."

"Who are you?" Taylor asked again.

"What's the difference. I could tell you that I'm a leading physicist, a Mossad agent, a fuckin' alien. I could tell you anything. Just call me Al."

"Al ... how would I die?"

"Fuck you. You wanna find out, you go there."

∞

Al had been silent after that. Fund-raiser done by six, dinner with the Mayor, quickie with the Mayor's wife, a full woman with the most beautiful laughter he had ever heard. By the time Melvin Taylor had crawled under the covers at the Waldorf, he had all but forgotten about the odd experience. He'd probably eaten something bad ... but Al had clicked in again just before Taylor had sunk into dreams. The voice had rambled on about many things, God, the world, good and evil ... This Al had countless interesting points of view, and this Al was also clearly an absolute psychopath. Taylor hadn't gotten much sleep last night. He had challenged Al's views, had attacked him when he could. As outlandish as it all had been, Taylor had enjoyed it. He rarely got to aggressively chew the basics without politics and diplomacy watering every good argument into a lame-ass compromise.

Now, standing by the window, looking down at the traffic, the President finished his single malt. He was solid as a rock. No doubt whatsoever.

"You may be trying to help ... you may also be threatening me. I don't know. And it doesn't really matter. I just know that you, whoever you are, are trying to keep me from that place. You are trying to stop me. I am President of the United States of America because nobody stops me. Nobody has ever stopped me. God knows, you may be right. But I can't help that. I can't sit here and wonder about what might have happened. If I do that, you rule my life. I am who I am because I don't let anybody rule my life. And that is why I will go to the hospital tomorrow."

"Mr. President," Al said, "you, Sir, are a moron."

"Been one all my life," Taylor said with a smile.

"Let me give you a little something to think about before I leave ... What if I knew that every single one of your staff thinks visiting Wilber Patorkin is a complete waste of everybody's time? What if I knew that your campaign people have asked you to cancel that visit in favor of a three million dollar fund-raiser? What if I knew that you've been considering just that since yesterday? What if I'm fuckin' with you? What if I only started talking to you to make damn sure that you do go to the hospital tomorrow? What if, Mel, what if I actually want you dead?"

"Looks like I'm up shit creek," Taylor said to the passing cabs down below and shrugged. This was okay. Whatever was going to happen tomorrow, it was fine. President Melvin Taylor was still the master of his own future.

"Who's up shit creek? What'd you do this time?" The President whirled around and saw Charlie Columbus, his two hundred and fifty-seven pound personal secretary, standing at the door. "Don't look at me like that, Mel, I knocked. So what's with the shit creek business?" She didn't wait for his answer, pushed the door closed and flopped her weight into the couch.

"Nothing. Just ... talking to myself."

"Maybe you should lay off the booze, Mr. President."

Taylor ignored the comment as he walked back to the bar, poured himself another one. "Charlie ... I would like to go to the hospital right now."

"Can't swing it. Want me to go over the schedule once more? You got more appointments than a friggin' Hollywood plastic surgeon tonight. Besides, what's so urgent about the hospital? The old fart dying or something?" She flipped through a dozen folders as Taylor sat down beside her. He seemed weary.

"I'm just looking forward to meeting the man, you know." Taylor smiled warmly at the thought of meeting this Wilber Patorkin. "The oldest man in America, Charlie. One hundred and fifteen years old, Charlie," he said, his eyes gleaming. "How could I pass that up?"

"Well, you're lucky we managed to fit it into tomorrow's schedule."

"Alright then. We go as planned. Tomorrow ... good."

Charlie heaved herself out of the couch, grabbed the first tie she saw. Taylor got up and patiently waited as she tightened a perfect knot. He slipped into his jacket when the door opened a second time.

Jimmy Weller walked in. Taylor knew that Charlie hated Weller's guts. She had once stated that, if character had a color, Jimmy Weller would be a rotting lime green with streaks of beige.

"Good Afternoon, Mr. President," Weller said with a put-on smile and a put-on air of confidence.

"What's up, Jimmy?"

"I thought you might like to know about this," Weller smiled proudly.

"What, Jimmy, what. Spit it out," Charlie said as she opened the door. Taylor nodded in her direction. Yep, time to leave, time for another fun event.

"Your approval rating, Sir. You are, as of ten minutes ago, at ninety-seven percent." The President stopped at the door, stood still.

"Ninety-seven percent, huh?"

"Yes, Sir. Highest approval rating of any president, ever, in all of American history. Ninety-seven percent. Congratulations, Sir."

The President seemed stunned.

"Mel. We really have to go," Charlie said.

"Shhhh," Mel Taylor said simply. He seemed to glow, he seemed to radiate energy. He stood as motionless as a statue, as if he were soaking up the country's ninety-seven percent worth of love and respect. The three stood in silence by the open door.

For a full minute.

Then the President spoke again with a wide smile.

"Well, we got three percent left out there. Let's go get them." With that he strode from the room, Weller at his heels.

Charlie closed the door and had to huff to catch up with the happily bouncing Prez.

GOD

Jerome and Jerry were walking back since, for some reason, the train hadn't stopped at Brooklyn Med. They had decided to walk instead of waiting for the next train in the other direction. Secretly, Jerry was glad that this would add precious time before he had to stand in front of Headnurse Griffin.

"I saw it."

"Jerome. Believe me, I know physics. It is simply impossible. Of course there is the subject of paranormal activities. But even if we're talking telekinetically advanced, for ex- "

"Tele-what?"

"Telekinesis, the ability to move objects by simply using the power of your mind."

"You saw it, too, didn't you?" Jerome casually said.

"No, I didn't." Jerry's answer was short and crisp. Impossible, after all, clearly impossible. Once you accepted things like that, anything was possible.

"Yes you did."

"No ... I don't think ... no, I did not. Our eyes play tricks on us all the time. I know about a lot of things, Jerome. And I don't have the slightest proof or acceptable explanation why I should have seen a set of dentures flying by."

"You can't explain it, you don't believe it?"

"Correct."

"What about God?"

"Doesn't exist, of course."

"Because you can't explain him?"

"Yes."

"But if you'd see him, you might change your mind, right?"

"Well, I think I would analyze -"

"You saw the flying teeth."

"Could have been anything that our eyes picked up."

They walked on, both of them thinking their own thoughts. Jerry suddenly realized that he was walking alone. He turned to see Jerome at the hot dog stand. The hot dog stand. Jerry was instantly reminded of the accident.

"What do you want on it?" Jerome called.

"Everything."

"Same for me." Jerome paid, packed the dogs and joined Jerry once more. They continued toward the hospital, chewing, trying to keep their clothes clean.

"I think there is a God," Jerome said with his mouth full. "Lots of shit happening I got no explanation for. They still happen. Me, I like to believe in just about everything I can't explain. Aliens? I believe it. That city that's supposed to be in the ocean somewhere - "

"Atlantis," Jerry mumbled in between bites.

"Atlantis, right. I believe it. The Loch Ness monster, Bigfoot and stuff, I believe it. And you know why?"

"No."

"Because it makes anything possible."

"But that's not realistic. You just - "

"Jerry, fuck it. If I believe in all of those things, then my world is wide open and much bigger than your world. I believe that anything is possible ... and that makes me feel good." Jerome finished his dog and carefully discarded the paper at the next trash can.

They continued on in silence. The hospital was already visible in the distance, a monstrous brick and glass structure four blocks down the avenue. They were about to cross another side street, when Wilber's dentures floated out from behind the corner and hovered right in front of their eyes. Both men stood still and gaped.

"You see it now?" Jerome asked in a hushed voice.

"What do you mean?" Jerry was staring straight at the dentures that were floating in place about three feet away from his eyes and Jerry was clinging to his sanity. The remainder of his hot dog fell from his hand and splattered his left shoe with sauerkraut. Neither man noticed.

"Jerry, come on. What do you see?"

"I don't know." It took Jerry a moment to realize that Jerome had approached the identified flying object. No doubt, dentures, flying dentures. Jerome carefully moved his hand around the teeth, above, below.

"No strings, Jerry. Come look."

Jerry's shoes were glued solid to the sidewalk. It required Jerome's gentle pull to allow him to move again. Now the teeth were just one foot away from Jerry's eyes.

"You see it now?"

"I ... I don't ..."

"Alright, touch it." Jerome had to grab Jerry's hand, lift it to the dentures' level, then let go of it. Jerry's hand was so close. He would simply need to release the tight fist his fingers were forced into, he would simply need to extend his index. His mind was racing. You open that hand, Jerry, the world as you know it is worth nothing. You open that hand, Jerry, the world becomes a great unknown. You open that hand, Jerry, you'll be scared shitless for the rest of your life. Don't touch it, Jerry.

It was as if Jerome had been reading his mind. "Jerry, just touch it. Then you'll know."

The fist loosened, then, in slow-motion the shaking index finger extended and finally and ever so gently touched the dentures in the air. The teeth didn't disappear, they just slightly retracted at Jerry's touch. It was as if the dentures had been waiting for this moment, for now they started moving again. They flew off swiftly in the direction of the hospital. One block, two blocks, until they were reduced to a disappearing dot in the distance.

Jerome picked up the hot dog leftovers dropped by Jerry.

"Looks like it's heading in the same direction we are."

"So ... there is a God?" Jerry was still staring ahead. Jerome was in the middle of cleaning off Jerry's shoe with the extra tissues he had taken from the stand. He looked up in surprise.

"I don't know. But I know one thing ... it's possible."

"Anything is possible," Jerry echoed quietly. Jerome got up, lightly patted Jerry on the back.

"Let's go."

Jerry simply nodded and followed Jerome. He kept looking left and right for the rest of the day, always half expecting to see more flying objects ... anything was possible.

COLD

Wilber stood at the open window, expecting the arrival of his teeth. It was incredible. He was able to actually see with the non-existent eyes of the object. It was as if he could simply turn on some tiny camera within those dentures. He had seen exactly where the dentures had been lodged in the sewer. He had seen the roach riding the dentures like some rodeo cowboy. He had seen the train conductor's perplexed look. And of course he had seen Jerry and Jerome staring at the flying teeth.

Wilber smiled proudly, thinking of Jerome. The boy was everything he knew him to be. He had a plain wisdom beyond his years. A wisdom he would pass on to Jerry. Good. Wilber had thoroughly enjoyed the moment with them, displaying the dentures for them, gently guiding them to some clearer points of view. Jerome. He had simply accepted the hovering teeth. Anything was possible. Well done, Jerome.

Freezing cold air swirled around Wilber's frail body, his gown flapping in the wind. Cold. A simple cold could kill you, Wilber. Wilber knew it wouldn't happen. Not now. It wasn't time yet. But he would die ... despite everything he knew, Wilber cried.

There would be no other life following this one. This part of his tremendous journey would be over. Time for something new, something final, something bound to be incredible, something way beyond even Wilber's considerable imagination. But that meant nothing to this life. The Wilber Patorkin life. This Wilber would never hear the birds of spring again. This Wilber would leave behind his every dream and hope and thought. This Wilber would soon be nothing but a vanishing memory in the minds and hearts of his friends.

The dentures ascended into view. They flew straight up, then floated a perfect curve through the window, did a playful double loop and landed in Wilber's outstretched palm. Wilber looked at them and realized that they sparkled cleaner than he'd ever seen them before. He placed them in his mouth, wiped his tears away. Still cold. But Wilber didn't mind. His tongue caressed the dentures. Life was good.

∞

A nurse, alerted by an icy draft in the hall, entered Wilber's room. For an instant she stood in the open door, gazing with astonishment at the sight of the skinny old man by the open window, encircled by a myriad of snowflakes that seemed to buzz around him like a tight swarm of friendly bees. The nurse rushed to close the window, then gently guided Wilber back to bed and tucked him in with extra blankets.

"I want to hear birds again," the old man mumbled to himself, his dentures clacking to the sound of his words.

"Sure you'll hear them. Soon. Spring is just around the corner, Mr. Patorkin. Just around the corner," Nurse Harper said and felt completely helpless saying it. The old man closed his eyes, breathing steadily. He was asleep ... He wouldn't make it. She was sure he wouldn't make it. No more springs for Wilber Patorkin. And the knowledge pained her more than she could hide. She lay down next to Wilber and took him in her arms. He was still freezing. She'd keep him warm.

Twenty-nine years as a nurse ... this felt good. She had almost forgotten how good it felt to help people. She had felt her life slip away. Helping people, for what? Her fervor had cost her the husband she had never met, and the children she had always wanted. She had sacrificed herself for a bunch of strangers. It was simply going through the motions now, her passion barely kept alive by the occasional open smile of a child or the rare gentle nod of a grateful face.

Nurse Harper pulled Wilber closer.

Helping people ... now it all came back to her. It was so right, her whole life was right. Holding Wilber, she realized that there was not one single uncertain thought in her heart. Life was clear, nothing missed. All the tears and all the pain were nothing compared to this ... helping people.

CHASE

"I chased the kid all the way into Chinatown."

It appeared as if Amanda hadn't moved, at all. She was still on her back, exact same position, eyes closed. Next to her, Frank was highly animated in telling his story.

He knew she was awake. Her hand in his moved with the flow of the story. So Frank went on, for the first time telling the secret he had kept to himself all these many years.

"I had the gun out and I kept switching it from one hand to the other because I was sweating and the trying to slip through my fingers. It was too fuckin' hot that day and the kid was so fast. But I wasn't going to let him get away. Running after him, staring holes in the kid's back, all I could see was the blood at the scene. The two Mexicans dead against the wall. Don't get me wrong. Those spics deserved the bullets in their heads. They had given up the right to live the day they had started selling in my neighborhood. But taking care of them was my job, the law's job. Not the job of the black kid running away from me now."

Frank felt Amanda's hand in his own. Her fingers were slightly curving, not holding on to Frank now. To Frank it seemed as if Amanda's hand was trying to shield the boy in his story.

"I had to get him, you know. My job, my pride, my reputation, the reputation of every other cop in the city. The more I ran the more faces saw me run. Some called, some just stared, some laughed ... nobody got in the way of the kid. The law was chasing the kid and so the kid was dangerous ..."

Frank took a deep breath, and glanced around the room at everything and nothing. His eyes stayed clear of Amanda.

"I would do it again. Same circumstances ... I'd do it again. I would chase that damn kid just as I did then."

There was a sudden and impatient squeeze of Amanda. Frank's head snapped around, but her face hadn't moved. Her eyes hadn't opened. Her firm grip was simply urging him on. The story, Frank, tell the story.

"We must have done every back alley in Chinatown. The kid was incredible and the more it seemed he was gonna get away, the harder I went after him. The streets were packed with Chinese, and yet it was as if the cop chasing the kid was running in a different world. No one seemed to notice us ... Then the kid ran into a clear back alley and tripped over a crate of rotting fish. I remember the stench, I remember the cool breeze in the shadow of the walls, I remember the ginger stray cat screeching, staring at us, then racing off on three good legs ... and I remember the kid falling. He didn't just fall. He had been running so fast that, when he tripped, his legs kept running above ground, kicking the air at least a half a dozen times before his body crashed against the brick wall. He was half unconscious, his nose bleeding badly, but he turned in a flash. Eyes wide open and the gun that had killed the two Mexicans was staring at my chest."

∞

Amanda knew what he was doing, it wasn't hard to figure. Frank had come to tell her the truth, a truth that he couldn't get himself to announce straight on. Instead he started telling her about Chinatown, about that truth. Amanda didn't mind the detour into Frank's past, into Frank's great secret.

∞

"The kid was so scared he didn't hear a word I said. He just kept shaking, half in fear and half in defiance. It was the first time I actually had a chance to take a good look at him. He had surprisingly thin, sharp features, hawk-like with a curved nose and glistening black eyes that held me in place. I think I was more scared than he was. But I had to make the move, he still wasn't listening, he still had the gun. It was just him and me then, I had to get the gun before people walked into the alley. Just a matter of time ... I shifted weight and was just about to carefully step forward, when the old man stepped out into the alley."

Amanda's hand was painfully gripping Frank's fingers.

"An old Chinese with a filthy apron dumped a load of leftover food into the trash. The kid didn't move a muscle. He must have been as startled as I was, but he kept his focus and his gun on me. There was no opportunity to jump in and wrestle him down. So we stayed as before, Mexican standoff, eyes locked on each other, three feet apart with our guns almost touching. The Chinese didn't disappear. I've always had excellent peripheral vision and I could clearly see the chink standing there, corner of my eye, not moving an inch. I told him I was a cop, told him to get lost ... nothing. The man did not move. He had, without apparent reason, become part of the standoff."

"What was the boy doing?" Amanda suddenly asked. Frank looked at her, flustered at the sudden sound of Amanda's voice. Still her face betrayed the fact that she was awake. No movement, not a hint of movement. Frank took a deep breath and continued.

"The kid was a jungle cat, fierce and cornered. But I was ready when he moved to run off again. I moved with him to cut him off ... and then it happened. I don't know whether any of this is going to make any sense to you. But it is how I saw it happen, felt it happen. When I moved to intercept, the kid's gun went off ... and then my gun did, too."

"You killed the boy?" Her voice was calm, not a trace of judgment. But all the same, clear conscience and all, Frank was afraid of her reaction.

" ... Yes. I aimed for his shoulder, Amanda. But when his bullet hit me in the chest ... The kid's gun went off again as he fell ... The next thing I realized was the old Chinese kneeling in between me and the kid ... and then suddenly the whole alley was flooded in brilliant light."

HELP

"Boy life going," the Chinese said.

Frank rubbed his burning eyes, his fingers leaving bloody streaks across his face. He just nodded, knowing the kid was beyond help. Frank desperately clung to his waking senses. You killed the boy, Frank. It isn't your fault. It is not your fault, Frank. He shouldn't have killed those men, he shouldn't have had the gun, he shouldn't have run from you. You just did your job, Frank.

"Your life going, too," the Chinese said.

"No. I'll be ... alright."

The Chinese was still on his knees and now Frank noticed what the man was doing. His two index fingers were drawing constant circles on Frank's and the kid's foreheads.

"What are you ...?" Frank was fading fast, the only thing keeping him was the old man's beautiful voice. I'm listening to a Chinese angel, Frank thought and in his delirium, he smiled.

"You want boy dead?"

"No. No, of course ... not. But I ..."

"Good."

"You want live?"

Frank looked at the black kid past the old man's knees. He had seen enough corpses to know that the kid was dead.

"He's dead."

"No. You. You want live?"

Frank stared into eyes that were dark and bottomless pools ... and suddenly he understood that his life was indeed draining out.

"Yes," Frank pleaded. "I want to live."

"Good," the Chinese said again. "Then I help." His fingers never stopped and Frank actually began to feel a glowing circle burning on his forehead. His eyelids were sinking under their own weight, yet he forced himself to keep them open. Look at the old man, look at everything, Frank. Stay awake, stay awake or die. Look at that face, the veins almost popping at the neck. Skin like broken leather. Apron all soiled, all colors ... red. Too much red.

"You're wounded!" Frank's intended shout was a mere whisper by the time it crossed his lips. The Chinese just looked down at him, smiling the smile of a thoroughly happy man. Frank tried to rise, tried to ... do something. But the circles continued and the continuing motion of the index on Frank's forehead kept him locked in place with what appeared to be absolutely no effort on the part of the old man.

"I had very good life."

"What are you ... " Frank struggled. "I have to ... hospital ... You ... " But the eerie peace in the old man's face seemed to make Frank's pleading urgency wholly out of place. Frank looked from the bleeding Chinese to the dead boy. The boy was transparent! And a fraction later the transparent hull of the kid was sucked into the index finger of the Chinese, leaving nothing but empty space on the pavement. Frank watched helplessly as a light charge traveled from that index finger up the old man's arm, through his neck, where it seemed to draw more power. Then the light descended the other arm and burst through the index into Frank's head. The light exploded in his brain and sent a paralyzing charge into every corner of his body. As Frank sank into unconsciousness, he had the strangest sensation of the light charge settling into him, like a cat making the spot by the warmth of the fireplace its own.

TWO

"I woke up three weeks later and found myself in that same back alley."

"I don't understand." Amanda was propped up on her elbows, eyes open, intensely watching Frank. Frank turned his head and his elated astonishment choked the answer he'd been ready to give. Amanda just smiled at him, squeezed his hand, then said impatiently "We're not talking about me now, Frank. What happened in that alley?"

"I ... Amanda, you ... " but her gaze allowed no argument and so he continued. "I don't know what happened. Three weeks later, same alley. And I was alone. There was no black kid, there was no old Chinese. There was just me ... or so I thought at first. Over the course of the next weeks I talked to every hospital, every morgue, every department, and every Chinese in Chinatown. The kid and the Chinese never reappeared, it was as if they had never existed in the first place. All I got was some rumors about a Chinese family that had apparently taken care of me for those three weeks. Of course I never found them either, I never got close to the truth."

"What about your wounds?"

"I wouldn't believe it but I saw it. By the time I woke up in the alley, the .38 bullet hole in my chest was healed. It was still visible, you know. But when I had it checked out by the department's doc, he insisted that the wound was at least ten years old." Amanda frowned. "I can't explain it, Amanda. All I know is this ... the Chinese did something. He kinda - I know it sounds nuts - I think the old man did the best he could under lousy circumstances. I think he knew that all three of us would die that afternoon. I think he somehow used his own life to save mine ... and, in a way, the life of the kid."

"In a way?"

"Yeah, in a way. The black kid's name was George Washington, and George Washington ... is me. I'm not crazy, Amanda. It's not like I'm some split personality psycho or something, it's not like that. But ever since that day back in Chinatown, George Washington has been a part of me. I know all about him, I know all about his family, his history, his hopes and dreams."

"You ... you can talk to the boy you shot dead more than thirty years ago?"

"No. I don't talk to him, I am him. Frank Wilkinson, George Washington, we are one since that day."

Amanda just nodded.

"And that's why I'm black, you know. I found out quickly what an incredible kid George was, is. And I realized that he was a much better man than I ever would be. That kid has love and pride like I never knew existed. So I chose him, over Frank Wilkinson. Never once regretted the choice."

"That's ... one hell of a story, Frank."

"I know. That's why I keep it to myself. Wouldn't want everybody to look at me the way you look at me now."

"I'm sorry. It's just that - "

"No problem, Amanda. You can look at me any which way you like ... as long as you promise that you do look at me on a daily basis for the rest of our lives."

Frank was as surprised as Amanda, when he realized what he'd just said. She slyly smiled.

"Are you proposing, Frank Wilkinson?"

"Well I ... Hell ... Yeah, I'm proposing." He bowed his head in an effort to simulate getting on his knees before her. "Amanda Griffin, will you marry me?"

Her hand caressed his cheek for a sweet moment.

"Yes, I will," she simply answered.

Frank rolled his wheelchair as close to the bed as possible. Then he yanked the wheels which tilted him slightly forward and brought his face close to hers.

They kissed and truth was there.

Amanda put one arm around his neck and pulled him close, head to head, ear to ear. Her shining heart battled against the tears that came despite her.

"I will never walk again, right?" she softly said into his ear. When he tried to jerk back in protest, her arm kept him locked in place. Head to head, ear to ear, side by side. She couldn't look at him, not just yet. "The truth, Frank."

" ... Paralyzed ... waste down," Frank finally answered. Amanda released her vice grip and Frank sank back into his wheelchair. He was amazed to see her smile at him.

"I guess I'm going to need some wheelchair instructions."

"I'm your man."

"Yes you are."

"I love you, Amanda."

Their hearts radiated with joy as they met in another laborious embrace.

GLOW

The nurse still stood next to Agent Wenker. Matter of fact he was sure she didn't even know she was standing next to him. She shook her head once more, pondering something. Wenker waited in polite silence for a long moment, but hey, the nurse seemed as off as Hutchinson had been before. This lady here was staring into space just as his boss had done a little while back. The difference was, this one was positively glowing, whereas Hutchinson had been pale as a worn sheet.

"Are you all right, Ma'am?" he said softly, leaning in her direction, yet without taking his feet even an inch off his post. The nurse looked at him, then smiled with the sudden nervousness of someone almost caught with a hand in the cookie jar.

∞

Jesus Christ, Nurse Harper thought. She hadn't given it a thought, not for an instant. She had been in there with the old man, in his bed, under the blankets. Just keeping him warm, of course, just helping ... but how this would have looked! She noticed with astonishment that she was blushing in front of the young FBI agent.

"I'm fine. Thank you for asking, though. I just ... working too much, I guess."

"How about him? How's he doing?" The agent nodded his head backwards in the direction of Wilber's room.

"Mr. Patorkin is one hundred and fifteen years old. He is ... he's doing as well as can be expected, I guess. I have to go now."" She left the agent without another glance and headed for the duty desk down the hall.

∞

Agent Wenker let his eyes follow the frazzled nurse for another while, then he settled back into focusing on the little cracks in the paint of the wall. Cracks. He wondered what might be behind them. Just a wall, or a doorstep into a brand new Narnia? Wenker loved fantasy novels, Lewis was good, but Tolkien was God as far as he was concerned.

His thoughts wandered once again into the room behind his back. What was it with the old man? Wenker couldn't help it, despite his bright logic and solid training, his possible answers to the old-man-riddle all involved wizards and magic and powerful spells. He was something special, the old man, that much was for sure.

Wenker suddenly realized how much he enjoyed this assignment. Standing guard outside a hospital room. This sort of duty was usually worth no more than a bunch of yawns and a static brain. But this time around it was clearly different. Wenker was alert, his mind racing with rampant imagination, his heart pumping with love and memories. He remembered people and places he hadn't thought of since childhood. He clearly saw his past, his friends, the little things that had shaped him into this man standing guard, here, now. Agent Wenker, with an 'e'. He smiled. All the lucky breaks had led him and kept him on the right track. A few more years of this. Maybe ten, ten more years worth of stories. Then he'd quit and write full-time. Write his first novel about a kid from Hoboken New Jersey who grew up to save the President's life. He had whole passages of the novel already waiting in his head. It would be a bestseller, better than all presidential thrillers combined. Wenker kept alert, his eyes wandering in deliberately slow circles. Watch everything. Be ready ... because he had the feeling that something big was going to happen. No idea what, no reason for it.

Just a feeling, probably nothing ... still.

WAIL

The door opened and Jerry walked out in front of Jerome. Both turned once more and waved back at the smiling Amanda and the grinning Frank.

"Thank you again for the visit, and the flowers, of course," Amanda called out to them.

"We'll try to come by again," Jerome said, hand on Jerry's shoulder.

"You do that, guys," Frank replied. "You do that. But don't wait too long, because this here lady's going to be back at the home real soon."

With a final wave the door closed and Jerome didn't have to look at Jerry to know what was about to come. Jerry had his chin on his chest and started sobbing. He stifled a wail with his hand and walked away quickly. Jerome followed to the elevators, where Doctor Rosenberg was waiting in white silence.

"Everything's okay, Jerry." No reply, Jerome shrugged. "Yeah alright, not everything's okay. But they're happy, they're okay with it, right?"

"She's a cripple because of me!"

"She's no more a cripple now than she was before. She's still Headnurse Griffin, the woman that'll laugh with you when you need it most and kick your butt if you don't respect the home. Only difference will be the new set of wheels."

Jerry stared at Jerome, sobbed again and let his head bang against the elevator buttons. The 'down' button lit up in reply.

Jerome gave Rosenberg a glance, but the doctor didn't even seem aware of them. An odd character, with his haggard face and long white beard he seemed out of place. No time, Jerry needed his attention.

"It's not your fault," Jerome continued. "Once and for all. And even if, Jerry, and I'm saying 'if', it were your fault ... maybe they would have never gotten this close if it wasn't for the accident. They're getting married, Jerry! I've never seen either one of them that happy, have you?"

Jerry sniffled, wiped his eyes and nose. " ... But how can they ... I mean it doesn't make any sense for them to be happy, I mean ... "

"Why shouldn't they be happy? Why should they let this accident make their life a tragedy? Life doesn't have to make sense, Jerry."

"Everything has to make sense," Jerry grumbled.

"Remember the flying teeth?"

"Yeah well ... "

The elevator arrived and Jerry moved to get in. Jerome held him back and pointed at the down arrow.

"We're going up to see Wilber, remember?" Jerome again looked to Rosenberg, holding the door open for him. "Sir?"

"Oh, no," Rosenberg said. "I'm going up, too."

Jerome let the elevator go and for a moment the three men waited in silence. Then Jerry spoke up.

"... Flying teeth, anything is possible, God and all that ... they're happy because of God?"

"They're happy because they choose to be." A second elevator door opened and this time they got in. "They're happy, Jerry, because of life." Jerome kept the door from closing and looked out at the doctor who hadn't moved a muscle. "You coming?"

Rosenberg looked at him earnestly.

"I'll take the next one, thank you."

Jerome frowned at the bearded man in white as the sliding door closed slowly shut.

BELLS

Most of the time he couldn't tell the future. But sometimes things were clear enough to know their future shape. And, once in a while, things were clear enough to be certain. Then Wilber could actually see, hear and smell them in great detail. One such 'thing' was the wedding of Amanda Griffin and Frank Wilkinson.

Wilber could see it now and knew with a dull pang that he'd never be there for the real event. It would be a lovely affair, held inside the magnificent rose garden at Romer Park near the home, with a reception at the home afterwards. Frank and Amanda would do the whole show, wheeling in front of the priest dressed in a black tux and a white gown. Best man Jerome waiting with the ring and 'brides maid' Jerry holding Amanda's embroidered train, making sure it didn't get stuck in the wheels. And there would be the bells. Amanda had it arranged that, although they didn't marry Catholic, the church at the near end of the park would ring their bells for the occasion.

Wilber could hear those bells as clearly as if they were sounding outside the hospital window right this moment. What a wonderful cacophony. Old bells and new bells, large ones and little ones trying to outdo each other in a marvelously deafening choir ... He was proud of Frank.

His friend had managed to come clean, gotten to her truth as well as his own, and had, in the process, even managed to arrive at an impromptu marriage proposal ... Wilber was tired, so tired. He still thought of Frank and Amanda, nodded heavily - and fell asleep without noticing it.

As Wilber's body rested, Wilber's mind was refusing to sleep. So much more to do, so much more to see, he thought for the umpteenth time. Despite everything he knew he desperately kept clinging to the Wilber life. His mind kept looking for places to keep busy, but it didn't roam the world anymore. Wilber had done plenty of that, enough to know that what truly mattered was close to home. Wilber's life, shining brilliantly, would have been stale without friends ... true friends. He had always known that friends didn't come in great numbers and accordingly his circle of friends had always been small. True friends were rare gems, true friends were lottery jackpots ... his mind slipped back to Frank.

Frank had told Amanda about Chinatown. But barely more than a glimpse of it all. He still had a million stories left to tell before his life with Amanda would be at an end. Wilber knew that Frank had lost his job just weeks after the shooting in Chinatown. His behavior had become erratic, frightening to both sides of the law. Acting like two different people, sometimes clearly acting 'black', he had ended up booted from the force ... and just months after that, his wife and kids had left him as well.

BLACK

Roaches. There had never been roaches when Alma was still around. Things were different now. Frank hadn't left the apartment for four weeks and three days, staring at the ceiling, still trying to make sense of what happened. Hell, trying to understand who the fuck he was!

He was fighting. Lost his job, lost his family. The unpaid rent and the potato-sized roaches were of no concern at this point. He was a white man, Goddamnit, a white cop with a sharp mind and clear instincts. He was a good man ... what the fuck was the black kid doing inside his head? Why was he being punished?

"I did my job! The kid killed those spics and I did my job. I chased him down. I would have taken him in, no rough stuff. It was an accident, an accident, you hear me, God?! Hell, what about me? I almost died, didn't I? Now get the fuckin' kid out of my head!"

A week later he found himself drunk by the side of the road on the outskirts of Frisco. He'd been ranting in the apartment, destroyed the whole place, screaming at the walls until the neighbors couldn't take it anymore. Enforced eviction. He had even known the cop who had shoved him out. Fucker. Goddamn motherfucker! What the fuck was he doing here? Where was he, why did he leave the city ... maybe because there was nothing left there. No reason to stay. Frank checked his pockets, thirteen dollars and sixty cents ... great. He sat down on the grassy slope as it started raining ... great.

He stared at the growing puddles. Once in a while those puddles were attacked by racing tires and the water would hit him in the face. Whoosh. He let it happen, kinda welcomed it. It slowly cleared his head. The less you have, the clearer things are, someone had said. No distractions ... Frank smirked.

"Guess that makes bums the brightest fuckers on the planet." But his sarcasm didn't take. No distractions, there was just this, the slope, the grass, the rain. And a bum sitting here with two people inside his head. Frank was surprised to learn that he was calm about it now. Calm. No distractions.

"Whaddaya know," he mumbled to himself and didn't even notice the Chrysler stopping next to him.

"Need a ride?" a voice asked. Frank raised his head and looked into the eyes of an elderly lady. Frank didn't say anything. He looked at the car, brand new, very nice.

Looked at the lady again. She was smiling and waiting patiently.

"You wanna give me a ride?"

"Sure. Where are you going?"

"That's a good question, Lady." And then it clicked, the answer suddenly there. "New York. I'm going to New York."

"I can take you as far as Sacramento, how's that?"

"That's great." He took of his jacket and put the dry inside on the seat, then he sat and closed the door. She turned up the music and drove off. "Thank you very much."

"You're very welcome."

They drove all the way to Sacramento in comfortable silence. Frank was looking at the passing landscapes, but didn't see a thing. He felt comfort in the sudden clarity of his mind. Black, he was black now. It really was very simple. Somehow the black kid had gotten into his mind and deeper still ... and now, having lived with two minds for some time, he finally got it. Frank knew that that black kid was without a doubt his better self. He knew all about Frank Wilkinson, and he knew all about the kid named George Washington. The two, no comparison. Frank would be black now, and proud to be.

Two days later he arrived in New York. He would look for Washington's relatives, his mother, his sister and her baby boy, and an uncle. See how they were doing, maybe even talk to them. He wouldn't be able to tell them the truth, either way they wouldn't want to hear it. But maybe he could just ... help them somehow. But less than an hour before Frank was to meet George Washington's mother, he got run over by a shiny New York City checker cab.

Messed up his legs for good.

His plans to meet the 'relatives' took a back seat to hospital and surgery. Painkillers played royally with his head and he ranted again, screamed and yelled a lot about being two people at once. That led to an extended visit and a great variety of ever increasing doses of drugs. Seventeen years later he was considered 'cured'. A thoroughly broken man, Frank was wheeled from the nut house straight to the Eisenhower Memorial Home. Up until that time, his New York experience hadn't really been all that much of a success.

Then his life suddenly veered towards the positive with the arrival of an old fart named Wilber Patorkin who quickly became the best friend he'd ever had. And then Nurse Griffin took over the home - and found a place in his dreams.

He tried to keep up with life outside the home. He got a card once from Alma and the kids. But they never made it to New York. And he kept informed about the Washingtons. They died away, one by one New York finished them off. George's mother died of cancer long before her time. His sister was shot and killed during a grocery store robbery that netted twenty-two dollars for two crack-heads who never made it past the age of seventeen. George's uncle ended up face down in the East

River, nine Colt 45's too many in his gut. That left the baby boy name Hakim.

Hakim Washington, shot in the head, killed with a single bullet from an Uzi. Killed by an eleven year old boy named Jerome. Frank had always known about Jerome. When Jerome had come to the Home a grown man, Frank thought about strangling him with his bare hands, thought about very slowly squeezing the life out of him. But instead he had decided to give him a chance. And the Jerome Frank got to know over time indeed deserved to live.

GUT

The limousine moved at high speed past blocked off traffic.

Brooklyn was sounding off a million angry horns. It was standing still because of the presidential convoy, making its way to the hospital. Brooklyn was pissed off.

Charlie sat deep in the burgundy leather and would occasionally mumble acknowledging sounds into her cellular. Just three people riding the presidential limo this time. Taylor, herself ... and the little butt-kisser Jimmy Weller.

Weller was riding with the Prez for the first time and it annoyed Charlie to no end. Wiener-boy clearly thought he had just been granted executive status.

Truth was, however, that no one else of rank and stature had felt like accompanying Taylor on this bullshit trip.

Money, politics, there was nothing to be gained from this visit. President Taylor knew this and it didn't bother him. He made it a point to do his own thing once in a while.

She looked at him. There, Taylor, the legend. She knew him so well.

Outwardly he looked completely at ease, legs spread wide, arms loose, no tension. But he was watching the fly-by Brooklyn a little too intensely.

Charlie knew that her boss was anxious.

Or scared, she suddenly thought ... nah. He was probably just excited about meeting the oldest man in the United States of America. She smiled at him.

President Melvin Taylor had a thing for greatness. He had never been a mediocre man, had never been satisfied with the norm, the regular, the average. With everything in his life he had aimed for greatness and had reached the highest post in the country. He didn't stop there, he continued to strive. He championed causes that money and politics had never dared to approach. He went out on every limb he could find and his willpower, his character and his charisma succeeded again and again. Every lost battle made him work not twice, but ten times harder. Greatness. Go for the most, the best. He worked harder and lived brighter than any president before him. Melvin Taylor was a great man, indeed. Great, and yet humble. And his trick to keep that humility lay, amazingly, in his love for greatness.

He had stood on top of the highest building, he had climbed Mount Everest as young man, he had hugged 'General Sherman', the largest tree, he had stood on the longest bridges and looked up at the tallest monument. He had been to see the biggest US flag, looked up at the largest tomato plant and had chatted with the tallest man on the planet. Greatness, in all forms and sizes, big, wide, tall, nothing too odd. President Taylor made it a point to meet greatness, look it in the eye, touch it, talk to it. It often reminded him of what more could be achieved. It kept him on solid ground. And not meeting Wilber Patorkin would be simply unforgivable. The oldest man in the United States of America. Now that was an achievement, a great achievement. Even if Patorkin turned out to be a vegetable, his age alone made the visit worth the President's while.

Then again, maybe there was more to him. Maybe Patorkin could tell him things, secrets of life. Either way, the trip was a must. Meeting greatness ... and defying that 'Al' voice. Taylor was scared. Fear, pure fear. He'd never admit it, he'd never show it, but there it was. Gut feeling. Stay the fuck home, don't go. All morning long his senses had screamed for him to call off the hospital visit. But he couldn't. He simply could not. Listening to instinct was one thing, giving in to some voice that had probably never been there in the first place was psychotic. Then again Taylor had no doubt that this Al really existed, he had no doubt that their conversations had actually taken place. All the easier the decision. He had to go.

"Your approval rating is holding steady, Sir."

Without a glance Taylor knew that Weller was looking up from his laptop with an eager smile, like a dog waiting for a bone. He didn't feel like handing out bones just now.

"Hmn," he simply replied. He kept looking out the window. Brooklyn, people of all walks. Down to earth people, proud people. Home, sweet home. Taylor loved this place.

"You're not gonna believe this," Charlie said. Taylor heard her put away her cell phone. Get yourself together, Mel. He turned to look at her.

"What?"

"We're all set, security, staff, schedule, all in place. Except for one thing ... " Charlie couldn't help grinning, forcing the President to frown.

"What?"

"Your man? Mr. Patorkin? Well, I assume you will want to talk to the guy, right?"

"Charlie, just spit it out, all right?"

"Alright, alright. Your Mr. Patorkin was brought to the hospital without his dentures. He apparently lost his teeth during the accident when they, get this, dropped from his mouth into a sewer hole. So anyway, the advance team requested for him to get a new set."

"Hutchinson may be an asshole, but he ain't no dummy," said Taylor.

"Right. So they bring a whole tray of brand new sets of teeth ... but what do you know - the old man opens his mouth and shows them his old dentures."

"The ones from the sewer?" Weller asked.

"The ones from the sewer. Exactly. And nobody's brought them to Patorkin according to the FBI. They're just back, out of nowhere, out of the sewer and back in his mouth."

"How's that possible?" The President listened with more interest and that listening slowly pulled him out of his reclusive mood.

"Ask him when we get there ... not that you'll understand a word he says, mind you. Dentures or no dentures, when he speaks it's all garbled, according to Hutchinson. Nobody understands a word he says, except for an old pal of Patorkin."

"So we'll have that guy there to translate."

"The FBI is against that, Sir," Weller suddenly said. "Agent Hutchinson wasn't very clear on it, but he thinks that Mr. Wilkinson may represent a serious security risk."

"Oh come on," Charlie said, rolling her eyes. "Frank Wilkinson is an eighty-five year old man in a wheelchair."

"Who struck and seriously wounded two people at the hospital," Weller insisted.

"Sounds like I man I'd like to meet," Taylor smiled.

"But Sir, I don't think - "

"Ah shut up, Jimmy," said Charlie.

The President stared out of the window again, the hospital came into view.

"Have Agent Hutchinson be in the room," Taylor said without looking at them. "If he thinks there's a risk, let him keep an eye on the man."

"An eighty-five year old wheelchair bound raisin ... that'll be a hell of a challenge for Hutchinson, Mel." Charlie was grinning. But her grin faded when no presidential humor came back in reply.

He didn't listen anymore. Not to Charlie Columbus, not to Jimmy Weller. Their usual bickering was drowned out by the deafening sight of the hospital. It was looming like an enormous white ghost. When the convoy stopped, the President was the first to get out. He planted his feet firmly on the ground and looked up. Yep, he was scared. That fucking 'Al' voice had him shit scared. Greatness, Mel. There's greatness waiting up there. Fuck Al.

He was about to take his first step toward the entrance when Al's voice froze him.

"Stupid move, Mr. President."

President Taylor started walking in silence. His face set, his jaw grinding down his teeth.

"You can still turn around, Mel," Al said.

Melvin Taylor continued up the steps.

"Last chance," Al warned.

The hospital's Chief Administrator was waiting by the open doors. There was a delegation of doctors and nurses. All cheers and smiles and handshakes.

President Taylor immersed himself and put on the show that was expected of him. Hell, he had always loved this part. He laughed, made jokes, patted shoulders. Then a glowing Clarence Wainright led the President of the United States into the building.

"You're a dead man," Al said.

Without hesitation, Taylor stepped inside.

BOB

„Bob who?" Hutchinson asked. He was very much irritated. This sucked, this wasn't the way it was supposed to work. He was advance detail, he checked and secured locations. Others were in charge of guarding the President. Now all of a sudden he had been ordered to be present during the visit. A welcome assignment under normal circumstances, an honor, even. But this time it meant he was forced back into the room with the old man. Back with the old man who had stolen his calm, his control. Right now that old man smiled at him with a set of brand new, wonderfully aligned and brilliantly white teeth in his mouth.

"Bob Redford, Pal," Frank Wilkinson answered. He looked from Agent Hutchinson to Nurse Harper. "Don't you guys watch movies? Those are Redford teeth. You know, any movie you see the guy in, his teeth are fuckin' perfect, just like that," he pointed at Wilber. "I mean, you guys ever see Jeremiah Johnson?"

"Who is Jeremiah Johnson?" Nurse Harper asked.

"We don't have time for this," Hutchinson spat. "President Taylor has just entered the building. Now will you please select a proper sized and decent looking set of teeth."

Patorkin looked at Hutchinson with infuriatingly warm eyes, completely ignoring his urgent request - then looking to the nurse.

"Jeremiah Johnson is a movie, Nurse Harper. Actually, quite a wonderful movie."

"It's a great movie, except for the teeth," Wilkinson continued. "The guy spends his whole life out in bumblefuck-nowhere-mountain. There's nothing but wilderness and snow and ice and bears and Indians his whole life long and Jeremiah's fuckin' teeth look great from beginning to end. I mean, come on!"

Thoroughly frustrated, Hutchinson took the tray of dentures from Nurse Harper and set them on the bed next to the stubborn old patient.

"Well okay, then pick another set. How about those? They look wonderful, and all natural, you see?" Hutchinson felt like a lousy salesman and hated himself, Wilber Patorkin and the world at large for it. "Pick one, will you? Brand new teeth, they're free, Goddamnit. It doesn't cost you a cent! How can you refuse an offer like that? Any one of these sets is worth a fortune and is obviously a great improvement over your old ones. Pick one. Go on, pick one ... please."

Patorkin removed Robert Redford and stuck another set into his mouth. He looked at himself in the little hand-mirror, then bared his teeth for the others to see. His pal Wilkinson laughed out loud, slapping his knees.

"Sean Connery!"

"Oh come on, that's ridiculous!" Agent Hutchinson put his hand to his ear piece. "The President will be here in five minutes. Five minutes, Mr. Patorkin. Please make up your mind."

∞

"My mind is made up, Mr. Hutchinson. Again, I do thank you for your effort, but I really am happy with my old teeth." He did a miserable Connery imitation in Nurse Harper's direction. "Thank you, Moneypenny." Then he took out Sean Connery and handed the whole tray back to the smiling Nurse. She left the room, leaving behind three men, one of them seething.

"Fine! Have it your way!" Hutchinson shouted and stomped past Frank. He tried to slam the door, but the stopper didn't allow him even that satisfaction. The door closed with a soft whoosh. Frank looked at Wilber.

"Not a happy camper. Looks like J. Edgar could probably use a little more of that thing you do."

"I'm working on it," Wilber said.

"Tough case?"

"Yep."

Frank glanced around the room, wheeled to the window. He could see the waiting limousines down below.

"The President of the United States ... you nervous, Champ?"

Wilber just smiled and shook his head. He couldn't tell Frank. He couldn't tell him that he was nervous. He couldn't tell Frank that he was worried, very much worried. The President was coming to see him ... and his meeting with Al was shortly thereafter. Al would be here. Had he planned it this way? Probably. Wilber had tried to reach Al many times now, tried to find him, read him. But there had been a solid block, Al making sure that Wilber would stay in the dark. What was Al's plan? Kill the President? Why? Why here? Why now?

"Can't fool this old fart. You're nervous."

"Well ... maybe a little."

UP

Clarence Wainright was happier than he had ever been in his entire life. He was riding the elevator with the President of the United States of America. His father would be proud for once. This would secure him at least a few weeks worth of love and respect at home. The hall had been packed with press and the quick interview and photo op had been brilliant. Wainright was sure his hospital would be headlining every major paper tomorrow. The Today show was going to be here later this afternoon to do a moving piece on patients who got to meet with the President. Too bad President Taylor had refused to allow press to cover his time with Wilber Patorkin. Oh well, can't have everything, Clarence thought.

∞

Jimmy Weller was hidden by the shoulders of the President. Suited him just fine. He was fairly grown up, but once in a while the unpleasant child he'd been caught up with him. He still loved making faces. He thought of how much he detested Charlie Columbus, he thought of what he could do to get her job. She could be booted, she was a fat pig and he would find a way to kick her ass. Hidden by the President, he contorted his face and stuck out his tongue at her. Felt good.

∞

Charlie was thinking chocolate. She loved the Waldorf where most things were excellent, service, location, staff. But the best thing, without a doubt, were the chocolates. She had been all over the world in all of the best hotels. But no pillow chocolates had ever come close to the ones the Waldorf staff lovingly placed on her pillow each night. Charlie silently sighed and smiled at the thought of another piece of chocolate waiting on her pillow.

∞

President Taylor waited for the light to reach the fifth floor. Instinct, premonition, Al's voice. Who knew. All he knew was that going up in this elevator was bringing him closer to his destiny.

He wasn't scared anymore, it was fine. He was here. And he was going to meet greatness in the form of Wilber Patorkin. He smiled as the elevator stopped.

AL

Wilber was sitting in his bed, propped up by several pillows. Frank brought him a glass of water.

"I didn't ask for water," Wilber said.

"I read your mind, buddy," Frank said with a light grin. Wilber nodded and drank eagerly. He was drying up inside. His body was getting ready to leave. Time is running out, Wilber. Just a few more days, just a few more days.

"Helllloooo!" Al's screaming voice.

Wilber didn't move, didn't want to worry Frank. They were still alone in the room, but Al was speaking. And Al was undoubtedly near.

"Frank. I'm just going to rest my eyes for a few moments."

Frank nodded understandingly and wheeled away to the window. Wilber leaned back and closed his eyes. Then he answered Al.

"Hi, Al."

"You know what's gonna happen, don't ya?"

"Death of a president?" Wilber said it casually and kept his dread hidden away from Al's senses. Wilber knew much about Melvin Taylor. The country had never had a better leader in all its many years. More than that, Melvin Taylor was a great human being.

"Bingo! But what you don't know is how I'm gonna do it."

"It doesn't matter," Wilber replied. "If he dies, then he was meant to die."

"You fuckin' prick," Al said with sudden fury. "What do you think your actions can alter the future and mine can't? What do you think you're better than me?!"

"Not better, Al ... just different."

"Sure. You're nothing but words. You can't make me stop, you can't change a thing, whatever you say. Besides," Al added with newfound calm, "who wants to change the future anyway. I live now, and I'm having fun now. And that's why Taylor's gonna kick the bucket today."

"He's a good man."

"Your good man's made the country a boring fuckin' place. For fun loving people like me that guy's the devil incarnate."

"Why are we talking, Al?"

"Why not?"

"Why are you here?"

"Why don't you read my mind?" Al said sarcastically.

"Al ... I can show you many things. Telekinesis is just a tiny spec of what I have learned. I can tell you - "

"And all I have to do is not kill Taylor, right? No deal. The President of the US of A is about to meet his fate and the name of his fate is Al."

"Do as you must."

"Thanks for your permission. How's it feel to be powerless, 'Champ'?"

"I wouldn't know, Al."

"Oh yeah? Then how's it feel to know that you're gonna die next Wednesday?"

"Seems like you've been reading my mind."

"Pretty boring crap, but you know how it is. Sometimes, when there's nothing better around, you even read the crappy papers. So how does it feel?" Al insisted.

"How does what feel?"

"Don't fuck with me or I'll kill your buddy Frankie over there as well. How's it feel to know that you'll be dead in four days?"

" ... Not good, Al."

"Scared about after?"

"No. Just sad to leave Wilber Patorkin behind."

"Truth is, you're scared to death that your theories won't hold. Truth is, you know that I'm right. There is nothing that follows. Absolutely beautiful black nothing."

Agent Hutchinson opened the door a crack and leaned in.

"The President is walking down the hall. Should be here in about sixty seconds. For God sake," he hissed at Frank. "Patorkin isn't sleeping, is he?!"

"I'm awake," Wilber said and opened his eyes. Hutchinson let out a sharp sigh of relief, shook his head and slid back out again.

"You ready, Champ?" Frank asked as he positioned himself protectively by the side of Wilber's bed.

"Sure." There was nothing to do but wait for Al's move. Wilber sat in silence, looking around the room, looking at his friend. Frank was nervously staring at the door, his hands sliding back and forth along the rails of his chair.

"Nothing you can do," Al said again.

"You could be so much more," Wilber replied.

"Fuck off, raisin face. He's dead."

" ... We'll see."

"We're still on for afterwards, right?" Al asked jovially.

"Three o'clock, cafeteria."

"Great," Al said and then his voice went into TV announcer mode. "And now, ladies and gentlemen, it's show-time!"

PIMP

Agent Frome waited by the duty desk on the ground floor. The President had passed, the crowd thinned. She waited patiently. She loved working for the FBI and had never once regretted joining the Bureau. There were plenty of successes and true satisfactions along her way, there were brushes with man hunts, serial killers, assassinations. Yes, life as an FBI agent had proven to be as thrilling and fulfilling as she had always hoped it to be. There were incidents she could share with family and friends, proud moments.

Then of course there were other assignments ... all of them classified, for different reasons. Those she kept to herself. She had to by law, and she did so out of conviction. Of course she couldn't tell her Mom and Dad about the time the Russian Foreign Minister had physically attacked the President. Negotiations hadn't gone according to the man's ideas.

∞

He snapped. He lunged across the table and reached for Taylor's throat. President Taylor reacted an instant late. As he yanked his chair back and stood up, the Russian Minister stayed glued to his throat like a leech. Taylor grabbed the hands and pulled the man across the table, then twisted and slammed a vicious Brooklyn back street punch to the Russian's solar plexus. Frome was the first agent to reach and aid the President. But Melvin Taylor had done the work for her. She didn't have to do more than pull the unconscious Russian out from under Taylor. The President smiled at her, thanked her for the assistance.

"Thank you, Agent Frome," Taylor said. She looked up at him and saw that smile he reserved for women only. She smiled back, while dragging the Russian.

"You're welcome, Sir ... Anytime." She couldn't help blushing and the President's eyes followed her for a moment. Then he brushed off his suit and addressed the stunned trade delegations.

"Ladies, Gentlemen. This is not the time for a break. We're in the middle of something big here. Both our countries have a lot to gain." He stretched and smiled.

"Now, I enjoyed the Minister's unusual negotiating style. If any of you wish to slug it out for a while, let's do it. Otherwise, please sit down again."

A medic stuck his head in the room and gave the President a signal. He nodded back. "Minister Ghorkin's fine and will be back in five minutes." He remained standing until every last one in the room had taken their seat again. "All right. Let's move on."

∞

Agent Frome had received a commendation and a nice little salary increase for having been there the instant it happened. There were many more unusual assignments, many more she couldn't tell anybody about. Her present job would probably be a bit unusual to some, incredibly foul to others. To Agent Frome it did not present a problem. She pimped for the President of the United States of America. One of her regular advance detail assignments included finding willing women for the President. It was a simple fact: This was how he worked, this was how he functioned. He was the best President anyone could have hoped for, and, important to Frome, he was a truly wonderful human being. So he screwed women like other people drank coffee, so what. That was his juice of life, and Agent Frome had no qualms providing it for him.

"Well, here I am," the pretty nurse said.

Agent Frome looked at her. She had talked to several women upon arrival at the hospital. Frome always kept it general, she knew what to listen for. At this point she could spot potentials immediately. A few specific questions filtered out trouble makers. She always looked for single, fun-loving, open-minded. Anyone obsessed with the President didn't qualify. She wanted women who loved a thrill, a good time, and nothing more.

This one was perfect.

"Nervous?" Agent Frome asked.

"Should I be?" Nurse Nelligan nurse answered coyly.

"Not at all," Frome smiled.

"Well yes I guess I am a little excited. It doesn't happen every day that I get to screw the most important man in the country. How is he, anyway? I mean, have you ever - "

"No, I haven't," Frome said a bit too quickly.

"Oops."

"Not a problem. Follow me. I'll show you where." Frome led the way to the elevators. Of course she had wondered about that. It was true that Taylor didn't dick around in the White House. He made sure to avoid relationship trouble. And sleeping with staff could cause problems ... still. He had done the odd secretary, but never once had the President made a move on her. She frowned lightly.

"Ehm ... Is this like, top secret?"

"Absolutely," Frome answered. "Your time with the President is for you, and for Taylor. Two people, one time, nothing more. You will keep this to yourself."

"Otherwise you'll kill me?" the nurse laughed.

"Only if you become a problem." Agent Frome stopped at the elevators and looked at Nurse Nelligan, not smiling.

"You're kidding, right?"

"Of course I'm kidding," Frome said, still not smiling.

∞

No problem, the nurse thought as they went up in the elevator. Who was she going to tell anyway, and who would believe her? Wow. Was she nervous? You had better believe it! President Melvin Taylor ... The whole country had heard rumors about him. She looked forward to the 'meeting'.

KILL

"And this is my friend Frank Wilkinson," Wilber said to the President. Taylor heartily shook Frank's hand and Frank was glowing like a bright summer night's full moon.

"Eighty-five years old, right? I've heard about you." The President winked and threw a punch at an imaginary foe. Frank blushed with pride. Four people in the room: Wilber, Frank, the President and Agent Hutchinson standing in the corner like a lamp that had lost its shade. Taylor grabbed a chair and sat by Wilber's bed.

"So what's with the teeth?" he said.

"You heard about that, too, did you?" Frank grinned.

"I hear most things," Taylor said. "I was told those dentures just appeared again. So what happened?"

"Magic," Wilber said with a smile.

"Why not," Taylor said, returning the smile. "Magic, fair enough. I thought you couldn't speak with your old teeth? Seems to me you're pretty clear."

"Well, Sir, I - "

"Guys, call me Mel, please." Frank wheeled his chair closer to the President, loving every minute of it.

"Alright, Mel," Wilber continued. "You see, since most conversations are not worth having, I just babble a little and the conversation usually stops. When I want to be understood, my teeth get the gum treatment." Wilber took out his teeth and showed the President the yellowish piece of gum stuck there.

The President smiled, not a bit taken aback.

∞

What a character, this guy. One hundred and fifteen years old, Jesus Christ the things the man must have seen. Every worry about Al's threat was gone for now. Melvin Taylor was completely mesmerized by the old man. Magic, indeed. Wilber Patorkin would qualify for Taylor's greatness category with his record breaking age alone. But there was more. Nothing that Taylor could know, yet something he could feel. Something strong, something powerful. What a character.

"Well I'm glad this occasion was worth the 'gum treatment'," he said and leaned forward. "I guess you wonder why I wanted to pay you a visit."

"Nope," Wilber answered.

"No?" Taylor looked from Wilber to Frank, smiling and puzzled. All he got from Frank was a blank shrug.

"I know why you're here," Wilber continued. "I know all about your interest in what you call 'greatness'. It's a little odd, if I may say so, but I'm glad it works for you. And I know it does work for you ... as for me being great ... well ... "

"How did you - " the President said with wide eyes.

"I read minds," Wilber said clearly.

∞

The President was stunned, and so was Agent Hutchinson in the corner. Of course! That's how the old fuck did it, screwed with his brain. Hutchinson glared at Wilber Patorkin. He would get the bastard as soon -

"That's not exactly polite," Wilber's voice suddenly said inside Hutchinson's head. "By all means, do speak your mind. But could you please keep it down while I'm talking to your boss?"

Hutchinson's body swayed like a willow in the wind. He had to grab the wall to keep from falling. His face didn't change, but his mind was shaking like a leaf.

"Sorry," he mumbled loud enough for the President to turn and frown at him.

"Did you say something, Hutch?"

"No, Sir." The reply came back crisp as always. The President looked back and forth between Wilber and Frank. Then he leaned in even closer to Wilber.

"I'm not sure I - "

"What can I say, Mel," Frank said, „You heard right. My buddy here reads your mind like you read the Washington Post."

Melvin Taylor's eyes were glued to Wilber's now. He was fascinated, he was terrified. Then it happened again.

A voice speaking to him from inside.

"Telepathy, Mel. I can talk to you and you can talk to me." Neither Wilber nor the President moved anymore.

∞

Frank and Agent Hutchinson were left with nothing but silence. Frank looked at the agent in the corner, but the weirdo seemed to be out of it, staring at nothing. Frank sighed and leaned back in his chair, glancing from silent Wilber to silent President Taylor ... Great. He'd just have to wait it out.

∞

"I know how this works," the President said to Wilber without using his voice. He suddenly appeared hard, a soldier's voice. "So how am I going to die?"

"Now I don't understand, Mel. What are you - "

"Fuck you, Al. No more games. Just tell me and do whatever you've got planned. I'm ready."

"You know Al?" Wilber said out loud, not realizing.

"Hey, we're talking again. Who's Al?" Frank stuck his head toward them again and waited for more.

"You're not Al?" Taylor asked suspiciously.

Wilber shook his head and went back to his inner voice.

"But I do know him. He's been talking to you?"

"Yes, just like you do now. Telepathy. Al told me that, if I came here today, I would die."

"But you came anyway."

"I had to."

"I understand," Wilber said, nodding his head.

∞

"You believe this shit?" Frank said with a grin. He looked to Agent Hutchinson and rolled his eyes. But the agent in the corner ignored him. Stuck up bastard, about time Wilber does a big number on you - you need it. With that he looked at the silent talkers again.

∞

Agent Hutchinson hadn't heard Frank. Agent Hutchinson was still staring at the wall. Agent Hutchinson was listening with painful concentration. Listening to a voice in his head, while part of him was fiercely struggling with his sanity.

"Hutch, this is God speaking," Al said earnestly to Hutchinson's mind. "You're wondering whether you're going crazy, I know. Let me calm your worries. You are hearing my voice, and you alone can hear me. Now listen to me and do not move. Listen to your God. I need your help, my friend. I know that you love your country. And I know that you love your President."

Agent Hutchinson had never felt this out of control in his life. The incident with the old fart was nothing compared to this. God was speaking to him. God! He couldn't move, besides, God had just told him not to. So he stood in place, still, a statue.

"Your President is about to go insane, Hutch. I know it doesn't appear that way, but you must believe me. Millions of lives depend on you. He will be at the Pentagon tomorrow, and he will push the button for no reason. Have faith in the words of your God. You, Hutch, are the savior of millions of innocent lives. You. Now, take out your 9 mm and kill President Taylor."

Agent Hutchinson fought hard, forced his hand to stay down, forced his fingers to stay away from the gun in his shoulder holster. But the voice kept pushing him, the voice of God. He was not crazy, he was not crazy! What if it was true, what if he could save all those lives? What if ... against his will his hand moved to the holster, gripped the pistol tight, but still refused to pull it forward.

∞

"Wilber?" President Taylor said inside. Nothing. Like a radio broadcast that had gone off the air. Only then did Taylor realize that Wilber Patorkin's eyes were closed. "Wilber?" he said softly in his own voice. Still, nothing.

Wilber Patorkin seemed asleep.

"It happens," Frank said, his voice a little shaky. "More and more often ... And, you know, every time he closes his eyes like that I'm dying a little. What if he doesn't wake up anymore?"

"Your friend is a remarkable man," Taylor said, putting a hand on Frank's shoulder.

"You have no idea," Frank replied. Both he and the President watched Wilber in silence. He was clearly breathing, steadily at first.

Then his chest heaved and he started drawing breaths faster and faster, as if he were running.

∞

Wilber was awake, Wilber was somewhere else, Wilber was busy. He had suddenly heard Al, heard him drill into Agent Hutchinson. Al had been subtle at first, kept the block up. Wilber would never have noticed a thing, if it hadn't been for the agent's struggle. Al had required more intensity than expected, and that was when Wilber had become aware.

"Kill him," Al ordered again.

"He's not God, Agent Hutchinson." There was nothing Wilber could do on the outside, nothing he could say. The agent was too close to breaking. A spoken word would be all that was needed for him to snap and kill everybody in the room.

"Kill the President. Do it or suffer eternal damnation."

"Do not believe him," Wilber insisted.

"All the lives that can be saved. Do it, Hutch, you must do it now." Al wasn't quite as steady anymore. He refused to acknowledge Wilber's presence, but his voice was already taking on darker shades of his ill temper.

"Take your hand off the weapon. Think of something good. Think hard and I will help you out of this." Wilber stayed calm, had to. He felt Agent Hutchinson release the grip of his pistol, when Al burst in again.

"Satan is tempting you, my friend. How easy it would be to let that man live. But the right choices are never easy. Be the man you can be, show me the courage within you and the angels will sing your name forever."

∞

Agent Hutchinson once more locked his fingers around his pistol. *Two voices. Two voices in my head. What can I do? What must I do? Please, God, don't make me do this. I can't kill the President, I just -*

"You must take this one life to save the lives of the many. There is no other choice, Hutch. Do not refuse your God. Do it. Do it now."

Agent Hutchinson tensed his muscles, about to pull and shoot ... when a storm of colors hit his every thought like a tidal wave. His mind was suddenly swamped with light and warmth and colors the likes he had never seen. The voices were mere background now, drowned out by the waves. Hutchinson glowed. The fingers let go of the pistol, the muscles relaxed, his arm went slack and lightly swung at his side like peacefully constant pendulums.

∞

"Goddamnit!" Al screamed.

"I couldn't let you do it, Al," Wilber said.

"You are so fucking boring."

"Wanna know what I did just now?"

"Ah fuck you ... See you at three."

With Al gone, Wilber opened his eyes again and saw two worried faces in front of him. Wilber's breathing steadied, at the same time he started pouring sweat. Breaking through Al right into Hutchinson's soul had been hard work.

"You alright, Champ?" Frank asked.

"I'll call a doctor," Taylor said, getting up.

"Sit down, Mel," Wilber said, his voice tired and creaky for a moment. "I'm fine, I'm fine. Just took a little nap." Taylor remained on his feet for a beat, frowning down at Wilber. When Wilber winked at him, he finally sat again. "Agent Hutchinson," Wilber suddenly called to the corner.

"Please, Agent Hutchinson, grab a chair and sit here with the rest of us."

Wilber pointed to a chair, motioned to the side of the bed. With his mind he had to gently steady Hutchinson's body and soul. Then Hutchinson was sitting by the bed, a silly grin on his face. President Taylor was looking at the agent quizzically. Hutchinson didn't see a thing, his President's frown meaningless. Agent Hutchinson was plain happy and nothing would be able to break that state for a while. He'd soon get used to his new self. Wilber smiled at Taylor.

"So what did you want to talk about, Mel?"

"Well you know, don't you?"

"I'm not reading your mind anymore. Wouldn't be polite, now that you know." Taylor smiled, then looked at Hutchinson's blissful grin again.

"Are you all right, Hutch?" the President asked.

"Great, I'm just great," Hutchinson responded pleasantly.

"You sure?"

"Absolutely, Sir," Hutchinson said. He looked at the President with an open smile. Taylor shook his head, then suddenly looked at Wilber again.

"I've never seen Hutchinson smile, ever. You wouldn't by any chance know what the hell is going on with him?"

"If anyone knows," Frank grinned, "Wilber does. I've seen shit you would not believe."

"Agent Hutchinson has had a little experience," Wilber said to Taylor. "Don't ask, Mel. I can tell you this. Agent

Hutchinson is a man of highest integrity, and a man who loves life."

The President finally took his eyes off Hutchinson, shrugged and turned back to Wilber.

"What do you know?" Taylor asked.

"There is nothing I can tell you. We are who we are, we have what he have. That's what we work with, Mel. You have learned much, given much, lived much. More than most people will in ten lifetimes."

"You actually know about reincarnation?"

"As I said," Wilber smiled. "There is nothing I can tell you. You have found your own truths and you will find your own future. Whatever there is to come, is your own to see."

"Thanks a lot," Taylor grinned and smirked at Hutchinson. "This guy won't tell me a thing, Hutch. Doesn't the FBI have ways to get people talking?"

"That would be the CIA, Sir," Hutchinson said with a smile.

"Hey, Hutch, you're developing a sense of humor," Taylor said with mock disbelief. Then he looked at Wilber and let out a little sigh. "Well all right, then. I'll find my own words of wisdom. What the heck. So I guess I won't know about my next life until I kick the bucket. Which, come to think of it, could be pretty soon if that Al character's been telling the truth."

"You don't have to worry about Al anymore," Wilber said. The President frowned at Wilber, his eyes went to Agent Hutchinson and back to Wilber.

"Don't ask, right?"

Wilber nodded. President Taylor got up and Hutchinson instantly followed suit. The agent went to the door and waited patiently, ready to swing it open.

"Got a bunch of crap meetings waiting," Taylor said. He took Wilber's hand and shook it firmly. He didn't let go for a while. "I thank you very much for your time," he said humbly.

"You are welcome, Mel."

"Anything at all I can do for you?"

"Nope."

"Still no words of wisdom?" Taylor smiled hopefully. Wilber looked at him for a long time. Their hands were still joined and the President obviously had no intention of letting go just yet.

"There are no limits," Wilber said.

Taylor, Hutchinson, even Frank, were hanging on his lips. But that was it, Wilber didn't add another word.

President Taylor nodded. Then he said goodbye to Frank as if they'd been buddies all their life. He finally strode from the room without looking back. Agent Hutchinson winked at Wilber, then followed his boss.

∞

"The President of the United States of America," Frank said, grinning at Wilber. "You should have shown him the flying furniture."

" ... I'm tired, Frank." Wilber half-smiled at Frank as his eyelids closed. He was already deep asleep when Frank took his hand and held it in both of his.

Frank watched his sleeping friend.

Frank died a little.

STAIRS

She waited on the 5th floor landing. The usually hectic staircase was deserted. Not a sound. They must have sealed it off, she thought. When Agent Frome had brought her here, she had been slightly irritated. Why here? Nurse Nelligan had expected to be led to a back room somewhere. Somehow she had had the romantic notion of the President bringing along his own private little pleasure dome. A picture of a desert tent in her mind, comfortable chaise-longue, velvet cushions, grapes, a Rudolph Valentino 'The Sheik' sort of thing. But Agent Frome had simply dropped her off here, staircase. Cold ground, cold walls, cold railing. Cold, white and sterile.

Nurse Nelligan had been here for more than thirty minutes now. It was as if the world around her had stopped. She didn't mind, she wasn't bored. As a matter of fact, the longer she waited, the more excited she got. She was imagining her immediate future with the President of the United States. How would they do it, which positions and where exactly. Melvin Taylor was a great looking man, this would be fun. Anticipation brought on a wicked smile.

"Come and get it, Mel," she said to the door an instant before the President walked in. He heard it and smiled broadly. As the door swung shut, she could see a secret agent planting himself outside. They would not be disturbed. Taylor sat down on the stairs and motioned her to join him.

"Please, sit down."

She did as told, and not knowing what to say or do next, she just waited. She glanced at the man. Yes, Melvin Taylor, the President. What a man ... what was he doing? Smiling at the stairs below, just a blank stare. After a moment his head came up and he turned to her.

"I'm sorry. You know, I don't usually do a lot of talking during these 'meetings'. But I just got to know this man ... it was quite an experience, I'm a little ... a lot to think about. By the way, I'm Mel." He offered his hand and she shook it.

"I'm Wendy."

"Nice to meet you, Wendy. Wendy as in Peter Pan Wendy?"

"That's why my mom picked the name. I didn't exactly turn out that way, though. I'm more of a mischievous Tinker Bell kind of girl."

"I'm glad to hear it."

They looked at each other, both loving the moment. This was all that counted. This moment, now. Wendy Nelligan was amazed by the perfect ease she felt. There was nothing unpleasant, nothing wrong here. Just two people talking, just two people looking forward to a little something more. She leaned in and kissed him.

∞

This is even better than usual, Taylor thought as his hands began to explore. He somehow felt that his mind was exploring, too. He didn't have a handle on it, didn't know what was going on. But it felt as if he could see her thoughts. Her mind wasn't cluttered and confused with layers of worries. Wendy Nelligan's mind was just in this one place, here, with him. She was thinking about the walls, the ground, the railing, places, positions. The President picked her up and gently pushed her against the railing.

"You must have read my mind," she whispered in between increasingly passionate kisses.

"I think so," he simply said and left it at that. He would wonder later. For now there was no reason to read anything anymore. Their bodies knew what to do and the fact that their minds seemed to caress as well only heightened the heat and lust of their lovemaking.

The moment he tripped, Taylor realized that he had never experienced a similar orgasm. The instant he fell, he knew that this was all there was, now, it couldn't get any better than this. The second his head connected with the landing below, the President understood that he had done good. The moment his neck broke he had truth, knowledge and wisdom.

He had lived his life to the fullest. No regrets. His life would be remembered as a life lived, not a life wasted.

When he died a split-second later, he suddenly knew what Wilber had meant. He could hear the old man as if Wilber had his head right next to his, his mouth close to Taylor's bleeding ear, on the cold hard ground.

"There are no limits, Mel," the voice gently said.

When Melvin Taylor's soul soared, he was not alone.

PLAY

The small apartment reverberated with the overjoyed laughter of exhilarated children.

Walt was playing with his seven kids. The whole building was probably shaking from all the tossing and yelling, Walter thought. He pushed the thought away, pushed every thought away. He picked up little Joseph, number five, and hurled him against the ceiling, then faked a knee-slammer and dumped the uncontrollably laughing boy onto the couch. Walt was sweating up a storm, he'd been playing on and off with all seven kids ever since the suspension had hit him squarely in the gut.

Suspended. Fucking pricks.

Wasn't his fault that the bus had shifted. How the hell was he supposed to explain what had happened? He couldn't, nobody could. What had happened wasn't possible.

There was nothing to do but tell that slime-ball inspector everything exactly as it had happened. Suspension had been phoned in less than half an hour later.

Fuckin' Wenderwiler.

Walt hurled number four. The helicopter move, Rebecca twirling up above his head, then let go. It was a moment his wife Gertrud could never watch. Even now, sitting pregnant in the corner watching TV, she closed her eyes for the perilous moment.

Walt ignored her, don't think, Walt. Gertrud, wife, number eight, suspension, no job, no rent, no place to live. He watched as Rebecca, arms stretched wide, sailed onto the battered couch, perfect landing. Need a new couch, no money, no job, number eight, don't think. Billy insisted on the same helicopter treatment and Walt obliged.

Twirling wildly, stop the thinking, concentrate. Not once in all this time with all these kids had Walt ever dropped one of them. He always ended the helicopter twirl with perfect timing, sailing them all back onto the couch, begging for more.

"Walt!"

He abruptly stopped, kept Billy up above his head, and looked at his wife. Her eyes were wide, disbelieving, her uncertain fingers pointing at the CBS news anchor.

"What is it?" he asked.

"President Taylor is dead."

"What?!"

"They just said it. An accident, fell down stairs at Brooklyn Medical ... broke his neck." Walt looked at her, then at the kids.

They were waiting in silence as he gently set Billy down. He simply motioned for them to wait in the other room. And all seven left without a word. When the door closed, Walt went to Gertrud and took her in his arms. She started sobbing instantly and he caressed her curls.

Worn out, new perm, no money, don't think, Walt. Don't think!

"I know how much you admired him," he said.

"I loved him," she cried softly into his shoulder.

There'll be another president, Walt thought.

"I know," Walt said.

They held each other in silence. Walt was still trying to keep his mind a bleached white. A dead president, so what.

Screeching bus tires kept streaking across his mind. Inspector Wenderwiler's face kept forcing itself into the blank. And dollars bills kept floating in the distance and disappearing forever from his grasp.

∞

Gertrud instead thought pictures of Melvin Taylor, her campaigning days for him when he had become a New York Senator. Yes, she had loved him. Truly. Nothing Walt ever needed to know.

∞

They both jumped when the doorbell rang. Walt carefully peeled himself from her fierce hug and walked to the door. He opened it, looking back at his wife, who was doubled over in grief for the leader of her country. Turning to greet the visitor, he was stunned to see Transit Authority Inspector Paul Wenderwiler standing there with a big smile.

"I'm not talking to you," Walt growled as he slammed the door. The doorbell rang out again. Walt and Gertrud exchanged glances. Walt's fists grew hard and unpredictable at his side. He ripped the door open again.

"What?!" Walt yelled at Wenderwiler. The fucker didn't seem impressed. Walt's glowing anger didn't seem to make the slightest dent in the peaceful smile of Paul Wenderwiler.

"I came to bring you good news," the inspector said.

"Did you quit your job?" Walt said, not hiding his sarcasm.

"Well yes, I did. But that's not the good news, Mr. Wirowsky. I came to tell you that your suspension has been rescinded. You're to report back to duty tomorrow morning."

Walt just stared at him. Gertrud walked up behind Walt, still sniveling, looking over her husband's shoulder at the man who had done his best to destroy them.

"He's not suspended anymore?" she asked.

"No, it's all been straightened out. Malfunction of left rear brake pads, case closed," Wenderwiler said pleasantly.

"There was nothing wrong with the brakes," Walt said, suspicion looming in narrowed eyes.

"I know that, of course. But that's what the record says anyway. Well I had to come up with something, didn't I?" Wenderwiler gave Walt a slyly disarming grin. "I really don't think you should worry about it anymore."

"So what did happen?"

"Nothing that's possible, I'm afraid. Nothing that would make sense on an inspection form, that's for sure. I really don't know. Look, I'm not a religious man, Mr. Wirowsky, but if I were to believe in God or guardian angels, well, something or somebody saved that kid from your bus."

"Well God sure didn't give a shit about the woman."

"Walt, please." Gertrud firmly held his arm as if to protect him from the imminent wrath of God.

"She'll be fine," the inspector said.

"Bullshit. I've been calling the hospital twice a day since the accident. Nothing's gonna be fine with those legs."

"I don't know about her legs. But I hear she's going to get married. Anyway, I should run." Wenderwiler held out his hand and Walt slowly reached out and shook it firmly.

"You really quit?" Walt said.

"I did, indeed. Time for something new. I'm opening up a landscape institute in Poughkeepsie. Took a bit to convince the wife, but now we're all packed and ready to go. I just have to find - " He stopped and looked across the cramped apartment. "How many kids do you have?"

"Seven. Why?"

"Going on eight, right?" Wenderwiler smiled at Gertrud. She self-consciously put her hands over her belly and nodded.

"What's it to you?" Walt asked darkly, his suspicion seeping back once again.

"And this is a three bedroom place?"

"None of your damn business." Walt said defensively. But gruff remarks couldn't shut down Wenderwiler.

"Well I've been trying to sell my house, you see. But no luck on such short notice. What can I say, I'm in a hurry to get to my new life. I get a six bedroom house, nice little garden, there's even a little pool tank in the back, nothing fancy, but still, if - "

"Good for you. Now look, I have to - "

"Do you want it?" Wenderwiler simply asked.

"What?" Walt and Gertrud asked simultaneously.

"I'm sure we could find an acceptable arrangement. At least come look at it. Here's the address, today at four?"

Walt stared at the business card that Wenderwiler held before him as if it were an unsafe bridge to an unknown place. He shook his head and was about to find the words for a decent rejection, when Gertrud grabbed the card.

"Four o'clock. We'll be there. Thank you very much, Mr. Wenderwiler." Gertrud shook his hand and smiled.

"Please, call me Paul. And don't expect too much, it's not exactly a palace. Now I must move on."

Walt suddenly took Wenderwiler's hand, shook it.

"Thank you," Walt finally said. With a wave Wenderwiler walked off toward his new life. They watched him walk down the hall and take the stairs instead of the creaky elevator.

A new life, Walt thought. He wasn't one to jump the gun. He was going to wait and react cautiously. See where the hitch was. Something was bound to be wrong. Nobody was just going to give them a break. Not in this life. Walt absently walked back into the apartment, when he suddenly felt his wife's eyes on his back. Walt turned.

Gertrud was looking at him with the most gloriously shining smile he had ever seen. Brimming with pure happiness, bursting with sheer love. They embraced in one fluid motion and with their kisses all of Walt's trepidations disappeared.

"A new life, Walt. A new life," Gertrud whispered.

Walt smiled. A new life. His wife, number eight, his job, crisp rays of sunlight streaking across the faded wallpaper. A new life. Yes. It was there. He could taste it on his wife's lips. He could feel it in his blood. A new life.

Meanwhile the seven children took turns at the keyhole, eager to witness, but quiet, careful not to make the magic of their parents disappear.

CUP

The cafeteria was busier than usual. Everybody was here, patients and staff. Nobody thought about working or being ill at present. This was the place to be, this was the place to talk. Not only was President Taylor dead, he had died in this very building, mere hours ago. Hushed conversations spread rumors across the hall. Loss and sadness found companionship in every face. Truth was, the cafeteria was a raucous mess.

Wilber sat alone at a corner table by the windows. Nobody was near him. Where there were clusters of people everywhere else, nobody seemed to even notice the old man. Wilber sipped from his cup again. Wonderful coffee. He had tasted many coffees across the world, American coffee was still the lousiest. Nothing like it, an enigma. Wilber emptied the cup, savoring every last lame and lukewarm drop, then set it down gingerly.

He looked at the people around him through a haze of dark green. He had never shielded himself before. But this time he had been forced to build the dark aura surrounding him now. Strangers and casually known faces alike had kept walking up to him, wanting to talk, wanting to share. All of them feeling a place of great peace with Wilber. He had done his best to be there for them, with them, but his being here had another reason.

Al. The current shield made him invisible to all but kindred forces. Al would see him.

But Al had not appeared yet and that left Wilber deeply distressed.

It was ten minutes past three o'clock.

He looked around again, eyes everywhere, but none were suggesting anything deeper, darker. No, Wilber didn't see Al, didn't feel Al. Anywhere. Maybe there's simply too much going on here, Wilber thought. Cafeteria, three o'clock. Usually, around Al's suggested meeting time, the place was deserted. Maybe this was it. Too many people. Too much confusion. Too loud.

"Al?" Wilber asked into the deep space of his mind. And, as expected, only silence came back like an echo. Wilber closed his eyes and searched some more. There was so much distress among these people, a collective cloud hanging over them like a death sentence. Wilber took a deep breath.

His dark green aura began to change colors, a bright mosaic of the warmest blues and reds and yellows. The aura expanded until the entire room was basked in its light. When Wilber opened his eyes, the aura exploded without a sound. Millions of aura bits and pieces seeped into every soul present. Wilber smiled. The change was instant. Wilber didn't brainwash. Wilber had not made it better for them. In this one instant, he simply gave them perspective, point of view.

The conversations continued without interruption. But invariably the words and thoughts and emotions found something positive now, a bright spot somewhere.

Within minutes the cafeteria would be empty. Life would continue, nurses would race, doctors would fix and patients would wait.

∞

Those roughly two hundred cafeteria people never knew, but the common bond of Wilber's little job kept them close for the rest of their lives. Soon forgotten were the faces from that day in the cafeteria, but the connection remained. They would met again, paths would cross, some soon and some years after that day. Some would bump into one another on the street, others would catch familiar eyes across a room. All of them with the powerful sense of somehow 'knowing the other', with a strong feeling of deja vu.

Invariably they would be drawn to each other like magnets. They would share, they would love, they would marry.

∞

"Got you another one," Frank said.

Wilber opened his eyes and looked at him. Frank set a fresh cup of coffee down before Wilber. The room was empty. They were all gone. Just Frank and Wilber left.

"Thank you, Frank."

"What'd you do this time?" Frank asked simply.

Around Wilber, nothing scared Frank anymore. He was surprised, yes, but not scared. Too many things had happened. Reading minds, Amanda, the bus, the flying furniture, his proposal, the President ... and now all the people had pretty much simultaneously left the cafeteria. He had been forced to wait by the side of the door until the stream of people had ebbed. Then, on entering the place, he had found just one person.

Who else.

"Oh, I just told them to get the hell out of here. Wanted some peace and quiet," Wilber answered with a little smile.

"I just bet you did. You probably gave the folks a cosmic kick in the ass or something."

"Hmn," Wilber replied.

∞

He knew what really was on Frank's mind. Wilber's death. No great mystery figuring that one, it was close, so close. He was thinking about it himself more and more often. But Wilber didn't feel like dwelling on it right now.

"Nervous about the wedding?" he said.

"Nah ... well, yeah, sure. But we're great. By the way, Wilber, I ... I talked to Amanda. And she's fine with the way she is, I mean ... the legs, you know. No need for any miracles, is what I'm saying."

"Okay," Wilber said, looking out the window.

"That's it, huh, 'okay'? ... Amanda says it's gonna be alright, but I don't know. Like last night I had a dream, I saw myself walking with Amanda. Both of us, walking down this path with rose bushes left and right. Both of us walking, you know? So I don't know, Pal. Maybe I expected a miracle anyway, you know. Maybe I wanted you to say 'Of course I'll make you two walk again before I kick the bucket, it's the least I can do'."

"Frank. You're young. So much will happen before your time comes."

"What are you saying? Are you saying I'm gonna walk again, with Amanda? Walk down that rose bush path together? Is that what you're saying?"

"I can't see your future, Frank. I just know that you are one of the brightest lights I have ever met in all my years."

"Great. So I got nothing to worry about, right? I'm a 'bright light' and that'll do it, right Champ? Well, sorry, Pal, but that doesn't do shit for two cripples."

∞

Frank found himself getting more and more riled up. What the fuck? Wilber was gonna die anyway, least he could do was help them. Least he could do was ... Least he could do ... Don't go, Wilber. Don't leave me. Frank pushed himself back from the table.

"I gotta go."

Yeah, get the fuck outta here, before you start crying like a baby. Get going, Frank, move it, he thought.

"I'll see you later," Wilber said.

That stopped Frank.

"How can you be so fuckin' casual about it? You're going to die tomorrow! You thought I didn't keep count? Tomorrow's the day, right?"

"Yes. Tomorrow's the day."

"And that's it?"

"And that's it," Wilber answered.

" ... What are you gonna do?" Frank asked, softer now.

"Same I always do, Frank. Go to the stop, spend the day."

" ... Can I come?"

"Sure, meet me at three."

"Three? But what if ... ?"

"I'll still be alive and well then," Wilber smiled.

"What time are they gonna let you get out of here?"

"Final checkup at four thirty. Jerome's picking me up at five. I'll be back at the home in time for dinner."

"Lucky you," Frank grinned.

"Yeehaa," Wilber answered, grinning back.

Wilber got up slowly and caught up with the waiting Frank. Together, side by side, they left the cafeteria.

Frank tried to keep the lump from his throat.

∞

Wilber was trying to do the exact same.

All the colors, all the light, all he had learned and all the infinite knowledge he would probably soon receive did not help one bit.

Tomorrow he would leave Wilber Patorkin behind, tomorrow this life would end ... and tomorrow Wilber and Frank would meet for their final time.

Wilber then let emotions flow and tears surged from his eyes, silent tears. He knew, without looking, that Frank was crying, too.

Side by side, alone, together.

Wilber wiped his cheeks.

Tomorrow ...

CHAPTER THREE

DEATH

WORDS

It was late night, Wilber was flat on his bed, eyes closed. To anybody's eyes the old man was sound asleep. But Wilber was in overdrive, dividing his energies. He had never liked to do that. One thing at a time, that's the way things were done right. But 'one thing at a time' simply didn't cut it anymore now that time was running out.

On the narrow table in the corner, an old typewriter was hammering away. Letters, words, sentences, paragraphs, chapters. Invisible fingers typed at great speed, phantom hands removed filled pages and replaced them with blank ones. Hundreds of filled pages already lay neatly stacked by the side of the typewriter.

None of this was necessary, not in the larger sense. Sure, Wilber knew that. But he didn't care. This Wilber Patorkin loved the life he had led, this Wilber Patorkin didn't want everything forgotten with tomorrow's last breath.

A great many things had happened in his great many years. He wrote it all down as it came to mind. A fairly complete record of his times, his family, his friends, his thoughts and feelings. One hundred and fifteen years worth of detailed memories ... he'd need more paper. Instantly, without even willing it, another part of his mind floated reams of paper from Amanda Griffin's office to his room.

Wilber also took time to say goodbye to friends. There were so many extraordinary people. He visited all of them. Victor, the Polish blacksmith; Harald, the German cartoonist; Maria, the Venezuelan prostitute - all perfect circles by the power of their own will. With many of them Wilber simply stayed for a while and said goodbye with his mere presence. He only spoke to those who were like himself, the people of the gift.

An Italian teacher with equal gifts sent his body to sit next to Wilber for a while. This was a simple task for any of them. A little practice allowed travel across enormous distances. Sarah, a bag lady in Brazil, wished him well for his impending journey. She sent him an astounding bouquet of colors, some new even to Wilber's mind.

They all envied him for his next and final step. He would soon reach the place every human soul imagined in a million different ways, and yet the place no human soul could ever truly see. Wilber would be there in less than a day, in Nirvana, Walhalla ... Paradise. Wilber deserved getting there, they all knew. Wilber had learned so very much. More than most of them would learn in ten more lifetimes. Everybody was happy for Wilber ... tomorrow he would reach his destiny.

Wilber kept his sadness to himself. Nobody seemed to even consider 'sticking around' as a suitable alternative. Nobody seemed to waste a second to think about Wilber Patorkin's life. Paradise, yeah, great ... but the closer tomorrow came, the less Wilber wanted to depart.

When all had gone and Wilber was alone again, he let his mind wander. And yet he kept circling around the same dilemma: Destiny, destination, final destination. The final stop - like a greyhound bus his soul had traveled the long route. Every stop another life, sometimes ahead of schedule, sometimes a bit late, no major accidents. A soul bus, yes, indeed. And on his way Wilber had taken on many passengers, taken them along for a while, shown them the sights. Buses, billions of buses going in every possible direction. Wilber had been part of the great ride for so long ...

"Why can't I get another stop!? What makes me so damn special?" Wilber yelled deep inside. He didn't expect an answer and, as expected, he didn't get one. Besides, he knew the answer, he knew how damn special he was. God ... was there really a God? Well he would know that, too, soon enough.

The novel of his memories grew and grew, as the typewriter kept hacking away. The more he wrote things down, the sadder he became. So much joy, so much pain ... life, lives. One more life, just once more. To see that first light of birth, to cherish that first embrace by a mother, to sink into the aching pool of first love, to -

"I don't want to go!"

... Nobody there to hear him. He was alone. Just an old man in the darkness of his room, on a crisply starched bed. Tears soaked his pillow. He wiped his eyes and blew his nose. Pull yourself together, Wilber. Might as well go with a damn smile ... Nothing to do but stick around and wait. Great.

Next stop: Paradise.

"Whoop-di-doo," Wilber mumbled.

NINE

The bed was made. Wilber's few belongings were stacked on a chair: Shirts, socks, underwear. Everything made ready for easy removal, the room prepared for the next occupant. It was nine o'clock and Frank, Jerome and Jerry were standing in the middle of Wilber's room.

"Where is he!?" Frank yelled at Jerome.

"Probably at the stop."

"Oh yeah? Did you take a look out the window this morning, Genius?!" Fear was clearly visible in Frank's face and Jerome kept his voice nice and calm. He and Jerry had a look out of the window.

"It's snowing," Jerry said.

"A lot," Jerome nodded.

"It's a fuckin' blizzard out there! There's no way in hell Wilber would make it to the stop. But I can just see him try anyway, I just know he'll do anything he can to get to that fuckin' stop one last time."

"One last time?" Jerome asked. "What do you mean, one last time?"

"Nothing. Never mind! We have to find him and if we don't find him we have to call the cops before he freezes to death, do you understand!?"

Jerome and Jerry looked at each other and gravely nodded.

"I'll go check the stop," said Jerome.

"I'm coming with you," said Jerry grimly.

Both men headed for the door and Frank stared at their backs. He yelled at them at the top of his lungs, as his fingers pointed furiously behind him to the window.

"He can't be at the stop, you morons! There's a fuckin' storm going on out there!"

Both Jerome and Jerry turned once more. Looked at Frank, then at the window. Maybe they had wanted to say something, but nothing came.

They just stared.

"What!?" Frank yelled in frustration.

Jerry simply pointed to the window, his eyes wide open. Frank gripped the right wheel of his chair and yanked it around. There were three birds on the window sill. All of them chirping happily. What are you so fuckin' happy about, Frank thought. And then he realized that the blizzard had gone. It had simply disappeared. The sun was shining bright, the sky was a clear blue and the snow was melting fast.

Jerry went to the window and, as he stuck out his hand, the birds flew off the and soared away. He looked back at Jerome.

"It's warm," he said softly. Jerome smiled and he opened the window wide. A fresh spring breeze caressed their faces.

"Must be in the 60's outside," Jerome said.

"That's impossible," Frank answered blankly.

"Nothing's impossible," Jerry announced proudly.

Frank stared from Jerry to Jerome, both of them smiling. Then he lightly shook his head at his own hysteria.

"Yeah, yeah, alright."

"You just call us if you need anything, Frank." Jerome nodded to Jerry and they left the room.

Frank still stared at the perfect spring day outside. Fuckin' Wilber was gonna give him a heart attack. Calm down, Frank, calm down. Else you'll kick the bucket even before Wilber does.

Wilber had given him a meeting time yesterday - three o'clock. There was no way in hell Frank could wait that long! He had come here this early to catch Wilber before his inevitable walk to the stop. But no such luck. Wilber must've left early. Frank imagined that Wilber had a few things left to do. And so, with a heavy heart, he decided to wait it out until his afternoon slot with the Champ.

TEN

What a day. A freak occurrence, as the meteorologists would exclaim all day long. Wilber had never changed the weather before, but hey, this was his final day so he figured he was allowed to splash a little. Not that the snow and the cold bothered him, but he expected a few people, and he wanted it to be nice and cozy for them.

He smiled the smile of a decided man. He had accepted his fate last night, accepted his upcoming final stop. And he had decided to make this final day a good one.

∞

What was she doing? Francesca Palocelli still couldn't believe it as she climbed down the stairs, huffing and puffing. She had tried the elevator - out of order. A clear sign if there ever was one. An omen. Don't do it, Francesca, don't go down there. But still her feet kept bringing her closer to that man across the street.

She shouldn't have looked out the window this morning. Strange weather. A blizzard. She had gotten used to seeing the old man down there at the bus stop. But then, after that terrible bus accident, she hadn't seen him anymore.

How that had made her sad, and how she had tried to reason that sadness away.

She really shouldn't have looked out of the window today.

∞

She stood by the window, frozen, her heart beating so hard it seemed about to burst through her chest. There he was! How the old man had managed to get to the stop in that horrible weather, she had no idea. The wind was strong, slamming hard flakes against the window panes. But somehow the storm didn't seem to quite reach the stop. It almost looked as if an invisible dome was protecting the stop from the winter storm.

And then, in the blink of an eye, the storm was gone.

That's when the old man looked up, straight into her eyes. Like an invitation. "Come on down," those eyes said. "Come on down and sit with me for a while."

Francesca tried to go about her routine then, tried to ignore the old man, tried to ignore everything she felt in her heart - it was futile. Her every thought was down there, at the stop. She finally put on her best dress, made up her face and tied her hair into a hurried but still elegant bun.

∞

And now she left the building and saw him looking at her. He waved and smiled. Almost against her will she waved back.

∞

Silence. Francesca Palocelli was sitting next to him now, just looking at him, waiting. She was a fine woman made old by an unkind soul. And yet that soul, the soul of her husband Antonio Palocelli, was still all she cared about. Still the question of his disappearance was clinging like a growing cancer to her every dream, every move, every hope.

'Not knowing' is the worst thing that can happen to you. And so Wilber let her know. He gently reached for her hand, but she shrunk away from the touch. He looked at her, again reached for her hand and took it - and this time she relaxed. Her mind opened up instantly and she saw

Antonio Palocelli. Wilber could feel her getting lighter as she watched the movie starring Antonio Palocelli, the man currently living in Phoenix, Arizona. He had another wife now, a vicious woman named Ursula. He had three more children with that woman, children that were as cruel as he.

"That's enough," she said sharply. And instantly the pictures in her mind stopped. She didn't bother finding out how Wilber had done what he had done, she just wanted to know one thing. "Was this real?"

"Yes."

"Why are you showing me this? So he's alive and raising another family? He's alive and has never even - " She choked down a heavy sob.

"You are a wonderful woman, Francesca Palocelli."

"Oh, shut up," she said bitterly, blowing her nose.

Wilber shut up. She eventually looked at him, blew her nose again and waved for him to continue.

"Oh alright, say what you gotta say."

"I'd like to let you in on a little secret, Francesca. Most couples are not meant to stay together. Most of their paths are joined for a while in harmony, running along in parallel lines. But most don't realize when their paths ache to change course. You see, ending a relationship is quite a natural thing, something that should happen a lot more often, as a matter of fact. People would be a whole lot happier."

"What, are you nuts!?" she said in wide-eyed fury. "There are such things as holy matrimony, eternal vows. They mean something! A holy bond for life, you understand? Life! I gave my life to that man! Marriage means everything!"

"No," Wilber said simply. "It doesn't. Priests, rings and papers mean nothing. What does mean everything, however, is what one truly believes. And once in a while two people truly believe in the same shared happiness, and once in a while those two people are soul mates."

"Why are you telling me all this nonsense?"

"Because you deserve happiness. Because if you give up the broken memory of Antonio Palocelli, you may find what you're looking for."

She stared at him and he could see the battle within her, even on her face. He didn't help, this part she had to do on her own ... and she did. Wilber watched the picture of Antonio Palocelli fade from Francesca's heart.

In the end all that remained of him was a distant, painless memory.

∞

When she walked away a few minutes later, Francesca forgot about her time with Wilber. She had a craving for food, rich, spicy Italian food. She would cook herself the best meal she had ever had. She felt great as she hailed a cab to take her to her favorite deli. So she couldn't really afford to take a cab, so what.

Her radiant joy spilled into the cab before her as she got in and slammed the door.

"Where to?" the driver asked.

"Balducci's, good man. Take me to Balducci's."

He started the engine and filed into the flow of the heavy midday traffic.

"That's a nice place. Pricey, though. You preparing something special, right?"

"No. Just a little dinner for myself," she said with a smile. She saw the driver glance back at her through the rearview mirror. She saw two gleaming eyes, sparkling, warm.

"Just for yourself, huh? That's a shame," he answered.

When a red light forced a stop, the driver turned around. And when their eyes locked, Francesca Palocelli thought, for just a moment, that she heard an old man's voice.

" ... and once in a while those two people are soul mates."

ELEVEN

He was fine. He was just fine. So what was he doing here? Why was he still in bed? Duncan Grey had got up at the usual time this morning, shower, instant coffee, the machine was too loud, a quick glance at the TV, news drifting past his eyes and ears, President Taylor's death the sole topic, repeating pictures of shocked hospital staff. A reporter claiming to have information on the President's final moments, something about a nurse.

Duncan had finished getting dressed, finished his coffee. And then, where he normally reached for the door knob, he had reached for the telephone. Just like that. Without giving it a thought, he had called in sick. Something he had never done before, straight out lied without the slightest hesitation.

After the call Duncan had taken off his clothes and had snuggled back into bed with his wife. The children were playing in the living room now. He could hear them, subdued. His wife had given him the odd glance. He had no explanation, just stayed in bed. Odd, snow storm this morning, now it was gleaming spring outside. Nathalie opened the door.

"Duncan?"

"Hmn?"

"Are you really alright?"

"Sure". He still stayed under the covers. Nice and comfy. He should do that more often.

"I don't get it."

"Neither do I," he said with a smile.

"Well if you're staying home anyway, you might as well come with us. We're going to the playground."

Duncan looked at her, blank for a moment. Then he nodded. Sure, why not. Playground was good. He really should do this more often. He rolled out of bed and gave Nathalie a sudden power-hug. She laughed and playfully tried to get out of it. He kissed her.

"Stop that!"

"Can't," he said in between kisses.

"Then get a breath mint, buddy." But he figured it wasn't that bad as the kissing continued and her body responded.

"So are we going to the playground?" she asked.

"Sure," he said and pulled her down onto the bed. Through her hair he spotted Nicky, Milo and Ellie at the door.

"Can we play, too?" asked Ellie.

"If we're not going to the playground, I wanna watch toons," said Nicky.

"Cool," agreed Milo.

Nathalie and Duncan smiled at each other, then got up.

"Alright let's go."

∞

"Hello."

Wilber turned, startled. A little girl stood right next to him. Shining innocence, not a cloud on her heart.

∞

Duncan and Nathalie were furious. The kids always left the house moments before them, and they always waited for them by the door. But when they came out this time, they only saw Nicky and Milo, busy inspecting a dead rat by the curb.

Ellie. Ellie was gone.

They raced off in both directions, she to the playground, he in the other direction. Duncan ran past the bus stop toward the church, where Ellie would play on the stairs sometimes. Maybe she was - Duncan stopped dead, whirled around and stared at the stop. There she was. There he was. And Ellie was sitting next to the old man, both of them looking at each other intently, both of them silent.

"Excuse me, I - "

For a moment Duncan wanted to reach for Ellie, hold her in his arms, a father protecting his little girl. But when he looked into the eyes of the old man, he suddenly remembered how often he had thought of him. How he had wondered and worried since he hadn't seen him anymore. The old man smiled at him. Ellie led her Dad to sit on the bench as well. So they sat there, Wilber in the middle. Silent for a moment.

"I ... I'm Duncan Grey. You know, I've always wanted to stop and speak to you. I'm glad you're all right. After that accident with the bus I thought that maybe you were - "

Ellie leaned forward and looked at her Dad.

"Dad, shhhhhh. It's okay."

Duncan frowned at her. Truth was, now that he thought about it, this wasn't awkward at all. Ellie was right, words meant nothing compared to this.

∞

When Nathalie arrived at the stop a few moments later, out of breath, both boys behind her, she couldn't believe her eyes ... and she didn't say a word. There was the old man Duncan had told her about so many times, sitting in between Ellie and Duncan. And the old man was holding their hands, just like that, in perfect comfort. A picture of absolute peace.

Nathalie could never explain why she did what she did next, nor did they ever talk about it in the years that followed. It wasn't meant to be pulled down into words. She stepped to the old man, bent down and hugged him, hugged him with all her might. Hugged him like she had always wanted to hug her father. The man she had never known, the man who had died in Vietnam the day she was born in Jersey City.

He was here now, her father was here in the hug of the old man.

∞

They stayed like that for a long time. Nathalie hugging Wilber. Wilber holding Ellie's and Duncan's hands. Milo on his Dad's knees and Nicky with his arm around Ellie. Framed by the poster boards of the stop. Most people just walked by, didn't notice, didn't see. Only few saw the whirlwind of colors surrounding the stop. Then the Greys left and went to the playground, had the time of their lives.

Wilber knew that this family of circles would glow long and rich and ripple into even greater lives. What a moment this had been, more precious and powerful than even he had imagined.

Michelangelo could have done a fine job of it. But it was over now. Gone.

He would never see them again.

NOON

Don't start crying, Wilber. You don't want to waste your final hours feeling sorry for yourself, do you? He did a lousy job convincing himself and he did cry for a while.

What was the point? What was the point of all of this? What was the good of all his lives, all his memories, if it was lost in Paradise? All his hopes and his wishes, his fears and his joys, his dreams and his losses, the memories of Frank, Amanda, Jerome, Jerry, Walt and all the others, the memory of the Greys and of his Paula. So much there, so much lost. Wilber wiped his nose and looked across the street.

He saw Henry 'The Fart' Barnum. And Henry wasn't running this time, he was walking with Tom Moorer. No bullying now, now fear, no anger, just two kids laughing.

∞

Seeing Henry almost get crushed by the bus had been like a massive jolt of electricity to Tom's heart. He had felt powerfully guilty for the days that followed, and eventually he had gone to Henry's house to apologize.

Tom had been about to knock when he had heard the voice, a man yelling at the top of his lungs, the words heavily slurred.

"Get in here and clean that up you fuckin' freak! You're a waste of space. Can you fuckin' believe it!? I'm gonna break your skull and nobody's gonna give a shit. Nobody's even gonna know you're gone. The world's better off without you, you stinkin' little - "

Henry's step-dad never got further than that. Because Tom had stepped in silently moments before. He had seen the man towering over Henry. The man had had his back to Tom, a bottle raised and ready to crack it down onto Henry's head. Bam! The fresh six-pack by the door had made for an excellent hammer. Henry's step-dad had been knocked out by beer before, but never quite like this.

Now they were laughing. About Henry throwing up on the man's shoes, pure fear rushing up. About Tom's perfect blow. They had picked the knocked-out man's pockets then. And the seven bucks bought them two burgers and some candy. Henry and Tom, Tom and Henry ... from that day on, friends for life.

∞

Wilber's eyes stayed with the two boys until they disappeared behind the church. And they, too, were gone. It was selfish to think of them all on his own terms. They would go on just fine without Wilber. They didn't need him. Wilber would go to Paradise and the world would keep on spinning.

He would be in that place soon, in Paradise, that place of surrounding perfection, that place of eternal peace, the place of boundless love ... it all sounded so damn boring to Wilber. He knew it was inevitable, and yet once more he started looking for ways out. What could he do? After all, he didn't ask for much, did he? He just wanted one more life, he just wanted to stay. On this planet, this world, with these people, with all the chaos. This place was wild, this place was fun. This place was without a doubt as different from Paradise as the Earth is different from the Sun.

What to do? How could he beat 'the system'? He couldn't kill, he couldn't be vicious, he couldn't look away when help was needed. He was who he had become by the paths of his many lives. And that made him ready for Paradise ... Wilber could just hear Frank, "Any way you look at it, Champ, you're screwed."

ONE

Today the 91 seemed less a public transportation vehicle and more Walt's private joy ride. He was singing and he didn't care about the looks he got from his passengers. Walt felt like hugging the world today, he felt like helping everybody, felt like spreading the lightness of his heart. But this sort of amplified happiness was clearly odd, if not scary, to the average New Yorker. Walt was performing to a practically empty bus. He had the radio on and sang along with Frank Zappa.

"Hey there, people, I'm Bobby Brown. They say I'm the cutest boy in town. My car is fast, my teeth are shiny. I tell all the girls they can kiss my - "

That's when Walt slammed on the brakes.

The old man - Jesus H. Christ, now wasn't that the topper, the icing on the cake. First he got unexpectedly promoted this morning, meaning a handsome raise. It was the company's way of making sure he wouldn't suddenly sue them for slander. After all, Wenderwiler had insinuated all sorts of scam stories for a while there. But Walt would never have sued them, ever. He firmly believed that the law was what was bringing this country down. Teachers afraid to speak out, doctors afraid to help, lawyers everywhere, law suits looming at every corner, it was strangling the country. Nobody seemed to be willing to stand up for his actions anymore. It was always 'Who can I blame, who can I sue, who's responsible?' Responsibility, Americans were in danger of forgetting to live that word.

The bus had stopped a good length beyond the stop. Walt opened all the doors, rose and arched his back with a crack.

"People! I hope you're not in a hurry, 'cause we're gonna be here a while." Only now did he realize that there was just a single passenger left, a stiff old lady wrapped in a faded coat and decorated with a brand new purple perm.

"Why?" she asked with a creaky voice. Walt, half way out the door already, stopped and looked back.

"What?"

"Why? I want to know why we are going to be here for a while, as you put it."

"Gotta say hello to an old friend."

"You can't. You have a duty, a schedule."

"I got a life, too." Walt clearly wanted to go to the old man, he would finally be able to speak to him. After all this time. But the old lady didn't let up.

"So do I. And I need to get to Franklin Avenue. It is your duty to get me there according to schedule. Otherwise I will report you."

"Oh come on lady, I'm always on time. Always. It's just this once, this one time."

"It is your duty," she maintained sternly. "I'm not going to report your frantic stop just now. I could have fractured a disk, you know. I'm not going to report this, if we continue now."

Walt looked from the lady to the stop. Through the window he saw the old man leaning forward. He was smiling at Walt, even lifted his hand and waved. Walt waved back, then his eyes went back to the woman with the purple hair.

"You have a responsibility."

"What?" Walt suddenly glared at her, anger in his voice. She didn't shrink back. Maybe she hadn't noticed.

"I said you have a responsibility. People in America seem to forget the meaning of - "

"I'm the most responsible guy on the planet, lady!"

"Then do your job."

Walt stared at her. Incredible, fuckin' incredible. She was right. He knew she was right. Do your job, Walt. Take the 91 and get back on schedule. He looked at the old man who was still smiling in his direction.

"Give me thirty seconds, alright?" Walt was almost pleading with her. She kept looking at him, then focused on her watch.

"Agreed. Thirty seconds, starting now."

Walt rushed from the bus and toward the stop. When he reached the old man, he already had his hand stretched out, ready for a quick shake.

"I'm Walt Wirowsky the driver of the 91, the accident, that was me and I was at the hospital, too, but you were in a coma and I just wanted to - "

The old man lightly clapped his hands together. Just once and it barely made a sound.

" - say hello because I've always wanted to stop before and never did. You know the schedule, gotta rush, but I just - "

"Please sit down, Walt."

"I'd love to but I can't I gotta - "

"You have all the time in the world. Have a look around."

All of a sudden Walt realized that he only heard his own heart, galloping like a race horse. Nothing else, not one other sound. No cars, no people, none of the city's usual noises. Dead silence. And then he realized that nothing was moving, either. Cars were in the middle of the street, frozen. A dog was pissing on the corner, looking stuffed. A fat woman was dragging her two children, her mouth open in the middle of an argument. And Walt had to reach for the bench and sit next to Wilber, when he saw three sparrows in flight, suspended in mid-air.

"What happened?"

"I gave us a little time."

"You did ... that?"

∞

Wilber nodded. He could hear Walt's mind spinning. Wondering what was going on, trying to make sense. Walt was recalling the impossible shift of the bus, now this. The common denominator between the two events was sitting right next to him. But Wilber noticed fondly that Walt didn't get scared. He was simply in awe.

"You can stop time?"

"Looks like it," said Wilber simply. "Never tried it before, but it works nicely, don't you think?"

"Has everything stopped? I mean, everything?"

"Yep."

"You stopped the whole planet ... just so we could talk a little?"

"Seemed like a good idea."

Walt leaned back, relaxed and smiled.

"This is great."

"So, Walt. What did you want to talk about?"

"I ... I ... Damned if I know." Walt stared at Wilber, then hung back his head and laughed out loud. "Nothing, I think. I ... I just wanted to say hello, find out your name, you know, small talk. You stopped the planet for small talk! You stopped the whole planet for Walt Wirowsky!" Walt continued to laugh. He was laughing so hard he had to get up. And he laughed even more when he saw the frozen lady in the bus, still staring at her watch.

Wilber took Walt's hand and they shook.

"Wilber Patorkin," Wilber said.

"Walt. Walt Wirowsky, proud to meet you."

„So am I, Walt, so am I."

Then Wilber let go and clapped his hands a second time.

Car engines roared, the dog sniffed his piss and waddled away, the fat lady yelled at her kids, the sparrows disappeared in a tree and Walt raced back to the bus. He looked back at the old lady, her eyes still on her watch. Then she sternly looked up.

"Twenty-eight seconds. Let us go then."

Walt nodded and got in behind the wheel. He started the engine and the bus slid back into traffic.

Odd. Twenty-eight seconds. Wilber Patorkin, the old man's name was. They had shaken hands. No time for anything else. Twenty-eight seconds. And yet ... Walt couldn't help feeling that he'd gotten far more than that. As if he had shared the bench with the old man, as if they had laughed together, as if the world had stopped for a while.

Crazy. Strange. Wonderful.

He wouldn't talk about it, how could he explain those twenty-eight seconds that somehow felt like so much more. For the rest of his life he would visit Wilber's grave once a year. He would tend the flowers, and he would remember the twenty-eight seconds. And the older he got, the more he seemed to remember ... or was he just adding to the story? Adding a little space to that long-gone moment in history? When he was eighty, he saw the frozen cars. When he was ninety, he saw the fat woman and her children. When he reached ninety-four, he saw the three sparrows, suspended in the air. And when he died a year later, all his children by his side, he remembered everything. The time with Wilber, the laughter, the suspended birds, the day when the planet had stopped. His children would never forget the smile on their father's face, the day he passed away.

TWO

He didn't know why and he couldn't see him anywhere, but Wilber knew that Al was on the way. He felt more then saw, large dark shoes that were crushing through fallen leaves. The shoes were walking a straight line through a park, through grass, through puddles, through mud and through people. The shoes seemed oblivious of everything and they seemed to have one clear destination. At the end of the straight line sat Wilber Patorkin.

It was two o'clock and suddenly Wilber thought about Frank. Frank would be here at three. What if Wilber was wrong about the time of his death? Or what if he had been right and now Al came into the equation and changed everything? What if he was dead on the bench when Frank showed up at three? The image sent a stab to Wilber's heart.

"Lighten up. I'm not going to kill you." With that, Franklin Rosenberg, Chief Surgeon at Brooklyn Medical Center, sat down next to Wilber.

Wilber gaped in genuine surprise.

"Who did you expect, Charles Manson?"

"You're Al?"

Franklin Rosenberg grinned. "That's me, good ole Al, your fun pal from the far side of the light."

"I must admit," said Wilber calmly. "I didn't expect you to be a doctor."

"Oh come on, what better way to play God?" Wilber looked at him for a long while.

"Mind if I keep calling you Al?"

"No."

"Why didn't you come to the cafeteria yesterday?"

"I wasn't in the mood."

"I see." Wilber left it at that.

"I see? That's all you have to say? You meet your nemesis after all these years and you just sit here like a sack of potatoes! Come on, Wilber. Let's have some fun, you and I. Let's fight the big one!" Al was up on his feet, waving his fists in front of Wilber, grinning, trying hard to keep grinning. Wilber didn't react, he just kept looking at his opposite. "Come on you lame fuck. You sit here like Buddha waiting for death to take you away - do something! You're still alive, you know!?"

"I'm going to miss you, too," Wilber said softly.

"Fuck you, Wilber, FUCK YOU!" Then Al sat down again next to Wilber.

"Why did you come?"

"Just wanted to say good-bye," Al said, his eyes straight on the building across the street.

"And maybe you wanted to find out a little something, too?"

Al looked at Wilber for a moment, then stared at the building again. "I already told you there's nothing you can tell me that I don't already know ... but if there's anything you want to get off your chest, feel free."

Then Wilber told him all he knew. All he had learned, all he had seen. All about his many lives, and all about the final place. Al listened, concentrated, eager for more. When Wilber was finished, Al looked at him for a moment, then he shook his head.

"That's it?"

"That's it."

"That's the great mystery? We live life after life until we're good enough to go to Paradise?"

"Simply put, yes."

"Sounds fuckin' boring."

"That's what I thought, too," Wilber said with a tired smile. Al smiled back, not an ounce of viciousness in his face. Then he shook his head again.

"You've been trying all these years to get me to change. For this? Thanks, Pal. But I think I'm just gonna go on being bad. Looks like that guarantees me a fresh life on Earth for ever after. I'd hate to go final. I can't believe you've been lying all these years. Acting like you know it all. But it looks like you know shit. You know as much about Paradise as every other bum on the planet. What a joke. What did you get for all your lies?"

"You came today."

"And now I'm leaving," Al got up, stretched, ready to go.

"You came for a reason."

"Have a nice death."

"You came to say good-bye to a friend."

Al stared down at him as he buttoned his coat up to the neck, the coat like an armor to keep Wilber out. Wilber struck out his hand for Al to take. Al didn't move.

"I don't have friends."

"You do now."

Al still didn't move, not a muscle. Moving even less than the suspended sparrows had moved before. And then the ice broke. Al reluctantly put his hand into Wilber's. They looked at each other, they shook. Then Al turned and walked away.

∞

He walked down the sidewalk, through the streets, into the park. Back the same way he had come from. But things were different now. He could smell the leaves, he could even smell their colors. He saw colors all around him. Colors the likes he had never seen before.

He tried to will them away, just as he was rubbing his hand against his coat, again and again. Where Wilber had touched him, a heat source seemed to be planted. Heat that tried to rise through his arm into every fiber of his body.

Franklin Rosenberg had files in his head, his brain like endless metal file cabinets crammed full of pictures. Pictures of every atrocity ever committed by mankind. Pictures of atrocities he made happen and pictures of things that happened to himself as a child. The life before this one. Then, too, had he been a Jew, but times had been different. Pictures of unspeakable horrors had been all he had seen then. At the camp. The camp where his mother had withered away, the camp where his father had fallen into the dust, coughing blood. Experiments, fear, torture, fear, torture, loss, anger, loss, hatred, loss, laughter, loss, fun, anger, fun, hatred, fun, death ... fun.

Franklin Rosenberg didn't realize that he had stopped walking. He was standing in the middle of a meadow. Crying ... Crying?! He wiped the tears away, furiously so, but they kept on coming. When he felt something move behind him, he whirled around.

The Dalmatian jumped up at him, sullied his coat. A puppy, yapping, happy, loud. A woman came running, yelling. Franklin Rosenberg didn't move, the dog didn't seem afraid of him. Just kept bouncing up at him. As if he could feel something, something that had changed.

∞

Godiva Spellman ran toward the old man. God, he was crying - and he looked just like Gandalf with that beard.

She kept yelling. She had named the puppy Willy, after Willy Wonka and the Chocolate Factory. He was a puppy, of course he didn't listen yet. A wonderful dog, very playful ... still, he had never acted quite like this before. It was is if that crying man had hot dogs in his coat pockets.

"Willy stop! Willy you leave that man alone, Willy!" She grabbed at the puppy's collar, but Willy was far too excited to let himself get caught. So he jumped and danced around the man, and she, trying to catch Willy, just had to keep jumping after him.

"I'm so sorry, he ... " I'm making a complete idiot of myself, she thought. "Willy stop, I told you to - " I can't believe I'm doing this. I must look like the biggest loser on the planet. Wait a second, don't I know this guy from somewhere? As she kept chasing the dog, she realized in glimpses that there was an interesting face underneath that beard.

∞

Franklin's tears kept on falling, soaking his beard as he watched in astonishment. A woman and a dog doing an absolutely bizarre dance around him. Godiva Spellman was her name, upper class, wealthy Jewish family she didn't care for. She had made her own way, Franklin knew. Taken none of her family's money, none of their grinding tradition, but all of her father's tenacity. She was ... a doctor, Franklin Rosenberg realized in amazement. And at this moment she was trying to remember where she had seen him before. He suddenly remembered. The last congress he had attended, his last speaking engagement seventeen years ago. She had been there, too. She had heard his final speech, telling the crowd of five hundred esteemed colleagues to go get off their golden horses and join the living. The speech where he had broken with his old life.

How things had changed since then.

∞

She had him, she finally had the little prick! Godiva Spellman held on to the dog and realized he was far stronger than she had expected.

"I am so sorry about this. I don't know what's gotten into him. He's never acted like this before. I'll certainly take care of your laundry bill. Bad dog! Bad dog!"

"It's all right," Franklin said.

" ... Why are you crying?"

"That's a long story."

Godiva Spellman suddenly looked at him in amazement. "Franklin Rosenberg. You are Franklin Rosenberg."

He just nodded and realized, to his surprise, that he was a bit embarrassed. Oddly, it was not exactly unpleasant, feeling embarrassed in the closeness of this woman.

"And you are Godiva Spellman."

"You know me? Why on earth would you know me?"

"That's another long story."

"I have all the time in the world."

He looked at her, feeling good, wondering for a moment. Then he saw himself with her, just a haze of things to come. Things would be good. Things would be very good.

THREE

He had been on hot needles all morning long, his butt constantly shifting in the chair, his nerves raw. He had screamed at an old lady who had just arrived at the home and he had felt unable to apologize. Wasn't anybody's fuckin' business if he felt like sitting at the entrance for hours and hours, not going anywhere. Just there, ready to go, but not going. The fuckin' clock on the wall by the entrance had been moving at the speed of a slow snail on a hot day in the desert.

When that clock had finally hit five to three, he'd gone full speed. That old lady shouldn't have been in the way. He had screamed her out of the way and had raced toward

Wilber. I could do the Olympics, Frank had thought while propelling the wheelchair toward the stop. Racing, faster, faster, only Wilber's face on his mind ... Oh no ... No!

Frank slowed down and came to a halt three feet from Wilber. He was afraid of going closer to his old friend, afraid of touching him. Wilber's head was slumped forward, he wasn't moving. What if I touch him and he still doesn't move, Frank thought. Agony rising in his throat, inching closer now. He can't be dead, he promised.

"'i Frank," Wilber's drowsy voice suddenly came.

Frank let out a silent sigh and said nothing. He wheeled himself next to Wilber, who now lifted his head and opened his eyes. He looks so old, Frank thought. He ...

"You're not reading my mind, are you?"

"Nope." Wilber smiled.

"So how are you?"

"Feeling good."

"And looking good, too," Frank said.

"You're a funny guy."

"Not half as funny as you." Frank stared at his shoes. "So how's this ... how is it gonna happen?"

"My dying, you mean?"

"Yeah ... that."

"Sometime soon I'll fall asleep ... and that'll be that."

"And you're fine with that?" Wilber thought for a moment and then nodded. "You're full of shit," Frank said.

Wilber smiled. He looked around, nobody was paying attention to the two old farts at the stop. He used the moment to float a large package from behind the stop onto Frank's lap.

"What's this?"

"It's my life, the life of Wilber Patorkin. I am leaving it in the good hands of my best friend."

Frank stared at him, tears welling up but he wiped them away. He opened the wrapping paper and saw the cover of a hardcover book. There was a circle and a line on the cover, nothing else.

"When did you manage to write a book?"

"Last night."

Frank stared at him, then just shook his head and let it go. "Am I in here, too?"

"You bet," Wilber grinned.

"Everything!?"

"Guess you'll just have to read it to find out."

Frank nodded and stole a glance at the clock on the church tower across the street. Time was flying now, rushing his friend away from him.

Wilber moved closer to the edge of the bench, as close to Frank's chair as he could get. There he put his arm around Frank's shoulder. Frank didn't shy away. Wilber put his head against Frank's.

∞

A bit of warmth, that's all he needs, Wilber thought as he closed his eyes. Frank Wilkinson, I'm going to miss you. His arm pulled Frank a little closer still.

A perfect circle ...

∞

Frank felt Wilber's head droop just an inch. He felt Wilber's hand slack away from around his shoulder and bump against the side of the bench with a thud. For a long while Frank stayed like that, not daring to move for fear that Wilber would fall. Then, ever so gently, he put his own arm around Wilber, their heads still together, both their eyes closed.

Frank silently cried.
He held Wilber tight.
Best friends in life.
Best friends in death.

∞

When Jerome and Jerry came by in the evening, they found Frank and Wilber in that exact same position.

Frank was wide awake and it wasn't an easy task to get him to let go of Wilber. Jerome gently and easily picked up Wilber's body, held him to his chest as if it were a baby.

Then, like a procession they went back to the home. Jerome first, bearing Wilber, followed by Jerry and Frank.

They put Wilber in his bed until the ambulance came to pick him up.

Frank stayed with him until the rear door of the ambulance swung shut and the red lights disappeared into the Brooklyn night.

CHAPTER FOUR

GOD

WIND

... It wasn't the light, it was the wind that came first. Just a feeling at first, then a distant sound. Coming closer fast.

Complete darkness.

Wilber woke and struggled to make sense. Where was he? What was this space, nothing but black in every direction. Couldn't be Paradise, could it? Wilber thought of Al, and how Al would roar with laughter if he knew Wilber to be here, in the middle of nowhere ...

I remember Al, Wilber suddenly realized. His excitement growing, he thought of everybody he had ever loved, hugged, cared for, spoken to or even simply heard of. His mind raced through every tiniest memory, hungrily touching on everything, just to make sure it was all still there. He thought of all the people in his final life, he thought of Frank and Amanda, Jerry and Jerome, Walt and Wenderwiler, Tom and Henry, he recalled the stop, he remembered President Taylor. He remembered absolutely everything! Nothing was lost, nothing, it was all still there. Wilber basked in his memories, let his childhood pass in front of him like an old movie, and he saw his Paula. He saw her in their happy days and he saw her in her death ... would she be here? Would he find his wife again, after all these years, in this place, whatever this place was?

"Paula?"

Nothing. No reply other than the wind, by now blowing like a horn, announcing the coming of a storm. From where? Again the question. Where am I?

Then he realized a change. Blackness faded as the wind blew stronger and stronger, blowing the black away. But still there was nothing. Not black anymore, yet still nothing but vast and empty space. Before Wilber had the chance to wonder, the nothing exploded. It exploded into brilliance. Sounds Wilber had never imagined possible, colors he had never dreamed of. He watched in awe and the beauty of it made him cry.

From far above he watched as the colors took shape below him. The nowhere gave way to an orb in space, an expanding orb that seemed vibrantly alive, bubbling with colors, fountains of colors, waves of colors. When the storm of infinite colors ebbed, Wilber discovered a world. A planet was there, below him where nothing had been moments earlier. Rivers made their ways through lush greens, mountains dug themselves out of the earth and stretched into the skies. Trees grew at an impossible speed, entire forests created in an instant.

Wilber's every thought was pushed aside as he witnessed the birth of a planet. Then the animals came, out of the waters, out of the caves, streaming into their new world. Making it theirs, their land, their home.

JOB

"Nice, ain't it?" a voice suddenly said next to Wilber.

Wilber whirled around but there was nothing. Only now did Wilber try to see himself, but there were no hands, no legs, no dentures, nothing at all. He felt himself far above the newborn planet, but he was nothing more than ... what? And where had the voice come from? And ...

"Who are you?"

"Wow. Now that's a truly original question. What do you think, Wilber? No really, tell me, what do you think?"

Wilber did think about it for a moment but couldn't come up with anything other than the obvious.

"Are you God?"

"Bravo! Yes. Yes, I am. Of course I am," the voice answered joyfully. And then it added, "And guess what. So are you!"

"Huh?"

"Huh!? That's all you've got to say?! You're God, my friend. You're the master of this universe. You're the creator of all you see below. You're the builder, you're the destroyer, you're the all and the everything. You oughta be able to do at least a little better than 'Huh'."

Flocks of multi-colored birds sailed past below. They look like rainbow clouds, Wilber thought. Lovely. The same instant brilliantly colored clouds popped up all around the planet below.

"Whoa, buddy, easy now! Don't you go around creating before you've had your little instruction."

"That was me? I made those clouds?" Wilber gaped.

"Yes, of course you did. Hello! Are you listening to me? I told you, didn't I? You're God!"

"Sorry," Wilber mumbled.

"And don't be sorry! We're never sorry. Being sorry doesn't do anybody any good. Never did. Never will. Waste of time. You should know about that. After all, you're here. If you fuck up, don't apologize. Fix it. That's what we do."

"We?"

"Oh yeah, right, right. Where was I? Instructions. Almost forgot. That spectacle down there, it gets me excited every single time. And when I get excited I lose my train of thought. Sorry about that, now let me - "

"I thought we're never sorry."

"Smart-ass."

"Sorry." Wilber started to enjoy himself.

"Listen Mr. Funny Man. We can go on doing this forever. And I do mean forever, infinity is our middle name. Or, you can just shut up for a moment and let me do my little spiel. What's it gonna be, Pal?"

Just listening might be a good idea at this point, Wilber thought. After all, he didn't know anything about this voice yet and maybe -

"I said shut up, didn't I? And don't you say sorry now!"

Wilber smiled an invisible grin into space.

"Thank you. Now then, let me see," the voice continued. "You've lived your final life, as you know. Bet you thought you'd be going to heavenly ole' Paradise. Well, fact is, my friend, Paradise is not a place, Paradise is a job."

Wilber listened intently, but couldn't help wishing he were down there on the planet, in the swarming midst of ongoing creation.

"Geez, alright then," the voice simply said. Less than an instant later, Wilber was standing in the midst of a luscious green meadow, rolling hills all around him as far as he could see. "Now, may I finally continue?" The voice sounded different somehow and Wilber looked around. To his surprise, he found himself next to a man in his early sixties. Thinning hair, dressed in jeans and sneakers, scarf wrapped around his neck. And he grinned at Wilber from under his bushy moustache. The man stuck out his hand and Wilber shook it.

"Richard Pinter, nice to meet you," the man said. "In my final life I was an acting teacher, great time, what a life. What a life! Didn't want to leave but it was my time."

Wilber now realized that he, too, was in his well known shape again. He glanced at his legs and gingerly tried to move. He glowed as he realized that he could bend his knees and bounce on his tiptoes without falling or breaking anything. Dropping the final remnants of the Wilber-Shuffle he suddenly bounced up and down, laughing like a child. Then he added a little dance, a dance from his youth and he momentarily lost himself in the steps. Wilber Patorkin dancing across the meadow, deer rushing past, nodding at Wilber, rainbow colored clouds beyond the horizon ... Richard smiled at Wilber and let him have his moment.

START

"I understand," said Wilber.

"I haven't explained yet," Richard shot back.

"Well, I'm God, aren't I?"

"Don't get cocky. There's always more to learn. As you yourself like to say, there are no limits. So there's a few questions you need to ask me, might as well start. Shall we?"

"So when our final life ends, we become God."

"And we get a little welcome present, a planet."

"Are there many of us?"

"Try counting the planets, Wilber."

"What comes after this?"

"Who knows. Who cares? All you need to worry about is this here and this now. Look around you. Don't think it's gonna be easy. Start slowly, think clearly, before you start creating. Trick is, don't go fancy. No seven-headed horses and some such. Simple things are best."

"No seven-headed horses. Okay."

"I'm serious, Wilber. If you go around - "

"Can I go back?" Wilber suddenly asked. Richard smiled at him for a long moment.

"I've had my acting school, you know. Had these fresh students walking through the doors every year. Their big eyes, their grand fears, their boundless hope. They would come to me, sit with me, play with me. I'd give them the odd clue here and there but basically they were learning about life all on their own. We were like family, better than family ... best time of all my lives ... Can you go back to your bus stop, to your friend Frank, to Earth? Of course you can. We can do whatever we please. And that, in a nutshell, is probably the toughest thing about this job."

"You have never gone back? Not once?"

"No. And neither will you. This is your home now, your love and your passion." Richard looked around. The planet seemed to have stopped its rapid growth. No more trees shooting up out of the earth, no more mountains rising, no more rivers bursting forth. The planet seemed ... ready. "That's about it. Standard issue planet. From here on out, it's entirely up to you. Remember, keep it simple. Well, gotta go."

Wilber suddenly felt anxious. "You're leaving?"

"What do you think, this is all I do? I got my own planet to take care of, you know."

"What if I have any more questions?"

"You're God," Richard grinned.

Wilber looked around. Excited he was, surely. But apprehensive just the same. What a task, what responsibility. "This is not going to be easy, is it?"

"Easy's boring," Richard answered. "Just remember to have fun." He gave Wilber a pat on the shoulder, then hugged him with all his might and disappeared into thin air.

∞

Wilber felt lost.

What now? Think, Wilber, think. What should you do? Was there anything that needed attending to right now? He did a three sixty, slowly scanning the lands. Everything looked just about right, for now. What to do? His face was grim. The task before him seemingly impossible ... then a smile spread across his face.

Out of nowhere it appeared. A bus stop, complete with poster boards, trash can and bench. Wilber walked to the bench, let his fingers glide over the cool surface and then slowly sat down.

When he leaned back, the radiance of his smile warmed the entire planet, his planet. And then it came to him, the name for this planet ...

... yep, it was just perfect.

THERE ARE NO LIMITS.

Made in the USA
Middletown, DE
26 May 2015